Other
Birds

Other
Birds

Sarah Addison Allen

ST. MARTIN'S PRESS
NEW YORK

First published in the United States by St. Martin's Press,
an imprint of St. Martin's Publishing Group

OTHER BIRDS. Copyright © 2022 by Sarah Addison Allen. All rights reserved.
Printed in the United States of America. For information, address
St. Martin's Publishing Group, 120 Broadway, New York, NY 10271.

www.stmartins.com

Book design by Michelle McMillian

Endpaper art: © Zaie/Shutterstock.com

Library of Congress Cataloging-in-Publication Data

Names: Allen, Sarah Addison, author.
Title: Other birds / Sarah Addison Allen.
Description: First edition. | New York: St. Martin's Press, 2022.
Identifiers: LCCN 2022010207 | ISBN 9781250019868 (hardcover) | ISBN
    9781250285805 (international, sold outside the U.S., subject to rights availability) |
    ISBN 9781250019882 (ebook)
Subjects: LCGFT: Novels.
Classification: LCC PS3601.L4356 O85 2022 | DDC 813/.6—dc23/eng/20220303
LC record available at https://lccn.loc.gov/2022010207

Our books may be purchased in bulk for promotional, educational, or business use.
Please contact your local bookseller or the Macmillan Corporate and Premium
Sales Department at 1-800-221-7945, extension 5442, or by email at
MacmillanSpecialMarkets@macmillan.com.

First Edition: 2022
First International Edition: 2022

10 9 8 7 6 5 4 3 2 1

To the memory of my mom, who taught me that food is love.
It was the first, and best, magic I ever knew.

And to the memory of my sister, who came before me
and illuminated the way.

Stories aren't fiction. Stories are fabric. They're the white sheets we drape over our ghosts so we can see them.

—ROSCOE AVANGER, *Sweet Mallow*

Other
Birds

Chapter One

T he empty wicker birdcage beside her began to rattle impatiently. Zoey gave it a sharp look as if to say they were almost there. It stopped.

She glanced at the cabdriver to see if he had noticed. The old fig-shaped man was watching her in the rearview mirror, his silver eyebrows raised. Several seconds passed and he continued to stare, which she found disconcerting because she felt his eyes should really be on the long bridge over the water. But he seemed to be waiting for her to respond.

"Did you say something?" Zoey said. He hadn't spoken a word since his *Where to?* when he'd picked her up at the airport.

"I asked if this was your first trip to Mallow Island."

"Oh," she said. "Yes." The birdcage rattled in disagreement, but she ignored it this time. It was her first trip. The first trip she could remember, anyway.

"Sightseeing?"

"I'm moving there. I start college in Charleston this fall."

"Well," he said, drawing the word out like a tune. "Don't hear of too many people moving to Mallow Island. It's mostly a tourist place because of that book by Roscoe Avanger. You know it?"

Zoey nodded, distracted now because the small sea island had just appeared on the horizon and she didn't want to miss a moment of it. It was rising from the marshy coastal water like a lackadaisical sea creature sunning itself, not a care in the world.

The closer they got to it, the more her excitement grew. This was really happening.

As soon as they were off the bridge, the cabdriver took a left and traveled down a two-lane highway that skirted the perimeter of the island. The water, dense with reedy vegetation, ended just inches from the pavement. But it didn't seem to bother the drivers of cars with out-of-state license plates. They zipped along confidently, following decorative metal signs that read:

THE MALLOW ISLAND RESORT HOTEL: 3 MILES AHEAD

THE SUGAR WAREHOUSE: 2 MILES AHEAD

HISTORIC TRADE STREET: NEXT RIGHT

Afraid he might miss the turn, Zoey was about to point it out to the cabdriver, but he'd already put on his blinker. She sat forward, not knowing where to look first. If she hadn't known that Mallow Island had been famous for its marshmallow candy over a century ago, Trade Street would have told her right away. It was busy and mildly surreal. The sidewalks were crowded with tourists taking pictures of old, narrow buildings painted in faded pastel colors. Nearly every restaurant and bakery had a chalkboard sign with a marshmallow item on its menu—marshmallow popcorn, chocolate milk served in toasted marshmallow cups, sweet potato fries with marsh-mallow dipping sauce.

Zoey rolled down the window, and a thick combination of salt from the Atlantic and sugar from the bakeries blew in. It was both strange and familiar. She wondered if the smell was bringing up a long-forgotten memory from when she was a little girl. She struggled to recall anything but, as with most things concerning her mother, her memory was more wish than real.

"Are you sure the place you're looking for is on Trade Street?" the cabdriver asked, braking hard when a dazzled tourist decided to cross the street without looking. Zoey had to put her arm out to stop the birdcage beside her from toppling over. Pigeon was going to be seriously pissed when Zoey finally let her out. "This is a business section, not residential."

Nervous that she might have gotten some detail wrong, Zoey rooted through her backpack to find the piece of paper on which she'd written the information. "Yes," she said, reading from the paper. "It's called the Dellawisp Condos. The building manager said the turn wasn't marked, but to go down the alley beside Sugar and Scribble Bakery and you'll find it." That was the hope, anyway. If this didn't work out, there was no backup plan. She'd be stuck here with no place to live this summer.

The cabdriver shrugged as they crawled down the street with bumper-to-bumper traffic. He found the bakery—a pink confection of a building with peeling white trim that looked like icing—and turned. The alley was darkly shaded by the buildings on either side of it, which didn't bode well for finding anyplace livable back here. Just when Zoey was beginning to think that this was a colossal joke being played on her, and that her father and stepmother were having a good laugh about it right now, the alley opened up and there it was—a beautiful old cobblestone building shaped like a horseshoe. A wrought iron gate was the only entrance. It gave the place an air of magical secrecy, probably bewildering anyone who happened to take a wrong turn down this dead-end alley.

It was smaller than Zoey thought it would be. Every story she'd ever heard her father tell of her mother had been prefaced by her love of money and her conniving ways of getting it, so this wasn't a place Zoey would ever have thought her mother would want to be—tiny and quiet and hidden. She felt a small thrill of happiness. Already she was learning something new.

"Huh. Who would've thought this was back here?" the cabdriver said. "How did you find out about this place?"

"My mother used to live here," Zoey answered, handing him some cash. Then she grabbed her backpack and the wicker birdcage and got out.

She purposely kept her back to the cab as it left. As soon as she could no longer hear it, she looked over her shoulder to make sure it was gone, then opened the birdcage. She felt Pigeon dart by her on angry wings.

Zoey took a steadying breath and walked to the gate, which bore a weathered brass sign that read THE DELLAWISP. She pushed it open and the hinges squeaked, piercing the silence. In front of her was a small, overgrown center garden. She stepped inside and followed a brick pathway lined with short trees bearing clusters of disproportionately large, bell-shaped blooms. They gave off a cloying scent like a bottle of dropped perfume. Her backpack brushed one of the trees as she passed, and suddenly a swirl of tiny turquoise birds flew out.

With a shriek of surprise, Zoey ran the rest of the way to the

U-bend of the building. She stepped onto the sidewalk in front of a door marked MANAGER. The birds, disconcertingly, landed on the sidewalk and began to hop around her.

They were exquisite little things, some no bigger than ring boxes. She watched as one found her shoelace and began to pull on it with its sherbet-orange beak.

"Please don't do that," she said, not wanting to move for fear of hurting it. "Can't you tell it to stop?" she asked Pigeon.

Pigeon gave a crisp coo from the garden, as if to say this move hadn't been Pigeon's idea, so Zoey was on her own.

Zoey knocked on the manager's door, her eyes still on the birds. When the door opened, she looked up to see an elderly black man in faded jeans and a khaki work shirt. He had a long white beard tied at his chin with a rubber band, like a pirate. The little birds seemed to take the open door as an invitation to enter and hopped past him into the office.

The man just stood there. His rheumy brown eyes, magnified behind square glasses, were focused on something over Zoey's shoulder in the garden. Zoey had to resist the urge to wave her hand in front of his face to find out if he could actually see her.

"Hi," Zoey finally said. "Are you Frasier?"

His eyes snapped to hers and he gave a rusty laugh. "I'm sorry, yes. And you must be Zoey. Welcome."

"Thank you." She pointed past him into his office. "Um, should they be doing that?"

He turned to see that the birds were on his desk, scattering papers and pencils. "Hey, come on now. Get off of there," he said, shooing them away as he opened a drawer and produced a set of keys. Zoey stepped aside as he herded the birds out and closed the door behind him. "They're a little spoiled, and bad for stealing. If you lose something, let me know. I keep a box of things I find in their nests."

"What kind of birds are they?" Zoey asked while the birds chittered complaints back and forth to each other as they hopped back into the garden.

"They're called dellawisps. They're native to the island. The man who renovated this building years ago found them nesting here, and he named the place after them. Not his most creative moment. But fitting, I suppose." He held up the keys. "Ready to see your place?"

Zoey nodded, wondering which of the landing units was hers. There appeared to be only five condos—two landing units each on either side of the U-bend, and one second-story unit perched above Frasier's office in the bend itself. A twisting metal staircase led to its balcony like a long curl of hair.

She was surprised when Frasier went to the staircase and began to walk up. She hurried after him, her backpack in one hand and the birdcage in the other. "This place isn't what I was expecting," she said as she followed him around the spiraling stairs.

Frasier stopped on the balcony and waited for her to join him. "The best things never are. I wish I could go back and see it for the first time." He watched her with his magnified eyes as she reached the balcony and took in the view. "This was the only structure to survive after all the houses on the island burned during the Civil War. The shops on Trade Street were later built in front of it, so it just sat here for years, forgotten by everyone but the birds. It was once horse stables. You can see where the stall doors were down there, where the patio doors are now. Your studio here was the hayloft."

Zoey turned to him with surprise. Her mother had lived in a *hayloft*? In her wildest dreams she wouldn't have come up with that.

At that moment, one of the glass-paned patio doors flew open and a woman in her forties with dark, greasy hair stepped out. She looked like she'd secretly raided someone's dirty-laundry basket. She was wearing a skirt over a pair of pants and what appeared to be three different shirts, badly buttoned, one over another. She stared up at Zoey with protuberant green eyes that made her seem slightly mad.

"What are you doing?" she yelled. "Who are you?"

"This is Zoey Hennessey," Frasier called. Zoey gave her a small wave. "I told you about her this morning. She's our newest resident."

"I don't like it! I don't like it one bit!" She pointed at Zoey. "No noise! Do you hear me? I'm trying to find the story I lost. It's in here somewhere and I can't concentrate with all this activity!" She turned and walked back inside.

"That was Lizbeth Lime," Frasier said before Zoey could ask. "You'll get used to her. We all have. The rest are a quiet bunch. Next to her is Charlotte Lungren. She's an artist. On the opposite side of the garden is Mac Garrett. He works nights. And next to him is Lucy Lime, Lizbeth's sister." At Zoey's obvious alarm that there might be another version of Lizbeth living here, Frasier smiled and said, "Don't worry. Lucy never complains about anything. She never leaves her condo."

"Never?"

Frasier shook his head. "She doesn't like being around people."

"Not even her sister?"

"Especially not her sister. She even has her groceries and prescriptions delivered." He turned to unlock the balcony doors.

"Speaking of deliveries, your boxes from Tulsa arrived yesterday. I had them put inside for you."

Frasier stepped in and reached for a wall switch. A crystal light fixture popped on, raining down variegated light. The building revealed itself to be like a geode—rocky on the outside but sparkling with unexpected decadence inside.

It was small, just one room. The furniture was covered with white sheets, but everything else she could see was lovely— the golden parquet floor, the whitewashed rafters, and the long kitchen counter on the far wall, which sported kitschy, pale pink appliances.

"I thought about uncovering all this for you, but I figured it was something you would want to do yourself." He handed her the keys. "If you have any questions, let me know. I'm here until five every day."

Pigeon flew in, bringing with her a wave of perfume from the strange blossoms on the trees. Questions. Yes, Zoey had questions. Tons of them. But the only one she could think to ask was "What are those trees in the garden?"

"Brugmansia. Some folks call them angel's trumpet. The man who renovated the place planted several different bushes and trees to see which kind the birds liked. He said it was the least he could do, since he had to evict them from their nests in the horse stalls. They liked the brugmansia best."

Pigeon circled the room restlessly. She moved the fragrance around like a ceiling fan. "The blooms have a very strong scent."

"Could've been worse." Frasier shrugged as he left. "They could have liked stinkweed."

A smile slowly formed on Zoey's lips as Pigeon swooped overhead. This was it. She dropped her backpack and the birdcage and immediately began pulling the sheets off the furniture in great sweeps. On one side of the room there was an over-the-top white leather sofa, a glass-topped coffee table, and two armchairs. On the other side were a white bed, a night table, and a tall chest of drawers.

Giddy with the possibility of all she might discover, Zoey started going through the drawers and cabinets.

But they were all empty.

The closet, too, was bare save for a set of pink sheets and bath towels.

Panic setting in, she took a second turn around the room to make sure, but there was absolutely nothing personal here of her mother's. Nothing. Not even under the mattress or between the couch cushions. There were no photos, no books with dog-eared pages, no half-written letters, no old address books, no clothes left in the closet. There was only this dust-covered furniture, new and impersonal, as if her mother had had the place redecorated just before she'd died twelve years ago.

Zoey sat on the stiff leather sofa and looked around, stunned.

To her right were the boxes Zoey had mailed a few days ago. They contained books and clothes, the only things she wanted to bring with her from her old life. She'd been told her mother's condo was furnished, so she'd left all her bedroom furniture behind in Tulsa. Earlier that morning when Zoey's Uber had arrived to take her to the airport, there had already been a charity truck idling in the driveway to haul it all away. Her stepmother, Tina, had timed it down to the minute.

Zoey hadn't been surprised. Tina had been talking about turning

Zoey's bedroom into a craft room for months. She even had a name for it. Wonderland.

I can't wait to get started on Wonderland.

That room is perfect for Wonderland.

Zoey, start packing so I can get to work on Wonderland as soon as you leave.

Zoey finally reached for her backpack and emptied its contents onto the coffee table in front of her. These were things she didn't want to risk mailing—her laptop, her tablet, her phone, important papers, and the small wooden box in which she kept the precious few items she had of her mother's.

She opened the box and took out the only photo. In it, Paloma was wearing red shoes and had a dark, high ponytail that rested like a question mark against the back of her head. With her short bangs and arched eyebrows, all she would have needed was a scarf around her neck and a bicycle with a basket and she would have looked like something from an old movie. Zoey didn't know when the photo had been taken. Zoey's father had only given it a cursory glance and told her he didn't remember when Zoey had asked years ago. But Zoey figured it couldn't have been long after Paloma had immigrated from Cuba. Zoey knew the story by heart. She used to recite it to herself over and over when she was a child, sometimes reenacting it in her bedroom. Paloma and her brother had been raised by their grandfather, who had been a birdkeeper. When he died, Paloma and her brother decided to leave Cuba on a small boat. There was a horrible storm, and her brother died. Paloma then drifted on the upturned boat for three days before a fishing boat found her. She looked so young in the photo, far too young to have been on her own, far too young to have taken up with Zoey's much older father once she arrived in America. Paloma had only lived here in South Carolina four years before Zoey's father retired and they all moved to Tulsa, where his family was from. But Paloma came back frequently to visit, sometimes for weeks at a time with baby Zoey, to this same condo Zoey's father bought Paloma as an extravagant gift early in their relationship.

Zoey got up and went to the pink refrigerator. She tacked the photo there with a promotional magnet bearing the name of a local appliance store. She hadn't eaten all day—she'd been too excited—so she automatically reached for the silver refrigerator handle and pulled it. She stared at the empty interior, realizing she needed to buy groceries and she had no idea where to get them.

She closed the door and leaned her forehead against it, suddenly feeling very alone.

But she could do this.

She *would*.

It was now after midnight, but Zoey hadn't moved from her sitting position on the balcony floor with her back against the stone wall. The humid air almost had a texture to it, and was unusually still.

God is holding His breath.

Her mother used to whisper that to Zoey in her mysterious accent when the wind abruptly stopped and everything went quiet for a moment, almost as if she'd made it happen. Zoey had a vague sense that her mother had been a great fabricator, as if to her there was no veil between what was real and what was not. It all existed together.

Zoey's four neighbors were all now home. She'd just watched the man with a night job, Mac, come in. Squares of light from his doors spread onto his patio. Across the garden, Charlotte-the-artist had already gone to bed, presumably with the young man she'd brought home with her earlier. Zoey had watched from the balcony as Charlotte had gestured for the young man to be quiet as they'd entered the garden. She'd pointed to Lizbeth Lime's condo, as if not wanting any noise to bring out her neighbor.

As for Lizbeth herself, she was still up, all her lights blazing. Her sister Lucy's lights were out, but the pulse of a small orange ember was flickering near her doors, as if Lucy might be smoking a cigarette inside alone in the dark.

Zoey knew she should probably go in and try to sleep. It had a been a long day. But being inside made her feel closed-in and lonely. And Pigeon was still out. She could hear the *whoosh* of her wings right now as she flew over the garden to peer into the low trees, curious about the dellawisps. Pigeon was very selective about whom she chose to honor with her presence. She was probably wondering if the little turquoise chatterboxes were worth the trouble to get to know.

Pigeon was obviously trying to make the best of the situation, but she hadn't wanted to move here. Judging by the years she tipped over glasses and stole trinkets belonging to Zoey's father and stepmother, generally trying to make their lives miserable, Pigeon hadn't wanted to stay in Tulsa, either. Sometimes there was no pleasing that bird. She nearly drove Zoey crazy on the plane that morning, perched on her head, pecking at her hair—hence Zoey's decision to make her stay in her cage on the cab ride. It made no sense to Zoey why Pigeon chose to travel with her instead of just flying herself here.

But then, an invisible bird made no sense by definition.

Pigeon swooped close by Zoey's head, nearly catching her hair. Zoey put her hands up to bat her away. Pigeon always did this when she thought Zoey was spending too much time in her own head. Pigeon believed in action, in being realistic, which Zoey had always thought was a tad hypocritical.

She heard Pigeon land in the wicker birdcage Zoey had put on top of the pink refrigerator. She cooed for Zoey to come in, but Zoey didn't want to. She was so wound up that it felt like a current was buzzing through her. She had the strangest feeling something was about to happen.

God is holding His breath.

Her skin prickled. She could almost hear the words, as if her mother were right beside her, whispering in her ear. It made her uneasy but she didn't know why. Hadn't that been the reason she'd chosen to go to college here? So she could move into this condo and feel closer to her mother, to have someplace to come to on breaks, someplace that finally felt like home?

At that moment, the patio doors to Charlotte's condo opened and the young man Charlotte had brought home earlier crept out. His skin was covered in swirls of tattoos that seemed to move in the darkness, like something alive. He pushed his long, straight hair out of his face as he strutted through the garden toward the alley gate. He walked like he was smiling to himself, like he'd gotten away with something. The dellawisps flew out of the trees and dive-bombed him when he got too close and he ran away, cursing softly into the night.

Pigeon cooed again and Zoey reluctantly got up and walked in, saying, "I think I'm going to try to make friends with them—Charlotte-the-artist and Mac-with-a-night-job and the Limes."

She wondered if she even remembered how to do it. Her last real friend had been Ingrid, in middle school. But surely it wouldn't be that hard.

Pigeon's silence told Zoey that she didn't like this idea.

"What else am I supposed to do this summer?"

Zoey heard Pigeon flap her wings impatiently as if to say Zoey probably should have thought about that before coming here. There were a lot of things Zoey probably should have thought about. Like how she was going to get groceries, for instance.

Earlier, she'd asked Frasier if there was a store within walking distance. Zoey had a car, one she dearly loved, which she'd bought last summer. But it wasn't scheduled to be delivered to her on the island for another few weeks. Frasier had directed her to a touristy specialty market down the street. Zoey had never bought herself real groceries before. The closest she'd ever come were the potato chips and white bread she bought at a convenience store on her way home from her after-school job at Kello's. Potato chip sandwiches were one of the few things she remembered her mother making for her. Her mother had had more money than she'd known what to do with in her adult life, but she'd always eaten like she was still a starving girl, lost on a boat trying to make her way to America. Zoey's father had been the very opposite of hands-on when it had come to raising Zoey after her mother died, but it now boggled Zoey's mind the basic things that supernaturally appeared when you lived with other people—things like salt and butter and soap and toilet paper. Zoey had been adding new things to her list all evening.

She went to the refrigerator to look inside again at the neat rows of Snapple and Orangina and the blocks of cheese and the softball-sized tomatoes she'd bought earlier. It was like looking in a mirror after a dramatic haircut and not quite recognizing herself. Who was this person with hard cheese in her pink refrigerator? When she opened the door, a shaft of bright light arced into the darkness of the condo. The small bottles of Orangina rattled but didn't mask the heavy *thump* that suddenly came from one of the units below.

Startled, Zoey closed the door and turned. She went back to the balcony and saw that Mac, a large redheaded man, had opened his door and was looking out into the garden, as if he'd heard the sound, too.

Something had just happened, something strange.

It left a quiet, ghostly feeling around them.

Zoey had spent too much of her life as an outsider to ever think of running to anyone when she was afraid. It wasn't that she was particularly brave, she just didn't want the disappointment of being turned away. But right now she felt a painful longing for something she couldn't name. She thought wildly of texting her dad, but he hadn't responded to her last text, when she'd told him her plane had arrived safely in Charleston.

She watched Mac step back inside and shut his patio doors, seemingly satisfied that nothing was amiss.

Before Zoey closed her own balcony doors and locked them, her eyes fell on Lucy Lime's unit. The ember of a cigarette was still glowing near the glass doors in the dark, as if Lucy was watching everything.

And Zoey had the oddest feeling that Lucy knew exactly what had just happened.

Chapter Two

Pigeon was knocking against the doors.

It felt like only minutes since Zoey had finally managed to fall asleep. She tried ignoring Pigeon, but that didn't work. If anything, the knocking got louder. She finally got out of bed and walked across the dark studio. As soon as she opened the curtained doors, morning sunlight flooded in, making her squint. She felt Pigeon zip by her.

The dellawisps were squawking in the garden, obviously upset about something. It sounded like a rain forest down there. No wonder her stupid bird wanted out. Pigeon was spectacularly incapable of minding her own business.

There were several voices below, almost drowned out by the dellawisps. Zoey was turning to go back to bed when she heard the crackle of a police radio add itself to the chatter, and that made her stop.

Police?

She stepped onto the balcony and looked down to see two officers talking to Frasier on Lizbeth Lime's patio. Dellawisps were flying around them. A few of the birds had landed on Frasier's shoulders. One was perched on his head like a fancy hat.

A clanking sound drew Zoey's attention, and she turned to see a man and a woman guiding an empty gurney through the garden. Frasier and the police officers stepped aside to let them enter Lizbeth's condo. The attendants looked relieved to be going inside, as it meant an escape from the cadre of little birds chasing them.

Zoey's brows shot up with alarm.

What had happened to Lizbeth Lime?

She immediately went down the balcony steps, as if she hadn't just accused Pigeon of being nosy.

Zoey reached the bottom of the steps and edged around the garden to Lizbeth Lime's patio. She chewed at a hangnail on her thumb while she waited for Frasier.

She was still in her shorts and T-shirt from last night. She'd been sleeping in her clothes since she was a child, when she hadn't truly understood what it had meant when her mother died. Her father had made it seem like Paloma had left on purpose in a fit of irresponsibility, as if she'd simply decided to go on a sudden vacation. Zoey began sleeping in her clothes so she would be ready to leave her father's house at a moment's notice when her mother finally returned. After her father remarried a year later, Zoey's stepmother would sometimes comment about this habit of Zoey's, which she found untidy—her own two tiny children from a previous marriage slept in very nice sleep things, after all. Zoey's father knew exactly why Zoey did it, but he would always shrug as if he didn't because he didn't like saying Paloma's name, and he knew his new wife liked it even less.

Frasier said a final word to the police officers and stepped off Lizbeth Lime's patio. He walked right past Zoey as if he hadn't seen her.

"Frasier?" she said, and he turned. "What happened?"

He reached out and patted her arm with a strong, bony hand. The force of it set her off balance a little. He was stronger than he looked. "Lizbeth died last night. But it's nothing you need to worry about."

Excepting her mother, Zoey had never known anyone who had died. Then again, she hadn't really known Lizbeth. She had only last night resolved to get to know her new neighbors, so it felt like she'd missed a train to somewhere important. "How?"

"She fell off a stepladder and a bookcase landed on her."

Wait, Zoey knew when it happened. She knew *exactly* when it happened. "I heard something last night!" she said. "A thump."

He nodded. "Mac said the same thing."

"Oh, right. Of course," she said, remembering that the redheaded man had opened his doors last night at the sound. "So it was just an accident?"

"Yes."

Zoey glanced over to Lucy Lime's condo. What was there to say? That Lucy had been sitting in her dark condo last night, smoking villainously after the thump? And what about Charlotte-the-artist's friend, the one who had left with such an air of secrecy?

"What about her?" Zoey asked, indicating Charlotte's patio. "Did she hear it, too?"

Charlotte herself opened her doors at that moment, looking sleepy and aggrieved. She was wearing the same strapless summer dress she'd had on yesterday. She stepped out almost in sync with the gurney being pushed out of Lizbeth Lime's condo next door. There was an unmistakable form buckled under a cover now. Charlotte automatically took a horrified step back. All three of them were silent as the attendants pushed the gurney out of the garden.

Charlotte turned to see Zoey and Frasier standing there. She looked too stunned to speak.

"Lizbeth died last night," Frasier said before she could ask. "Excuse me, I have some calls to make."

After he walked away, Charlotte finally spoke. "How did it happen?" Her voice was hoarse, as if she'd just woken up. She put her hands to her head and twisted her wispy blond hair into a topknot.

Zoey took her question as permission to step onto her patio. From the distance of her balcony, all Zoey had gleaned yesterday was that Charlotte dressed like she bought her clothes in vintage shops and drove an old powder-blue scooter. But she was even more interesting up close. What Zoey had mistaken for tattoos on her arms and legs was actually henna. Some of it was dark brown, as if done recently, but some was lighter, almost the golden color of Charlotte's skin, like an impression left in sand. Her face was narrow, her eyes were large and blue, and her blond eyebrows were feathered into unruly wings at the tails. She was *fascinating* to look at, like a piece of art you had to stare at a long time before it made sense. "Frasier says a bookcase landed on her in the middle of the night," Zoey said. Charlotte's eyes kept sliding over to the police officers. "Does that sound odd to you?"

"Odd?" Charlotte repeated, as if Zoey's words were processing just a second too slow. "No. She was always moving things around in there."

"Did you hear anything?"

"No. I got used to the noise. And last night I was . . ." She paused. "Sleeping deeply."

"What about the guy you were with?"

That got Charlotte's attention. "Is he still here?"

Zoey shook her head. "I saw him leave around one this morning."

"Oh. We're just friends," she said awkwardly. Then, without another word, she stepped back into her condo and began to close her doors.

"Wait," Zoey said, startled by how quickly their encounter was over. She held out her hand. "I'm Zoey Hennessey. I just moved here. I'm in the studio."

The woman shook Zoey's hand distractedly. Her skin was cool to the touch. "Charlotte."

"Nice to meet you!" Zoey said as the doors closed on her.

She stared at them for a moment, disappointed. Then she turned and looked out at the garden, wondering what to do with herself now.

With a sigh, she walked away.

———

Charlotte, listening from inside, heard Zoey finally leave. She slumped against the wall.

Just minutes ago the sound of voices in the garden had been a strange enough occurrence to wake her. No one at the Dellawisp stopped to chat. They didn't want to risk the wrath of Lizbeth Lime, resident busybody and, unfortunately, Charlotte's next-door neighbor. She knew whoever was out there was going to make Lizbeth go into full-on crazy-neighbor mode soon. Charlotte had gotten up and quickly walked into the living room, where she'd left Benny sleeping on the couch last night, to warn him not to go out or he'd find himself on the receiving end of an epic tirade.

But Benny had already left.

And Lizbeth was dead.

That was one too many things to process with a hangover.

She needed water. A lot of it. She left the doors and walked through the living room with its old stone floors and exposed ceiling beams. It was furnished with only a squashy yellow couch and chair she'd bought at a charity shop when she'd moved here. Furniture had never mattered to her, and this place was beautiful enough on its own. She sold everything every time she moved, anyway. It was the real estate that mattered most. She always bought a place outright, however small, when she moved. It wasn't exactly the bohemian lifestyle that teenaged Charlotte had once dreamed of, but she'd never been able to totally overcome her need to have a place of her own so she wouldn't have to be reliant on someone else for a roof over her head, like her mother.

The quilt she'd covered Benny with last night was crumpled on the floor by the couch like a ball of patterned paper. She bent to pick it up as she passed, and it made her head swim. She and Benny had spent the previous evening drinking and sharing their misery over the rent increase at the Sugar Warehouse, the artists' enclave where they both worked. Unable to afford it now, they'd both been forced to give up their booths. Yesterday had been their last day. Benny, a wood-carver she'd only ever spoken to in passing, had unexpectedly offered to help her bring home her boxes of henna supplies, because it would have taken her several trips on her scooter.

She'd gotten caught up in Benny's drunk enthusiasm about banding together to find space somewhere else on the island to do their art. But Benny wasn't here now, and she didn't know what that meant. She didn't have his number. She wasn't even sure he had a business card. Maybe he was out doing something charming like getting orange scones from one of the bakeries on Trade Street. He'd be back, she told herself, and then they'd scout out some new places. It felt good to at least be together with someone on this.

Life goes on.

She'd survived worse.

In the small galley kitchen, which was white and serene and probably her favorite part of her condo, Charlotte took a glass from the cabinet and filled it with tap water. Her leather backpack was open on the counter. It didn't register at first as she drank. But then she lowered the glass from her lips and set it on the countertop with a click, an uneasy feeling coming over her.

She reached into the backpack and brought out her work pouch wallet. She zipped it open, holding her breath.

It was empty.

She immediately emptied her backpack and sifted through everything, frantically at first, then more deliberately, making absolutely sure.

Benny, who obviously held his alcohol better than she did, had taken her money.

She ran back to the front doors and opened them. The police officers were still on Lizbeth Lime's patio.

The female officer turned to Charlotte. Charlotte smiled. When it came to the police, she never wanted to call too much attention to herself. She stepped back inside and closed the doors, willing her heart to stop racing.

Whenever she moved, all the money from the sale of her previous home went into buying a new place, for that one security she allowed herself. With everything else, she lived hand to mouth. She needed the money that had been in her backpack. This was the first time in her life she'd ever been able to support herself wholly with her henna, something teenaged Charlotte had always dreamed of. She'd been working longer hours and saving for weeks since finding out about the rent increase, so she would have something to live on until she found a new space to work in. She'd had a cushion. Now that cushion was significantly less soft.

"Bastard, bastard, *bastard*!" she whispered, every muscle tense with the effort not to cry. She was *through*. She'd cried too much these past few months, ugly, shuddering cries that left her gasping for breath, because of her breakup with Asher—the only bad thing that had come out of moving to Mallow Island. Her mother had cried like that, and it had always struck Charlotte as selfish and overly dramatic. There had been much more devastating things happening during her childhood, yet all her mother could do was cry for herself.

A lifetime of trying not to be like her mother, and look what she had turned into.

Just another desperate, cash-poor artist with a broken heart.

———— ••• ————

Frasier, sitting in his office, could hear the birds outside start to calm. The police must have finally left. He waggled his head a little. Old Otis, the eldest of the dellawisps, was still perched in his hair. Otis swayed, but didn't move. He must have fallen asleep.

The desk in front of Frasier was littered with sketchbooks and colored pencils. Drawing was a medium he'd taken up later in life and all he drew was birds, over and over, usually in the heat of the day when it was too hot to be in the garden. The wall in front of him was covered in sketches of the dellawisps, so many of them the papers overlapped, forming a decoupage of turquoise birds.

He stared at them for a while; then he took off his thick glasses and rubbed his eyes. What a morning.

He was at an age now where the people he'd once known outnumbered the people he presently knew. After passing away, sometimes his friends would visit him before leaving this earthly world. It had been happening all his life, and what had been a terrifying experience for him as a boy no longer surprised him. It was usually just a brief encounter—a sparkle out of the corner of his eye, a gust of wind in an airless room, a particular scent.

But there were some, out of fear or confusion or unfinished business, who stayed with him longer.

And of course Lizbeth would be one of them.

She was here in his office with him and he sensed her impatience, like she was wondering where something was.

"I don't know where he is," he said to her, hoping she was thinking about her son, though more than likely she was still wondering where that blasted story of hers was. "I'll find him, but I doubt he will come home. Not even now."

But Lizbeth wasn't listening. In death, as in life, she was singularly the worst listener he'd ever met.

Before her son Oliver had left for college a few years ago, Oliver had asked Frasier to check on Lizbeth regularly. Despite Oliver's complicated relationship with his mother, despite the fact that he couldn't get away fast enough, he'd still been worried about what would become of her once he was gone.

Lizbeth had moved into the Dellawisp when Oliver was just three years old, so Frasier had watched him grow up and had helped raise him as best he was able. Lizbeth wasn't one anybody would ever call maternal. Still, Frasier had hoped he and Lizbeth would share how much they missed the boy during his check-ins. But it had soon become clear that Lizbeth had no interest in talking, or listening, to Frasier about anything. Once Frasier had finally caught on to this, he'd begun amusing himself by telling Lizbeth great daily fictions about once being shipwrecked with the Queen of England, or the time he joined a band of burglars all dressed as Santa who pulled off the largest heist in history on Christmas Eve at the Mall of America. Once he'd even told her that he was madly in love with her and asked her to run away with him to a nudist colony on Corsica.

She'd never heard a word. She'd been too busy sorting and cataloging and murmuring to herself, "I know I saw it somewhere."

She'd spent most of her time trying to find things. Over the past few years, it was the story she wanted Roscoe Avanger to write about her, somewhere in her maze of boxes. Once a week Frasier would clean Lizbeth's kitchen and her bathroom, but the rest was hopeless, which was a shame. Though small, these unit interiors were exquisite. Frasier would take out anything spoiled, rotten, or mildewed so there wasn't a smell or an infestation the other residents could complain about. They already had plenty of things to complain about with Lizbeth. She used to write down everything she saw them doing, sure it was a crime of some sort. She would hand him sheets upon sheets of notes about them, which he always threw away.

He'd known something was wrong the moment he'd entered her place this morning. It had been unnaturally still, no shuffling of papers, no kinetic Lizbeth energy permeating the space, bouncing around with nowhere to escape. He'd found her under an over-turned bookcase containing hundreds and hundreds of copies of Roscoe Avanger's famous *Sweet Mallow*. He'd finally managed to push the heavy oak piece off of her, cursing his age because he could have lifted it with a single finger when he was younger, but cursing *that damn book* even more. But it had been too late. She'd been dead for hours. He'd lowered himself onto a stack of books beside her and taken his phone out to call for help. The quiet had been unnerving while he'd waited, so he'd told her a story about stumbling across a diamond mine in his grandfather's backyard when he was a boy.

Frasier finally put his glasses back on and pushed his wheeled desk chair across his small office to the filing cabinet, past the clip-boards he had tacked to the wall with work orders, birdseed de-liveries, and a lost-and-found list of the things the dellawisps had stolen. They were funny little thieves. Most people thought they were a nuisance, but he enjoyed them. It had taken him all his life to understand this, but even unlikable things have worth. It was how, after all, he'd learned to live with himself.

He took out the file with Lizbeth's sister Lucy's name on it, then pushed himself back to his desk, Otis still swaying on his head. He went through the papers until he found Lucy's phone number. She hadn't answered her door when he'd knocked earlier, but that wasn't unusual. She never answered her door.

"I didn't really find a diamond mine," he told Lizbeth as he dialed. "But that thing about the Queen of England? Absolutely true." He felt Lizbeth shift around restlessly. "What, you don't believe me? She still sends me birthday cards."

GHOST STORY

Lizbeth

Lucy. Lucy. Lucy.

Why is he calling my sister? She doesn't care about me.

Frasier needs to go find my story. *That* will bring Oliver home, if he's so worried about that. Then they'll both discover the truth about Lucy and they'll finally love me for everything I ever had to put up with. They'll never love Lucy. That will show her.

Even this last thing can't be all about me. How fitting. My first memory isn't even my own. It's about *her.* I remember sitting alone in the back of a strange classroom while Lucy was up front with our parents by the blackboard. The teacher was expressing concern about Lucy's unruly behavior. Our father was rubbing Lucy's back with a single finger, almost seductively, like he was spelling out letters on her skin. He'd always loved her best. But she was ignoring him and staring out the open windows, a look of practiced boredom on her pale, lovely face. I remember watching closely, highly suspicious of her calm demeanor (having fallen for it before with bruises as the consequence), and seeing that she was surreptitiously heel-kicking her chair leg with such force that her shoe fell off. She kept kicking until tiny drops of crimson appeared on her white sock.

When you grow up with a sister like Lucy, so beautiful and so troubled, you desperately try to find ways to shine by comparison. She was bad in school. So I excelled. She crawled out her bedroom window at night to meet boys. I never dated until Oliver's father. My entire life became defined by Lucy, like when you can't remember the real meaning of a word so you explain its opposite. But even though I succeeded at the things she failed at, including *being a mother,* I never got the same attention. After Oliver was born, I think my own mother even wanted me to be *grateful* to Lucy, as if she nobly walked the path in front of me like a warrior and took all of life's nasty arrows to her chest, just so I would know when to duck.

But there was nothing noble about Lucy. I have always *despised* her, despised the way her problems seemed so much bigger than everyone else's. I had problems. What about me?

Anyone who has led a life like Lucy's would be dead by now. *She* should have been the first to go. But, no. My beautiful blond sister inherited our father's hearty genes, capable of withstanding almost anything. Me, I inherited our mother's fatal curse for unhappiness, doomed to be attracted to things that never loved us back.

And now look what's happening. Frasier is worried about *her.*

I'm the dead one.

I wish I could touch my things. That always brought me comfort. But I can't touch anything now. What am I supposed to do? Just wait here?

There are two other ghosts here. I see them peering out the windows. One of them used to live here at the Dellawisp, but I never liked her. The other one is an old woman who used to live down the street from me in my old neighborhood on the island. Her, I liked. She used to feed me corn bread on her porch. How odd that she's here. She's trying to get my attention to tell me something, but I'm ignoring her. I'm not here to make friends.

But it looks like I'm going to have to put up with both of them for a while, because I can't seem to go anywhere except where Frasier is right now. It's the only connection I feel. But I'm sure when my story is finally found and Oliver comes home, he'll want me. He and Frasier were always so close, in their own little club, leaving me out. But once they know everything, they'll regret not feeling sorrier for me.

And they'll hate Lucy for every reason I never told them.

Chapter Three

That night, her second at the Dellawisp, Zoey lay in bed in the dark, unable to sleep again. She was scrolling through Instagram, her face illuminated by the light of her phone.

Her stepmother had posted an update. Tina was one of those people who lived on social media, and everything she posted was beautiful. She had a certain reputation for it. Her Instagram profile read: Tina Hennessey. Wife to Alrick. Mother to twins Casey and Douglas. Former Miss Oklahoma. Philanthropist. Amateur Decorator.

Suddenly, Zoey put her phone down and stared into the darkness. Great lumps that were her mother's couch and chairs stared back at her. She thought she'd heard something outside. Silent seconds ticked by. Had she imagined it?

She got out of bed and walked across the studio. Pigeon rustled in her cage on the refrigerator, cooing sleepily like an exhausted nanny for Zoey to go back to sleep. Zoey ignored her and went to the balcony doors and opened them. Sea mist, briny and heavy, was covering the garden, smothering her view. It was so thick she almost missed it, the brief flicker of light.

If she'd been a cat, her tail would have twitched.

She stepped forward and leaned over the railing. The shine of a flashlight beam was breaking through the mist, moving around the periphery of the garden. It disappeared underneath Zoey's balcony, and Zoey held herself still. It reappeared on the other side, walking toward Lizbeth's condo.

Someone was sneaking around, just one night after Lizbeth Lime died!

Her bare feet were moving down the metal staircase before she was even aware of it. Once she reached the ground, she skirted along the wall where the mailboxes and Frasier's office door were located, following the light as it shone back and forth over Charlotte's and Lizbeth's doors. But then the flashlight clicked off and Zoey stopped. There was the sound of hurried footsteps coming near. She barely had time to take a few steps back and flatten herself into Frasier's office doorway before someone walked right by her, so close Zoey could smell the cigarette smoke. She sensed the person stop just feet from her, and Zoey held her breath. Finally, the person ran away.

Zoey waited to hear the squeak of the garden gate or the closing of a patio door, some further indication of retreating movement. She heard neither.

Was the person waiting for her from some short distance?

She finally decided to make a run for her studio. She took the steps two at a time, then shut and locked the doors behind her. Pigeon rustled in her cage, still asleep.

"The *one time* you don't wake up," she whispered to Pigeon.

She lifted the curtains and looked out.

The mist was moving like someone taking a deep breath and blowing it away. It cleared enough for her to see that Lucy Lime was smoking inside by her doors, the orange ember of her cigarette glowing then dimming like a pulse with each drag she took.

F rasier! I think someone was trying to break into Lizbeth's condo last night."

Frasier stopped on his way to his office, a paper cup of coffee in one hand and an old-fashioned metal lunch box in the other. He also had a brown envelope tucked under his arm. He looked up at her on her balcony. Morning sunshine winked off his large glasses.

"They had a flashlight," she added at his confused expression.

"Ah," he said. "You probably saw headlights. Sometimes cars from Trade Street make a wrong turn down the alley."

She quickly walked down the steps as he spoke. "No, you don't understand. It was definitely a person."

"Did the birds wake up?" A few of the dellawisps had landed on the sidewalk in front of his office. They hopped around impatiently, as if they had something better to do.

"No."

"If they didn't stir, then it was nothing. They're a fairly reliable alarm system."

"Or it was someone who knew enough not to walk *through* the garden, and instead to take the longer way around it," she pointed out.

Someone, she'd concluded, like Lucy Lime.

Frasier studied her with his cloudy eyes. "What are you doing this summer, Zoey?"

She hesitated, feeling suddenly emotional. It seemed a lot to unload on him, how she'd always imagined her mother's condo to be like a time capsule and *that* was what she thought she'd be doing this summer—falling into the soft, comforting history of her dead mother. She was still trying to process the fact that what she knew might be all she would ever know, and there would be no guidance on where she came from or where she should go from here. "I can't do much of anything until my car gets here," she said. "And school doesn't start until August."

"How would you like a job?" he asked.

She'd quit her after-school job at Kello's used bookstore to come here. That job had been her escape from long evenings spent alone in her bedroom in Tulsa. She'd never fit in with the family created by her father, Tina, and Tina's children. And it had made everyone happier, including Zoey herself, when she'd finally stopped trying. But she hadn't thought she would need that kind of refuge here. She'd been wrong. "What kind of job?"

Frasier unlocked his office door and set his coffee and lunch box inside. He also set inside the mysterious brown envelope he had tucked under his arm.

"Follow me," he said as he walked away. The dellawisps immediately flew behind him, trailing so closely they made him look like he was giving off turquoise exhaust. Zoey brought up the rear, not entirely sure if Frasier had been talking to her or the birds.

He went straight to Lizbeth's door. The birds stopped just short of the patio, as if they'd been chased away from it often enough to be wary. Zoey caught up with him as he produced a key from his jeans pocket. He touched the key to Lizbeth's lock, but the doors creaked open on their own, as if the handles hadn't caught.

"That's strange," he said. "I thought I locked up before I went home yesterday."

"I bet it was the person I saw last night," Zoey whispered, a tad more dramatically than she intended.

Frasier shook his head patiently. "No one in their right mind would want to be in Lizbeth's place." He pushed the doors open the rest of the way. "Come. I'll show you why."

She followed him in. The place was absolutely packed with cardboard boxes, stacks and stacks of them, going all the way to the ceiling. A single trail snaked between them into a dense, ominous recess. And the *smell*. An unwashed odor hit her like a physical force.

It was hard to imagine someplace this small holding this much stuff. It gave Zoey a panicky feeling, as if left alone she might never find her way out of this maze of floor-to-ceiling belongings. Sweat popped onto her skin. It was almost like Lizbeth could still be in here somewhere, lost.

She felt Pigeon zoom in and land on her shoulder. She bit Zoey's ear, hard, wanting her to leave. Zoey shrugged and Pigeon flew away, landing somewhere high on a box and causing some papers to float down like leaves.

"Roscoe Avanger is the executor of Lizbeth's estate, such as it is," Frasier said, turning to watch the papers flutter down. "At first he was going to have the whole place gutted at once, but then decided to see if there was a story, or story notes, or *something* in here."

"Roscoe Avanger," Zoey repeated. "The writer?" *Sweet Mallow*, his legendary and only book, written fifty years ago, was set on Mallow Island.

Frasier nodded. "Lizbeth worked for him."

"Are you saying he wrote something new? And it's in *here*?"

"No," Frasier said as he walked back out to the patio. "Not exactly."

"What do you mean?" she said, close at his heels, grateful to escape the claustrophobic feeling Lizbeth's condo was giving her. The sweat on her skin evaporated in the sunlight and made her shiver.

"It's a story Lizbeth always said she wanted him to write. It probably doesn't exist, but it's important to her. It *was* important to her. Was," he said, flustered that he'd just referred to her in the present tense, as if she were still here. "It shouldn't take more than a week or so, depending on how much you want to work on it every day. Do you want the job?"

There was no use thinking it over. Of course she wanted it. "Yes," she said, and immediately wanted to tell someone. But the only person she knew who would be remotely interested in this Roscoe Avanger connection was her old boss at the used bookstore, Kello, and he was ridiculously anti-technology. He didn't even have a phone at the store.

"All right. Don't throw anything out until you've gone through it. Every box." Frasier looked back into the condo with a deep sigh. He had a sinewy vigor to him, but seemed somehow more fragile this morning. It occurred to her that maybe the shock of Lizbeth Lime's death had rattled him to his bones, and he was grieving. She felt embarrassed for not acknowledging it sooner.

"I'm sorry," she said. "About Lizbeth, I mean. Did you know her well?"

"I knew her a long time. That's not quite the same thing." He handed her Lizbeth's key, then walked back to his office. The della-wisps followed him until he closed the door.

They looked lost for a moment, then seized on their next distraction.

Charlotte had just emerged from next door, bringing her blue scooter with her. She walked into the garden toward the gate, ostensibly because the narrow pathway around it was too small for the scooter. The birds, predictably, dive-bombed her. A fat one landed on the seat and chirped like a crabby backseat driver as she pushed.

Pigeon cooed in a dignified way at their behavior, from somewhere on the low stone wall separating Lizbeth Lime's patio from Charlotte's.

"Charlotte! Hey, Charlotte!" Zoey called. Charlotte turned her head and Zoey could see the split second she considered ignoring her. Unhappiness was undulating off her in waves. Zoey beckoned her back. "Come look at this."

Charlotte gathered herself together and pushed down the kickstand, leaving the birds to descend upon the scooter.

Zoey led her to Lizbeth's doors.

"My God," Charlotte said. Her words disappeared inside as if they were another thing for Lizbeth to collect.

"You said you could hear her moving things around. Did you know about this?"

"I had no idea," Charlotte said as Zoey studied her. She was wearing a short, flowered sundress and black bicycle shorts. Her hair was twisted up and she had on a pair of silver aviator-style sunglasses. She turned and Zoey could see herself reflected in them. Zoey's short, dark hair was falling on her forehead, which looked like the bangs her mother used to wear. She liked that glimpse of her. Aside from her coloring, there was very little about her that Zoey thought resembled her beautiful mother. "Why are the doors open?" Charlotte asked.

"When Frasier went to unlock them just now, they were already open," Zoey said. "He thinks he forgot to lock them yesterday, but I saw someone sneaking around here last night. He gave me a job clearing all this out. Lizbeth worked for *Roscoe Avanger,* did you know that? Apparently, he wants some story idea Lizbeth was going to give him. Isn't that amazing? Roscoe Avanger might finally be writing something new!"

Out of that deluge of information, Charlotte focused on what was, to Zoey, the least interesting thing by far. "Wait. Frasier gave you a job?"

"Yes."

"That's great," Charlotte said, walking away. "Just wonderful."

Surprised, Zoey followed her. "What's wrong?"

Charlotte reached her scooter and lifted the kickstand. The della-wisps flew up into a cloud. She pushed the scooter toward the alley without another word, and eventually Zoey stopped following.

Chapter Four

This was the last thing Charlotte wanted to do, so of course the one day she would have welcomed traffic, there was none. It took only ten minutes on the coastal highway around the island for her to get to the Sugar Warehouse, the name of a colossal warehouse left over from the heyday of the candy trade when ships would bring in loads of sugar for the candymakers.

There was no practical use for the warehouse after the trade dried up on the island during the Great Depression, so the building fell into disrepair. Eventually it became so far gone that everyone seemed to be waiting for it to simply fall into the ocean. Enter wealthy Margot Tulip from Charleston. She bought the warehouse and, to everyone's surprise, instead of tearing it down and building a hotel she turned it over to her son Asher—a lackadaisical man with failed ambitions of becoming an artist. Asher renovated it and rented out booth space dirt cheap to an eclectic group of local artists that he liked to consider his tribe, even though he had more money than any of them would ever see in their lifetimes. Restaurants and coffee shops soon moved into the spaces facing the piers, and presto change-o. Instant tourist attraction.

Charlotte had phoned several fellow artists from the Sugar Warehouse yesterday after discovering Benny had left with her money, but none of them had returned her calls. She'd finally resorted to calling Asher at his office. Unlike with the others, she wasn't surprised when he hadn't responded. They hadn't spoken in months. Now she had no choice. There was the little matter of the missing seventeen hundred dollars she'd had in her backpack. She had a square reader on her phone for credit cards, but many customers still paid in cash. And if she had cash, she always, always carried it with her. She wanted to be able to touch it, to know it was still there. It was an old habit since running away.

Once she reached the seaside parking lot, she took off her helmet. The day was hot and hazy, with long white clouds stretched across the blue sky like pulled taffy. She stared out at the water, letting the wind blow across her damp face and hair. She'd spent the first part of her life not even knowing how to swim. Now she couldn't imagine not being near an ocean. It was wide open for all to see, not forested and hidden like the camp in Vermont where she'd grown up.

She finally screwed up her courage and walked into the cavernous Sugar Warehouse, with its concrete floor and a roof so high the steel ceiling beams faded into darkness, where gulls nested. Large hanging fluorescent lights brightened the building, which was divided into row upon row of booths occupied by artists selling, chatting, and creating—woodworkers, potters, painters, photographers, doll makers, even handmade-clothing designers.

The information desk was directly to the left of the entrance inside, and she went there and told the receptionist that she wanted to see Asher. She needed him to know that there was a very good reason for her call yesterday. And it wasn't because she wanted her booth back, or wanted *him* back.

When Asher finally appeared from his office, her hand involuntarily gripped the helmet she was carrying.

"Charlotte," he said, all business as he walked over to her, "what can I do for you?"

She'd been working here for nearly a year and a half before he'd ever spoken to her. Her henna booth had been close enough to the information desk that she could watch him come and go. Something sparkled around him, an irresistible sheen of confidence, with his dark curly hair and those garishly bright polos he favored. He would sometimes wink at her when he noticed her attention, but that had been it. He winked at everyone. But then, for a reason that only became clear later, one day last winter he'd walked over to her to watch her work. He'd talked to her clients as she drew, charming them so much they left her large tips. Between clients, he would touch the designs on Charlotte's arms while asking about each of them, holding her eyes just a little too long.

And that was all it had taken.

It always happened this way. She would be alone for years, because protecting herself from anyone who could hurt her was what teenaged Charlotte had always wanted and she owed that to her; then along would come someone like Asher who showed her where all her cracks were.

After that fateful day, her sheer craving for him had been unbearable as she'd waited every day for the warehouse to close early during its winter hours. When everyone had left, she would go to Asher in his office and they would spend all evening making love. Occasionally she would convince him to come back to the Dellawisp with her, but Asher had never once taken her to his own home in Charleston. He'd never asked her personal questions, never asked about her past. She'd almost forgotten she had one, which had been a heady feeling.

"I called you yesterday," she said.

"I know. I've been busy."

"It was only because I need contact information for Benny, the wood-carver who had the booth across from mine."

Asher crossed his arms on his chest and rocked back on his heels, considering the request. "Why would you need Benny's contact information?"

He was going to make this hard. She tamped down the urge to bean him with her helmet. "Obviously, because I need to contact him."

"But why?"

"That's my business."

"I saw you leave together yesterday. He helped you move."

"Asher," she said with a sigh, "the sooner you give me his number and address, the sooner I'll leave."

Asher smiled slightly, a smile that met his gray eyes, a quirk of his facial musculature that always made him seem sincere. It was an amazing thing to watch, how quickly he could turn on the charm. "Maybe I don't want you to leave."

But she felt no stirring of desire anymore, which, perversely, gave her hope. Because how much easier would life be if she never felt longing for anything ever again? For a woman who wanted no connections, she still found herself caught up in them with men, and they were always like this—burning hot then just as quickly burning out. Maybe Asher had cured her. Maybe it was all out of her system and she could finally be the person teenaged Charlotte had wanted to be. "So, how far along is Paige now?" she asked.

He took a small step toward her. "You know it's not the same with her."

Actually, she didn't. Asher had known his fiancée Paige was pregnant when he'd started seeing Charlotte. It was *why* he'd started seeing her. In his man-child world, he thought falling back on old habits meant he didn't have to face his future responsibilities. But Charlotte hadn't even known there *was* a Paige. "That won't work now, Asher," she said. "Not everything is that easy, even for you."

He leaned in and said softly into her ear, "Oh, Charlotte, you were very, very easy."

She pulled back and stared at him with disgust.

From behind her, Charlotte heard a voice say, "Asher. Paige and I just got back from her doctor's appointment. She's in the coffee shop. Go join her."

Charlotte turned to see an older woman with bleached society hair standing there. She was wearing a short A-line dress and beige heels—something since arriving in South Carolina Charlotte had come to think of as the Wealthy Southern Woman Uniform. Asher smiled at his mother and kissed her on the cheek as he passed.

Margot waited until he disappeared before turning to Charlotte. "Can I help you with something, Charlotte?"

Okay, she would try this again. "I need contact information for someone who used to work here. Benny. He had a booth across from mine."

A flit of suspicion crossed her face. "Why are you looking for him?"

Not wanting to get into the details with Margot any more than she did with Asher, she said, "He helped me move. But I can't find something important now, and I need to ask him if he knows where it is."

Margot seemed to consider that. "You don't need his contact information," she finally said. "He's working here at Usher's Woodworks now."

Charlotte frowned. That didn't make any sense. If he already had another job here, why did he talk about finding space somewhere else with her? And was he really stupid enough to think she wouldn't find him right back where they'd started?

She turned to walk away, but Margot caught her by the arm with her tanned, veiny hand. "I don't apologize for Asher, ever. I know the kind of man he is. I'm married to the kind of man he is. But I have a grandchild on the way any day now, and I'll protect that, even if he won't. I know what it feels like when someone betrays you. You'll get past this. And you'll get past it even sooner if you never come back here."

It was such an absurd notion that rich, in-control Margot, who'd had the privilege of choices all her life, could teach Charlotte anything about surviving betrayal. Charlotte had survived her childhood. Margot would never know the strength it had taken to do that. Charlotte extricated her arm.

"I'm already past this," she said, walking away and grabbing a directory off the desk as she went.

She checked the directory and located Usher's. It was one of the larger booths, selling handmade chairs. But it looked like they were now including smaller cash-and-carry things like figurines. Benny was sitting at a long table with some other wood-carvers, carving his signature birds. He was young and handsome, but he had roughed himself up in that way pretty men sometimes do when they want to hide their prettiness—long hair, scrawny beard, tattoos. He'd seemed like such a nice guy, a little immature maybe, but not capable of stealing.

What was he doing back here?

When she stopped in front of him, he looked up and the color left his face. She stared back, waiting.

"I was trying to make you feel better, okay?" Benny leaned in and said quietly. "We all know what Asher and his mother did to you. I just wanted to make you see that you didn't need this place, and that you were going to be fine. You can get work doing your henna anywhere. I didn't want to tell you I'd already been offered a space to share here."

What Asher and *his mother* did to her? She shook her head with frustration, not understanding, and not wanting to. "I don't care where you work, Benny. I just want my money back."

He pushed away from the table and indicated she should follow him out of the booth. "What money?"

She stopped and tourists broke around them in the wide aisles. "The money you took from my backpack before you left my condo in the middle of the night."

"I didn't steal any money from you!" He flicked his long dark hair over his shoulder with a nervous jerk of his head.

"Fine, Benny. I'm calling the police." Of course she wouldn't, but he didn't know that.

"Charlotte, I swear. I was just doing you a favor. Asher and Margot worked with everyone who got the notice of the rent increase and couldn't afford it. We share space now, or work for other companies. But not you, because Margot wanted *you* out."

She looked around immediately, as if she might see proof of this. But the place was too big. She knew how important it was for artists to be where people could easily find their work. Thanks to Margot, they'd closed ranks.

That's why no one had called her back.

She'd never been particularly intimidated by Margot, not like some of the other artists here. Not that she didn't understand a healthy respect for the person to whom you paid rent, but the past decade of her life had been one of constant movement, so if things ended, fine, she would just move on.

But leaving and being kicked out were two entirely different things.

She suddenly had to get out of there. In fact, she couldn't leave fast enough. She had to find her bearings. Benny jogged after her. "Charlotte, I didn't steal a thing! I left. I got attacked by those birds. I got in my truck. I drove away. That's it. Wait, wait." He got in front of her and walked backward, facing her. "There was a woman standing on the sidewalk near the alley to your place. I don't know if she was homeless or if she lives there, but she looked rough. She was smoking a cigarette, real shady-like. I didn't lock your door behind me. Maybe it was her. Maybe she came in and stole your money."

That made her stop. "What did she look like? No, never mind. I don't want to know," she said, and pushed past him.

Ultimately, it didn't matter who took her money.

It only mattered that it was gone, and she couldn't do a damn thing about it.

Chapter Five

The sun was beginning to set, slanting shadows across the room as Charlotte lay on her bed. She was listening to the music Zoey was playing next door as she was cleaning out Lizbeth's place. It was such an odd sensation, having music at the Dellawisp. Charlotte was actually beginning to enjoy it. But then, without warning, the music stopped. Zoey must have finished for the day.

The sudden quiet made Charlotte's bedroom feel as if it had been plunged underwater. Even the small glass ball ornaments she'd hung by fishing wire from the ceiling gave the impression of air bubbles floating to the water's surface. It was folklore Charlotte had grown up hearing, how these glass spheres called witch balls had been used for centuries to protect homes against ghosts and evil spirits. Her artistic mother used to replicate them out of grapevines, the only thing she had to work with. She would tell customers about their mystical properties at the roadside stand where the camp sold maple syrup and the meager amount of vegetables they managed to grow.

Charlotte now collected them, and the symbolism wasn't lost on her.

She was trying to protect herself from the ghosts of her past.

She reached for her phone on the nightstand to check her bank balance again, but stopped herself. She knew what it was. And she knew how long it was going to last. She grabbed the remote control instead and turned on her small television, just to fill the quiet.

A few moments later, she rolled over and gave a muffled scream of frustration into her comforter, beating the mattress with her fists for good measure. But even a good temper tantrum didn't help.

Only one thing would.

She made herself lean over the edge of her mattress. She felt around for the low basket she kept under the bed and pulled it out.

She hadn't taken anything with her when she'd left Vermont when she was sixteen except the bag of money she'd stolen from the camp, a few clothes, and this diary. Moving as much as she did wasn't easy. Traveling to a new city sometimes caused anxiety so intense she couldn't catch her breath. So she kept this diary to reread when things were hard. In it was a long list teenaged Charlotte had made of places she'd wanted to live and rules she wanted to live by when she finally ran away. It never failed to make her feel better that she could check off so many of them now. It reminded her that it was all worth it.

She flipped through the thin pages covered in loopy, girlish cursive, lingering longest on the pages about Pepper Quint.

I braided Pepper's hair today and told her she should never cut it because it was so beautiful. I wish my hair looked like hers.

I told Pepper that I wanted to be a henna artist because it was the most beautiful thing in the world. She didn't know what henna was, so I told her. We checked out a book about it from the library and hid it so Minister McCauley wouldn't see what we were reading. We spent all day practicing drawing on our legs so that our jeans would cover our work. She was really good at it. Way better than me.

I cried today after my session with Minister McCauley. He hit me when I told him I knew he was a fake. Not hard. But still. He hates that I know. I told my parents what he did, AND THEY TOOK HIS SIDE. But when I told Pepper, she hugged me and gave me an orange she'd brought home from school lunch. Later, I let all the air out of his car tires. I don't know how Pepper has stood it here all these years. She never thought about leaving until I came along. This is the only place she's ever known. She thought it was normal. But it's not. I've finally convinced her that it's NOT normal. I wish my parents had never joined The Church of McCauley. I wish we had never moved here to the camp.

The diary was the story of two girls—Pepper, who had always lived at the scraggy camp where the followers of Marvin McCauley resided, and who didn't know how to have her own dreams, and Charlotte, who had moved there later with her family, and who had nothing *but* dreams.

Charlotte had made it out of that life.

Pepper hadn't.

Tucked into a makeshift envelope glued to the back cover of the diary was a photo their seventh-grade teacher had taken for the school yearbook. Neither Charlotte nor Pepper had been able to afford the yearbook, and Minister McCauley wouldn't have let them keep it anyway, so Mr. Hartman had given them this photo at the end of the school year. They were standing by the windows of the classroom, their arms around their shoulders, two thin, scruffy girls who looked happy at that moment, that single moment.

Charlotte turned on her side and put the photo on the pillow next to her. The glass balls above her shimmered, casting light on the girls.

Her eyes slowly closed. She was caught in that never-never land between sleep and waking—not here and not there—when she thought she heard something beyond the murmur of the television. A click. Then another. Something like a doorknob unlocking and turning, but then being caught by the interior dead bolt. Her brain wanted to wake, to tell her someone was trying to break in. But her body was too far gone into exhaustion, and she fell into a deep, dreamless nothing.

◆

When Charlotte opened her eyes the next morning, the first thing she saw was the photo on the pillow beside her.

She always got maudlin when she thought of Pepper. Or maybe being maudlin made her think of Pepper. Either way, she was sick of wallowing.

There was music coming from Lizbeth's place next door again. Zoey back at work. Charlotte rolled over and stared at the ceiling. The witch ball ornaments were swaying slightly in the cool air blowing from the AC.

She sighed and rubbed her eyes.

Then realized the AC wasn't on.

So why were they moving?

She opened her eyes again and saw that the balls were now still. She must have imagined it.

With a good night's sleep came some clarity about her next steps.

Number one, she needed to scout out new places for a henna table. Pronto. Number two, Zoey. She never socialized with neighbors. There was no point, giving how often she moved. But Charlotte was ashamed of how standoffish she'd been yesterday. None of this was Zoey's fault. Charlotte owed her an apology.

She got up and put the photo and the diary back under her bed. Then she dragged a chair to the center of the bedroom and untied one of the witch balls. She jumped down and walked next door.

Lizbeth's patio now had an arsenal of cleaning supplies stacked by the doors, which were wide open. Inside, Zoey's back was to her. She had on shorts, a T-shirt, yellow rubber gloves, and purple plaid rain boots. "Stop bothering me! You're acting like those birds outside," she was saying over the music. "It's none of your business if I want to do this. But if you're that concerned, I'll be done faster if you quit knocking things over."

Charlotte looked around to see who she was talking to, but no one was there. She knocked on the doorframe.

Zoey turned and Charlotte saw that she was wearing a white cupped face mask. Zoey put down the box of magazines she was holding and pushed the mask to the top of her head. With her pixie-cut hair, arched eyebrows, and ears that stuck out slightly, she looked like a very tall elf. She was so fresh, so new to the world. It almost hurt Charlotte to look at her.

"It looks like you're already making a dent," Charlotte said. Zoey had cleared a good ten feet of boxes away from the patio doors. It wouldn't be long before she reached the doorway to the bedroom, if the layout was anything like Charlotte's condo. But who knew how much was in there?

"It's *all* paper," Zoey said, as if she couldn't believe her good fortune. She peeled off her gloves and turned down the music on her phone. "Weird stuff like old receipts and newspapers and junk mail from decades ago. I haven't even found any furniture yet."

Charlotte held up the glass ball. It was the size of an apple and was one of her prettiest, graduating from clear on top to a bubbled lavender color on the bottom. One of the glassblowers at the Sugar Warehouse had made it. "I came over to give you a housewarming gift. Welcome to the Dellawisp."

Surprise registered on Zoey's face. She stepped out onto the patio and took the ball from her. Sunlight caught the three strings of glass suspended inside and made them shimmer like icicles.

"It's called a witch ball," Charlotte said, stuffing her hands into the pockets of her cutoffs. "Those thin glass strings are supposed to catch spirits that come into your house and trap them inside the ball, protecting you from them. If the ball breaks, it means you have a particularly strong ghost. Not a bit of truth to that, but it makes a nice story."

Zoey looked around for a place to set it, deciding on an industrial-sized box of recycling bags. She stepped back and admired it. "Did you make it?"

"No." Charlotte shrugged. "I just collect them."

"I love it. Thank you."

"It's also an apology. I'm having some issues, but they have nothing to do with you. I just lost my job," she said, deliberately not mentioning her missing money. Zoey had seen Benny leave that night, and she didn't want her to make the connection and go to the police herself. "Yesterday, my first thought was that Frasier should have offered *me* the job cleaning this place out. But he didn't know. So why should he ask me? I feel ridiculous."

"Don't feel ridiculous," Zoey said without missing a beat. "I'll go tell him I changed my mind and that you offered to take over. I'll even help you. For free."

"Don't worry about it. I've got everything under control." Heaven forbid anyone think otherwise.

Zoey studied her. "Where did you work?"

"I had a booth in the Sugar Warehouse, on the other side of the island. I do henna." She took her hands out of her pockets to show her, just so those dark eyes would stop boring into her own.

"I had henna done once at a street fair outside the bookstore where I worked in high school," Zoey said. "Vines, all down my fingers, like that. Only not as pretty as yours."

"Vines symbolize perseverance," Charlotte said. "Flowers mean joy. The sun represents eternal love. And the moon, here, is the power of change." She pointed to her knee. "Birds are supposed to be messengers between heaven and earth." She indicated a peacock on the other knee. Birds had always been her favorite to draw. Then she touched a circle on her leg at the hem of her cutoffs. "This is a mandala. It represents the universe."

Zoey looked impressed. "I had no idea it all meant something."

Charlotte put her hands back in her pockets. "In all my years, I've never encountered something that didn't mean anything."

Her phrasing seemed to give Zoey pause. "How old *are* you?"

"A lot older than you," Charlotte said. "Twenty-six."

"That's not *a lot* older," Zoey said with a laugh. "I'll be nineteen in a few weeks."

Charlotte smiled for the first time in what felt like forever. Nineteen had once seemed exotic to her, too, being *so very close* to twenty. "So what brings you here? Are you in college?" she asked. The island had a big seasonal tourist economy, so half the summer workforce consisted of college kids.

"I start my freshman year at the College of Charleston in the fall."

"Well, I'll leave you to this."

"Wait," Zoey said, before Charlotte could turn to go. "Did you happen to see anything last night, or hear anything unusual?"

Charlotte suddenly remembered the sound that had tried to penetrate her layers of exhaustion as she'd fallen asleep. "I thought I heard a doorknob rattle. But I was probably dreaming. Why?"

"You weren't dreaming!" Zoey said. "Lizbeth's patio doors were open again this morning, just like yesterday. And I know I locked up."

"Maybe it was Frasier."

"I already asked. It wasn't him." Zoey made a tiny gesture, like she didn't want anyone but Charlotte to see, indicating the two units across the garden. "Do you think it could be *her*?"

"Lucy?" Charlotte asked, and Zoey nodded. "No. Now, if you were accusing Lizbeth, I wouldn't be surprised. I can't tell you the number of times I found her trying to peer in my patio doors when she thought I was gone."

"Still, we should probably make sure our doors are locked until we know what we're dealing with."

"Don't worry about Lucy," she said, reaching out to squeeze Zoey's shoulder. The gesture was very unlike her and she felt embarrassed for doing it.

"Then who could it be?"

Charlotte thought about it. "Maybe it was someone who heard about Lizbeth's death and wanted to get a look at her condo to make a quick offer based on the state of the place. It happens all the time. People are ghouls."

"How would they have a key?"

"If a door isn't bolted from inside, a handle lock is pretty easy to pick."

She could see that Zoey was dying to know how she knew this.

But before she could ask there was the sound of a door opening across the garden. Zoey turned sharply, obviously thinking she had magically summoned Lucy, the Boo Radley of the Dellawisp, with only the power of suggestion.

But it turned out to be the larger-than-life redheaded man next door to Lucy. Zoey visibly deflated. She was young enough to think that drama was something you had to run toward. She had no idea that drama doesn't need to be chased. It knows exactly where you live.

"Do you know him?" Zoey asked as the man walked out, back first. He always wore his hair styled in a mod pompadour, short on the sides and long on top. And he dressed like a hipster in old hiking boots, cargo shorts, and untucked plaid shirts. But there was something about him, just in the way he moved, that made Charlotte think he was an older soul covered in a younger man's skin.

"That's Mac. I think he works at a restaurant. Sometimes when he cooks it makes the whole garden smell like . . ." She hesitated while they watched him walk to the mailboxes.

Zoey looked at her expectantly. "Like what?"

"Home." But it didn't, really. At least not the place she ran away from. That place had smelled like mud and sweat and the peculiar scent a roof gets when it's so wet it's about to collapse. This man's cooking smelled like what home *should* smell like.

"He looks like he would be nice," Zoey said as he reached the mailboxes. He dropped his keys and bent to pick them up.

"Are you interested in him?" Charlotte asked. "I bet he's old enough to be your dad."

"My dad is seventy-three. He's thirty, tops," Zoey said. "I just meant, since we all live here, shouldn't we be friends?"

There was no good way to respond to that without diminishing

Zoey's enthusiasm. Charlotte could only hope that she was going to move into a dorm in the fall. There she could make friends her own age in that cloistered collegiate universe where everything was new and theoretical. Where the real world was years and years away.

Suddenly, there was a crash and they turned to see that Zoey's witch ball had rolled off the box and shattered on the concrete patio.

"Looks like you have a ghost," Charlotte joked. "Here, I'll get it."

As Charlotte grabbed a broom that was on the patio, she could have sworn she heard Zoey mutter, "*Pigeon!*"

Chapter Six

Mac Garrett heard voices as he stepped out of his condo, so he closed his patio doors quickly. Lizbeth Lime was always skulking around, looking for something to report. It took him a moment to remember that she was gone.

He turned to see that the voices belonged to two women standing on Lizbeth Lime's patio. He didn't recognize the one with dark hair, but the other was his neighbor Charlotte. Her long flyaway hair was down today, and her blue-jean cutoffs afforded him a view of the tan designs fading on her skin. He didn't know what the designs were. At first he'd assumed they were tattoos, but over the years he realized that they changed week to week, which was a source of endless fascination. Was she drawing on herself? Or was someone else doing it? Why?

Mac had lived at the Dellawisp nearly eight years, longer than anyone other than the Lime sisters, who had given off such an air of permanence that it felt like they'd been here since the beginning of time. He remembered when Charlotte had moved in two years ago, remembered the exact spring day. Several rangy men in sandals had helped her move in some old furniture, and afterward they'd had beers on her patio until Lizbeth had come out and yelled at them. Two years was a long time to put up with that.

Instead of walking to the alley, Mac decided to detour to the mailboxes in the U-bend of the building next to Frasier's office. He rarely got physical mail, but it was a shameless excuse to get closer. As he pulled his keys from his pocket, he tried to hear their conversation.

His keys suddenly slipped from his hand and fell to the sidewalk with a clatter. He looked over to find the women looking at him. He bent, his knees popping, and picked up the keys and unlocked his box. Surprise, surprise. Nothing was there. He stood there longer than necessary, leaning in so the door to the box hid his face from them. He closed his eyes with embarrassment. He hoped they hadn't realized he was eavesdropping.

After a few moments, he finally closed the box, revealing the dark-haired girl now beside him. He gave a start.

"Hi," she said. She was carrying a box of magazines. It appeared to be so heavy she was bowed back from the weight of it. "I'm Zoey." She awkwardly held out one hand, trying to balance the box with the other.

"Mac," he said, shaking her hand gently so as not to tip her over. She was younger than he'd assumed from a distance. She was nearly his height, six feet, but as thin as a cat's whisker.

"Do you work in a restaurant?" she asked, apropos of nothing. He was on his way to run a few errands this morning, so he was in street clothes, not his chef's whites.

"Popcorn." When she looked at him blankly, he added, "I work at Popcorn. It's in the Mallow Island Resort Hotel."

"Charlotte said your place smells really good sometimes." She nodded back to where Charlotte was now sweeping something into a dustpan on Lizbeth's patio.

Mac and Charlotte had never spoken beyond the polite things about the weather that neighbors say in passing. He never thought she'd paid him much mind, *but she noticed when he cooked.* He realized he was staring at her and looked away. The girl saw, though. He felt his face grow hot, which he knew was apparent despite his thick, vivid-red beard. *Never* not *know what you're feeling,* Camille used to say. It was the curse of his fair, freckled skin.

"What's happening with Lizbeth's place now?" he asked by way of distraction. "Are you moving in?"

"No. I just moved into the studio. Frasier gave me a job cleaning Lizbeth's place out," she said. "Do you know anything about her sister?"

"Lucy? I hardly ever see her. But I don't think she and Lizbeth got along. They never spoke, at least not that I saw."

Zoey shifted the weight of the box and stumbled back.

"Here, I'll take that," Mac said, pocketing his keys and lifting the box from her.

"Thanks. It goes in the recycling dumpster," she said. She followed him out of the garden and into the alley. There, he hoisted the box into the Dellawisp's blue dumpster, which was nearly full.

"Lizbeth must have had a lot to recycle," he said, clapping the dust from the box off his hands.

"You don't know the half of it. I'm getting a workout carrying this stuff out here."

"Well, don't blame Frasier. I'm sure he couldn't put the dumpsters nearer to the building without incurring the wrath of Roscoe Avanger."

Zoey looked at him curiously. "Why would Roscoe Avanger have a say in it?"

"He was the one who bought these old stables and saved them from being demolished a few decades ago."

Zoey turned to look at the gray cobblestone building. "It was *Roscoe Avanger* who renovated this place?"

Mac nodded. "And he always buys back the condos when the owners want to sell. I gather he feels a little territorial."

"Ha!" Zoey exclaimed, turning back to him as if he understood. "I knew it wasn't someone sneaking around to get a look at Lizbeth's condo to buy!"

"Excuse me?"

"Nothing. Sorry," she said. "I didn't know any of this when I moved in. I inherited my studio from my mother."

"Then you should read the book Roscoe Avanger wrote about the Dellawisp, if you can find a copy."

"*Sweet Mallow*? I have a copy. But I don't remember this place being in it."

"Not *Sweet Mallow,* the other one. The little nonfiction one. *Dancing with the Dellawisps.* It's about his renovation of the property and giving the birds a permanent home in the garden."

"I had no idea Roscoe Avanger had written another book!"

"I'm pretty sure it was only sold on the island. I think he self-published it," Mac said. "I never read it, but Frasier illustrated it. He told me about it once when I asked about the drawings of the birds on his office wall." Zoey didn't respond, obviously still thinking about the book, so he figured that was his cue to leave. Sometimes it was hard to tell. He envied people with a natural ability to walk in and out of conversations. Camille used to say it was because he kept waiting for people to say goodbye, when he knew good and well that saying goodbye was not a prerequisite for leaving. "Well, it was nice to meet you."

There were six parking spaces reserved for the Dellawisp residents in the lot between the back of Sugar and Scribble Bakery and the front gate to the garden, but only Mac with his Chevy Tahoe and Frasier with his beat-up work truck parked there. He walked toward his SUV, but Zoey called his name and he turned.

She pointed to his left shoulder. "You have some flour, right there."

He didn't have to look to know it wasn't flour. "It's cornmeal. Thanks."

Quit it, Camille, he thought crossly as he brushed it off.

It was after midnight when Mac got home from work. He stuck his key into his door lock, but paused with a strange feeling of being watched. He turned and looked around. No one was there. Then he thought to look up and saw Zoey sitting on her balcony, her long legs dangling over the ledge. That studio had been unoccupied as long as he'd lived here. He'd always wondered why.

It was late and he almost called for her to go to bed. But he couldn't have been much older than she was when he'd moved out on his own. *We got wings we can't see*, Camille used to say. *We were made to fly away.*

Zoey waved at him. He smiled and waved back before opening his doors. He stuck his leg in first in case Fig tried to run out. She'd never shown any interest in life outside the condo, but he didn't want to take any chances.

He flicked on the light and tossed his keys on the coffee table. Fig lifted her head from the couch and meowed in her croaky little voice.

"Hello, beautiful," he said.

The only calico hair Fig had left was on her belly, which she rolled over and let him scratch. The upper half of her body was a road map of old scars, her ears burned down to tiny leaves. When he'd first brought her home, he'd left the radio on for her for company while he was at work before he'd realized she was deaf.

Three years ago, Fig had been badly burned behind the hotel. One of the dishwashers at Popcorn had tossed a cigarette at her, not realizing she'd had gasoline and oil on her from sleeping under cars in the employee parking lot. The dishwasher, Nigel, had taken off his shirt and doused the flames, then came running into the kitchen saying, "I didn't know! I was just trying to scare it away!"

Mac had stopped what he was doing and grabbed the cat from Nigel. He'd been feeding her scraps for months and everyone knew it. Without a word he'd walked out and driven to an emergency clinic in Charleston. Nigel never came back to work. Several people said Mac had scared him, scared him with the look he'd given him. Mac didn't know what look that had been. For a long time he'd assumed it had been anger, until he'd run into Nigel a year or so ago. Nigel had apologized again and said, "Man, that look you gave me. I still can't get it out of my head. It was like I'd killed your grandma, like I'd taken your heart out of your chest."

After weeks at the vet, Fig had been well enough to be released, so Mac had brought her home to the Dellawisp. He'd been hiding her from Lizbeth Lime and Frasier ever since. Pets were expressly forbidden in order to protect the bird population in the garden. But it wasn't as if Fig had the agility or even the desire to catch any of those birds. Frankly, he was more worried about what those crazy birds would do to his sweet, fat cat if Fig ever wandered outside.

He went straight to the shower to wash the kitchen smell off him. When he got out, Fig was sitting on the bathroom mat. She hopped into the tub and drank some of the water left dripping from the faucet while Mac dried off.

After putting on pajama bottoms and a T-shirt, he went to the couch and sat heavily. He turned on the television and flicked through the channels as he rubbed his aching knees. A few minutes later he thought he heard something. He hit the Mute button on the remote. There was a creak coming from the garden, like the gate was opening slowly. He waited to hear if it was Lucy Lime. She never came out during the day, but sometimes he heard her leave at night. When he didn't hear the sound of her door closing, he got up and pulled the curtains back. The footpath lights in the garden were hidden by ferns and Knock Out roses, giving the area a muted green glow, almost like being under the sea. He saw a shadow move near the two units on the other side.

He thought of Charlotte alone over there now that Lizbeth was gone. Lizbeth had been a pain in the ass, but if something was going on, right or wrong, she'd been the one to notice and take action. He'd taken that for granted for years. He opened the doors and stepped out. The birds were rustling in the low brugmansia trees, chirping halfheartedly as they wound down to sleep. A faraway car puttered down Trade Street. Other than that, it was the quiet that only one o'clock in the morning can bring. He watched the garden for several more moments, but there was no movement. He looked up to see if Zoey was still on her balcony, but she had obviously gone to bed. He had the feeling now that she had been waiting up for him before going inside, like she was looking out for him.

He suddenly wondered why she had asked him earlier about Lucy. He looked over to her unkempt patio next door. The few times he'd actually seen her, Lucy looked rough around the edges, but in a defeated kind of way. It was as if life had thrown her one too many curveballs she wasn't able to catch, so she had resigned herself to simply getting hit. He'd never thought there was anything dangerous about her.

Get yourself back in here, he imagined Camille saying.

He stepped back in and sat on the couch again. Fig jumped up and settled on his lap, purring. He zoned out for a while in front of the TV, until he was nearly asleep. But he never let himself sleep anywhere other than in his bedroom, not since Camille died five years ago and he began waking up covered in cornmeal.

The first time it happened, it was easy enough to dismiss. He was a chef whose specialty was dishes made with cornmeal inspired by Camille, so he thought he'd probably brought it in with him on his clothes from the restaurant. But then it happened again the next night. He dismissed it again, this time as the stress over Camille's death making him sleepwalk into his own kitchen. But then it happened the next night. And the next. Weeks passed, every morning the same, waking to his bed sprinkled in cornmeal. His girlfriend at the time—a high-maintenance beauty named Evalina who had worked at the front desk at the hotel—began to freak out about it when she stayed over. She hated the way the cornmeal would stick like dandruff to her hair. She told him to stop doing it, and she'd gotten angry when he told her he couldn't.

He said good night to Fig, who knew by now that she wasn't allowed in his bedroom while he slept. He closed his bedroom door behind him and took a fresh white bedsheet from the stack he always kept on the leather armchair in the corner. He flipped the sheet over his bedspread, where it floated in midair for a graceful, cloud-like moment before covering the bed. He crawled under the covers, pulling the sheet over his head.

When morning rolled around, he woke up and gently slid out from under the covers.

Sleepily, this routine now five years old, he gathered the edges of the top white sheet and went to the bathroom. There, he shook the cornmeal that had fallen on him during the night into the bathtub. He ran water and watched it wash down the drain.

He turned and looked at himself in the beveled mirror over the bathroom sink. His hair and beard no longer looked red. Finely dusted in cornmeal, he looked like a very old version of himself.

He sighed and turned on the faucet at the sink.

GHOST STORY

Camille

Sometimes it feels like I'm almost gone. Weightless. Floating. It re-
minds me of the first time my brother John took me to Wildman Beach.
It was an hour's walk, and he didn't want his little sister tagging along
and slowing him down. All my young life I could smell the ocean from
our house, which was smack-dab in the center of the island, tempting
me like hot pie in an oven. That, combined with the allure of doing
something up until then only John had been allowed to do, made
me full of brattiness. When I pouted, watching John set out on dark
summer mornings, my mama used to say, "Use your imagination and
you can be there any time you want." But I didn't want to imagine
it. I wanted the real thing. Turns out, the real thing almost killed me.
Mama finally made John take me when I was eight years old. John
knew I couldn't swim, but he still dragged me into the water that first
time, saying the only way to learn was to go out as far as possible and
make my own way back. *If you really want to come back,* he said, *you'll
fight it.*

I nearly drowned. John pulled me out and I had no breath and everyone thought I was dead. But I *did* want to come back—to my old dog Goodnuff, to my beat-up baby doll Mosey, and to my mama and her corn bread, which was waiting on the kitchen table, just dry enough to crumble into a glass of milk. I was a fat baby, so that feeling of weightlessness when I almost died was scary. I was used to weight keeping me grounded, every step a comforting reverberation of the earth coming through my bare feet.

I don't mind this weightlessness so much now, not like I did then. I'm just waiting to finally be let go. In a way, it's nice to be remembered, nice that someone in the world still needs me, still needs at least the memory of who I was. That's what keeps me here.

My Macbaby keeps me here.

He was the biggest surprise of my life. Because I never set out to keep any children until he showed up on my doorstep. I never had any of my own and I was okay with that. I had lots of brothers and sisters and nieces and nephews, so I'd seen too many births and I'd seen too much baby poop. When I grew up, all I wanted was to leave that behind. I liked children okay. They could be cute and funny as all get-out. But I didn't like how they took so much of you. I knew women who had too many mouths to feed because they couldn't keep their husbands off of them. And I knew childless women who faded away to nothing because they thought they were only worth something if they had a baby. And all these women, they had pieces of them missing. They'd be walking down the road and I could actually see holes in them where the sun shone through. I never knew why they seemed so normal, so happy to have all those holes, until Macbaby.

He found my body after I died, and I wish to God I could have changed that.

I never wanted to put that burden on him.

I'd been cooking corn bread in my kitchen when I just slipped away.

As easy as can be. I was ready this time. Macbaby would come to check on me every few days after he moved out. He would take me to the grocery store and all my doctors' appointments. That day he came in with all the fixings for a millionaire pie I told him I wanted to make for our Sunday dessert. He found me on the floor, covered in cornmeal like snow. I was gone, or so I thought, until I heard him cry, cry like I never heard him cry before, and that brought me right back to him, where I've been ever since.

One day he'll be ready to let me go. Until then, I'm here, weightless but not unhappy, waiting to be released like a wish or a balloon, floating up to that place where hope goes.

That's the difference between me and that Lizbeth. She doesn't have the right holes.

She's avoiding me and the other ghost here, even though I know she recognizes me from when she was a little girl here on the island.

She needs help understanding the right reasons to stay.

And the right reasons to go.

Chapter Seven

Frasier was sitting in his office staring at the still-unopened brown envelope on the desk in front of him, where it had been all day yesterday, when there was a knock at his door.

"It happened again!" Zoey said, and for a moment Frasier saw her mother very clearly. He'd known Paloma, of course, those few short years she'd lived at the Dellawisp. He remembered her volatility, the way she would fling her arms around when she was riled, and the incessant fights she and Alrick Hennessey, the man who would eventually father Zoey, would have here. Alrick had bought the condo for Paloma and set her up here away from prying Charleston eyes when Paloma was younger than Zoey was now. Paloma had known more than a teenager should have known about what it took to survive. She'd been charming and calculating. She'd had to be. She was alone in a foreign country with only the ghost of her dead brother for company. Zoey didn't seem to have any of her passion or survival instincts, and given that she'd grown up under the thumb of Alrick Hennessey, he hardly wondered why. But witnessing her frustration right now, he considered that he might have underestimated her.

Without another word, Zoey turned and walked away. He was in need of a distraction from the brown envelope, so he went with her.

She reached Lizbeth's patio and waited for him. "Look, it's unlocked again," she said, indicating the door that was open a sliver. "I know I locked it when I was through yesterday. I swear. This makes the third day it's happened. Why is someone sneaking around here? What does it mean?"

He pushed the door with his finger and it swept open easily. He jiggled the doorknob, then bent to examine the handle. Aside from some obvious scratches that could have been there forever, it seemed fine. He looked into the condo. The stone floor was slowly widening in an arc from the boxes that had already been removed, and it brightened the place like dawn breaking. Little bits of Lizbeth were slowly leaving. He didn't understand why that made him sad. He hated this clutter. He was glad to see it go. "Has anything been disturbed?"

"The boxes I was working on yesterday haven't been moved. But as for the rest of them, I wouldn't be able to tell. I'm not going into the back until I've cleaned out the front, in case of an avalanche."

"Did you see someone with a flashlight again last night?"

"Well, no." She crossed her arms over her chest. "But I was tired and went to bed earlier than usual, just after Mac got home."

"Then I think the logical explanation is that there's something wrong with the handle itself. I'll replace it soon. Carry on. You're doing a great job."

She looked slightly mollified as she picked up a cardboard milk box that was sitting just inside the doors and held it out to him. "While you're here, could you tell me what I should do with this?"

"What is it?"

"Just some things I thought were important enough to save," she said, still holding the box out. He didn't know why he was reluctant to take it. "They're the only things I've found so far that haven't been junk paper."

He looked in the box and saw that it contained a cheap-looking framed print of an abandoned fishing boat on a beach, a necklace with the word "Duncan" written in bent-wire cursive, and a glass vase he immediately recognized as the one he'd given to Lizbeth, full of cheap grocery-store flowers, for her fortieth birthday. That she'd kept it was no surprise, it was the guilt he felt for the pitiful gesture it had been, so last-minute, so late in the day, and how absolutely thrilled she'd been to get it.

"No one wants these things," Frasier said, more brusquely than he intended.

"Not even *Lucy*?"

"The only person who wants something in here is Roscoe. And he's looking for something that probably doesn't exist."

"But it doesn't feel right, throwing these things away," she said.

There it was again. That confusing sadness. "All right. Use your best judgment, and Oliver can make the final decision."

"Who is Oliver?" she said as she set the box down.

He thought of the brown envelope in his office. "Her son."

"She has *a son*?"

"He hasn't been home in years."

"Is he coming home now?"

"I seriously doubt it. Carry on." He walked back to his office before she could ask any more questions. The dellawisps had gathered in front of his door, hopping around, waiting for him. When he entered, old Otis tried to hop inside with him.

"Not now, Otis," he said, and Otis was very vocal about his displeasure as Frasier closed the door on him.

Lizbeth was hovering near his filing cabinets. She'd always wanted to go through them. She'd wanted to know everything about everyone who lived here. If he hadn't locked his door every night before going home, he felt sure she would have come in and taken all the resident files and put them in her boxes.

He sat down at his desk and stared at the envelope, stroking his long, wiry beard. He had pulled some strings to get the information he needed quickly. He knew a PI in Charleston he used to go to school with on the island. Like many boys here at the time, Robert could have easily gone down a criminal path. He was retired from the police force and now used his uncanny snooping skills to catch cheating husbands instead. He and Frasier would get together for beers every once in a while. They would talk about rough boys they had grown up with, most of them long gone now, and in silences they would exchange looks of the same guilty relief that they'd survived relatively unscathed.

Frasier reached for the envelope. He tore it open and pulled out a single piece of paper.

The only thing written on it was ten numbers.

He grabbed his phone and dialed before he lost his nerve.

NORRIE BEACH, CALIFORNIA

Oliver awoke suddenly and tried to puzzle out the reason why.

A nightmare? A muscle cramp?

Whatever the reason, he was wide awake now. He slowly extricated himself from Garland, who had wrapped herself around him in her sleep like a vine. He went to her window and opened it and took some deep breaths. The early-morning air was strangely sweet. The scent reminded him of the brugmansia trees that were probably blooming now on Mallow Island. It made him stagger back. He went directly to her shower and stayed there for half an hour, trying to wash away the smell.

He never should have agreed to this, a week with Garland at her father's house in quaint, moneyed Norrie Beach. Several of Garland's friends were here, too, but they didn't have to worry about finding a place to stay now that they were out of their dorm rooms. They already had apartments in cities where jobs were waiting for them. And if by some chance those plans fell through, they could always go home. They had a soft place to land. Oliver didn't have that luxury, yet here he was pretending he didn't have a care in the world. He'd had several interviews before graduation, even one good offer in San Diego, but Garland told him her dad was going to give him that job at the Rondo, so he would definitely be moving to Norrie Beach. He should be looking for a place to live right now, but Garland had the whole week planned down to the hour. He had no idea what he was going to do when the week was up. Sleep in his car, probably.

But it would be worth it. He wanted that job at the Rondo more than he wanted anything.

He told himself it was because it had won so many awards for its environmentally friendly practices. Who with a major in hotel management and a minor in environmental science wouldn't want the Norrie Beach Rondo? He didn't want to believe it had anything to do with the fact that the resort looked like something from the Old South—white columns, big porches, fat trees. He didn't want to believe it had anything whatsoever to do with Mallow Island.

Until he'd set eyes on the Rondo, nothing about this coast had ever reminded him of home. That was the very reason he'd chosen to come here. He and his mother had been like opposite ends of a magnet, repelling each other. The force of her had pushed him so far away only the Pacific Ocean had stopped him. The school therapist he'd seen his freshman year in college when he'd been struggling to find his footing told him to be prepared for triggers eventually. He could get away from home physically, but getting away from it emotionally would be harder.

Later that morning, bleary from lack of sleep, Oliver stood at the brunch table, looking things over. Garland had given the housekeeper specific instructions on what should be served. For whatever reason, this week was very, very important to her. He took a *pain aux raisins* and a cup of coffee and walked through the open French doors with their white curtains flapping in the chlorinated breeze.

They were all there by the pool—Garland, her best friend Heather One, her second-best friend Heather Two, her gay male best friend Roy, and her straight male best friend Cooper. This was how she referred to them, like they were all dolls in her dollhouse. They were thin and tan and draped on lounge chairs like silk, their hangovers from last night barely having time to register with the mimosas now slipping down their throats.

"Did you change your perfume?" Oliver asked Garland as he sat beside her.

"No," Garland said, putting her wrist to her nose. She had dark red hair, wide-set eyes, and a small nose that didn't quite fit her face. According to Heather Two, who he suspected didn't even like Garland despite being her second-best friend, she'd had a nose job when she was seventeen. "Why? Don't you like my perfume?"

"Yes. No. I mean, of course I like it," he said quickly, knowing he couldn't afford to get on her bad side. The Rondo was at stake. Every single thing he owned was stuffed in his car, which was parked in Garland's garage right next to her father's Range Rover, the keys to which her father had hidden too well for Garland to find. She'd lost her license two years ago. "I just thought I smelled something different earlier."

"I think you smell wonderful," Cooper said with a wink from his lounge chair to the left of her.

"That's because you're always sniffing around her," Roy said in his imperious way. His face was to the sun and he barely moved his lips.

Cooper barked like a dog.

Garland laughed and threw a lounge pillow at him. "Animal."

"Have you heard from your dad?" Oliver asked.

Garland rolled her eyes and adjusted the tiny triangles of her green bikini a little farther apart, which drew Cooper's attention to her breasts immediately. Oliver wondered if he should feel more concerned by Garland's flirting with Cooper, the way her eyes would slide to him when she thought no one was looking. Did Oliver even have the right to feel jealous? He and Garland were sharing a bed (something of a surprise when she'd shown him to her room when he'd arrived yesterday) but not yet sleeping together (again, a surprise, as she was fairly aggressive and obviously used to getting what she wanted). "No," she said. "Thank God."

He had only met Garland two months ago, when he'd driven to Norrie Beach for that interview at the Rondo. He'd thought it had gone well, despite nearly sweating through his only suit. Garland had approached him in the lobby afterward, introducing herself as the owner's daughter. She had invited Oliver to lunch, and then she'd stuck like glue to him, her reasons still a mystery. She had visited him several times before he graduated, sneaking into his dorm at his tiny college near Ridgecrest, the one he'd chosen based solely on the fact that it had been the only one he'd applied to on this coast that had offered him a full scholarship. Sometimes she'd want to make out, but mostly she'd wanted to wax on about her two years at UCLA before she'd flunked out. She would take dozens of selfies of them together to send to her dollhouse friends, wanting them to believe, for whatever reason, that she and Oliver were closer than they really were. So Oliver now found himself in the untenable position of not knowing how to maintain her interest, because he didn't know where it was coming from. She held the Rondo in front of him like a carrot.

"But you said your dad was coming home soon?" Oliver asked.

"Who knows?" Garland shrugged. "The stepmonster will probably keep him at sea for weeks just to spite me."

"We should join them! They're sailing near Greece, right?" Heather One said, sitting up in her lounge chair excitedly. Oliver tensed. Oh, God. He didn't have the money for an overseas trip. He didn't even have a passport. Until he'd come to California, he hadn't traveled anywhere except that one time he'd driven Roscoe Avanger to a resort in Palm Beach, Florida, where Roscoe was giving a keynote speech. Roscoe had broken his foot and had asked Oliver to take him. It was the first time Oliver, then sixteen, had ever stayed in a hotel. It had changed his life, knowing that places like that existed, great bastions of comfort and cleanliness. He hadn't wanted to leave, to go back to his mother's madness.

"Uh, *no*," Garland said. "I get quite enough of the stepmonster at home, thank you very much. She doesn't even know she's doing me a favor."

"Yeah, she's such a bitch," Heather Two said, seeing her chance to move up in the pecking order. Heather One blushed with embarrassment.

Garland made no secret of her hatred for her stepmother, Jade. They were constantly at war over Garland's father's attention. From what Oliver could gather, Garland's father played them against each other, and used their mutual resentment to get what he wanted. Garland wanted people to believe she was like her mother, a gentle little East Coast socialite who had died when Garland was ten. But Oliver knew her hotelier father by reputation, and he thought Garland definitely favored him. Not that Oliver would say as much to her. He tried to say as little as possible. Just last night at a trendy, monumentally expensive restaurant in Norrie Beach called Symbiotic, Garland had laughed at him while they were all having a boozy kickoff to their week together. "My quiet, *gorgeous* little Oliver," she'd said. "Why don't you say more with that accent? All you do is watch, watch, watch, like you're taking notes."

Cooper had laughed and made a toast to him in a mock–Southern belle accent. "To gorgeous *little* Oliver." Later, Cooper had picked up the tab for all the booze, but not the food, and Oliver had had to surreptitiously check his debit card balance on his phone to see how much was left from his college job as a front desk clerk at Motel 6. A job he'd quit to come here.

Heather Two had nudged him under the table and whispered, "Don't worry. My treat." And that, if anything, had made Oliver feel worse.

"Whose phone is that?" Garland asked as everyone by the pool reached for their devices at once. "Is it mine?"

"No, it's mine," Oliver said, setting aside his coffee and pastry and taking his ringing phone out of his shorts pocket. He'd been waiting to hear from the Rondo for weeks, checking the website several times a day to see if the environmental manager's position was still listed. When he looked at the screen, he recognized the area code, but not the number. He debated whether or not to answer. He pressed Accept and put the phone to his ear, not saying anything in case it was her. He hadn't heard a word from his mother in four years, when he'd changed his number and deleted his contacts.

"Oliver?" the voice on the other end said. "Oliver? This is Frasier," he added unnecessarily, because Oliver had recognized his old friend's voice right away.

"Frasier. Hello." He didn't ask how he'd gotten this number. Frasier had his ways.

"Son, there's no easy way to tell you this. Lizbeth has died. I'm sorry."

Oliver stilled. The smile that had started to form from hearing a familiar voice faded. He stared straight ahead at the diamonds of morning sunlight dancing on the blue surface of the pool. The others were unabashedly listening. He tried not to show his shock, tried not to show anything at all.

"Oliver?" Frasier asked at his silence.

"Yes, I'm here." He cleared his throat. "How?"

"It looks like she fell off a stepladder and a bookcase landed on her."

It was always going to end this way, with her world falling down around her. Oliver hadn't been able to save her, and he hadn't been able to make her get help, no matter how hard he'd tried. He'd just been a child, so much smaller than the responsibility he'd felt. "Do you need me for anything?" he asked.

"No. But there's the matter of the condo. Not the contents, of course. She always wanted that to go to Roscoe, lucky sod," Frasier said. "It's being cleaned out as we speak."

"I don't want anything," he said.

"You want to sell?"

He hesitated, trying to hold on to the thread of the conversation. "Sell what?"

"The condo."

"It was hers? I thought . . ." He thought the great Roscoe Avanger was just letting her live there, free of charge, because she worked for him and he felt sorry for her and Oliver.

"It was in her name," Frasier said. "She owned it. It's yours now. Do you want to sell?"

"Wh . . . Yes."

"Okay. I'll be in touch. Give me an address where I can reach you."

"I'll text you," Oliver said, not wanting Frasier to know he didn't have a permanent address, that he felt in such dire straits. He was supposed to be thriving away from Mallow Island. "Is this your cell number?"

"Yes. Are you all right, son?"

"I said goodbye a long time ago."

"I know you did." Frasier paused. "Are you okay out there in California? Are you still in school?"

"Just graduated. Look, I have to go."

"Right. I'm sorry, Oliver."

Oliver hung up, and then he texted Frasier Garland's address. He'd ask her to forward anything to him when he got his own place.

"Who was that?" Garland finally asked when it became clear Oliver wasn't going to explain the call.

"An old friend of my mother's from home," Oliver said, putting the phone back in his pocket and picking up his cup of coffee, but not taking a sip. His hand was shaking slightly. "He just found out I graduated."

"My sweet Southern boy from Mallow Island," Garland said. "Take me there one day."

Oliver didn't respond.

"Oliver's mother died when he was ten, just like mine," Garland told the others. He'd never said that. She'd just assumed it, creating her own narrative from what little Oliver had told her. He'd never talked about his mother to anyone but his school therapist. And only Frasier ever knew how bad it was, living with her.

While their voices floated around him, Oliver stared at the pool water, his eyes behind his sunglasses watering because the sun was so bright.

No other reason, he told himself.

No other reason at all.

Chapter Eight

Charlotte had gone to bed intending to get up first thing in the morning to look for new places on the island to do her henna. Yet here she was, still in bed, staring at those damn witch balls so long that her eyes felt gritty.

Zoey's music suddenly fired up and Charlotte blinked out of her stupor. Time to get rolling. She was just wasting time. She got out of bed and found some clothes, and then she grabbed her backpack and walked to her blue scooter in the living room. She always kept it inside at night for fear of how easy it would be to steal, thus robbing her of her only mode of transportation. Sometimes she truly longed for a car, but this had been the crazy mode of transportation teenaged Charlotte had dreamed about. She was about to push up the kickstand, but stopped.

She really, really didn't want to do this.

Not yet. Not today.

She set her backpack down and followed the thumping bass next door instead. She knocked on the doorframe and Zoey looked up from a box she was going through.

"Hi. Want some company?" Charlotte asked, because *I want some company* was so much harder for her to say.

"Of course! Come in," Zoey said. "Lizbeth's door was unlocked again this morning. You didn't hear anything again last night, did you?"

"No." Charlotte stepped forward to take a seat on an orange crate beside her.

"I think it's Lucy. And if it is her, then why?"

"Don't worry about Lucy. She's harmless."

Zoey looked dubious. "But how do you know? How does anyone know? No one ever sees her. Oh! You'll never guess what Frasier just told me. Lizbeth has *a son*."

"Huh. I didn't know that." She had trouble imagining Lizbeth as a mother, though she didn't know why. Women who had no business being mothers had children all the time. Look at her own mother.

"Frasier said he's not coming home."

"Some people are happier leaving the past in the past," Charlotte said, reaching out and pulling a box to her. She lifted the flaps and looked inside. "So hidden in all this paper is supposedly a story?"

"That's what Frasier says. Want to go digging for treasure with me?" Zoey asked.

Charlotte hesitated. She knew, deep down, that she wasn't going to find another place for her henna on the island. *The* place for arts was the Sugar Warehouse. The only place with a higher tourist draw was Trade Street, and its allure was primarily the sweet shops, bakeries, and restaurants occupying the old buildings where the island's marshmallow candy was once sold. She wouldn't have to try very hard to get a waitstaff job, but that was a last resort. So she was going to have to look for space off the island. And if she had to leave the island for work, she might as well move to another city on the list in the diary and spare herself a commute. It was a slippery slope, all leading to one place.

Someplace that wasn't here.

She was feeling emotionally spent, and when that happened the real her, the one who craved permanence and connections and simply *being still*, started peeking through the cracks. She hated the thought of leaving hot, sweet Mallow Island. She'd been here for over two years—longer than she'd spent anywhere since leaving the camp in Vermont—and she felt settled here, if that was indeed what this feeling was.

Just for today, she would allow herself not to think about moving again. She would sit here with her earnest young neighbor and go through boxes.

She would think about leaving tomorrow.

"Okay, I'm in," Charlotte said, and grabbed a pair of rubber gloves and a mask.

She started out thinking that each box was going to contain something fascinating but, other than the odd trinket, it turned out to be the same old thing. Just useless paper. Nothing that looked like a Roscoe Avanger story. Zoey said every piece had to be handled in case the story was actually story ideas written on random bits of paper, but how anything one of America's most celebrated authors wanted wound up in a box in Lizbeth Lime's condo, Charlotte wasn't sure. This was a place you put something you wanted to lose, not find. After a while, Charlotte would groan dramatically when she opened a box only to find decades-old flyers for yard sales and lost pets that Lizbeth had obviously ripped off telephone poles and collected.

But Zoey was fascinated with it all. She would laugh when she came across boxes of Lillian Vernon and Harriet Carter catalogs from the 1990s, or stained menus that looked like they'd been salvaged from Trade Street restaurant dumpsters. And when she found a box of Lizbeth's diaries written in her teens and twenties, it was like she'd found a vein of gemstones. Charlotte thought it was the most interesting thing by far to be uncovered and wanted to read them, but Zoey respectfully set them aside in the box she had reserved for Lizbeth's son, even though she said he wasn't coming home and hadn't asked for anything to be saved.

A few hours later, after opening the third box in a row of junk mail addressed to at least seven different past residents of the Dellawisp, most of whom had once lived in Charlotte's condo, Charlotte shook her head and said, "I need a break. How about you?" Zoey, deeply absorbed in going through a box of restraining orders taken out on Lizbeth by the same businesses on Trade Street whose dumpsters she'd raided, didn't respond. Charlotte nudged her. "You've been listening to the same song on repeat for hours."

"Oh, sorry." She peeled off her gloves and turned off the music, a song by the National about starting a war.

Charlotte got up and stretched, her shoulders feeling a familiar ache, one she usually felt after being hunched over for hours in marathon back-to-back henna appointments during busy summer months. "It's late. We should have lunch."

"Together?" Zoey said, surprised.

Charlotte laughed. "Yes, together."

"I have some things I bought at the corner market. Do you want me to bring them down?"

"Sure."

Zoey darted out, as if afraid Charlotte might change her mind.

While Zoey ran up to her studio, Charlotte moved their orange crates outside to Lizbeth's patio, then turned a box upside down for a table.

She was cleaning her hands with some wipes when Zoey came back down with a shopping bag. She stopped by Charlotte's patio and pointed to the table and chairs there. "Can we sit here?" she asked.

Charlotte had purchased the patio set at the local Goodwill when she first moved in, thinking of afternoons like this, softly fragranced with salt air and the sweet scent of the brugmansia blooms, exactly the kind of Southern coastal summers you read about in novels. She should have noticed the big clue that none of the other residents had patio furniture. She was about to shoot down Zoey's idea, but stopped herself. "I was going to say that we can't because Lizbeth will come out and yell at us for making noise if we sit here," she said, walking over. "It's going to take some time to get used to actually enjoying my patio."

"She must have been lonely," Zoey said as she and Charlotte sat down, "with only those boxes for company."

"I suspect her boxes made her happier than people did."

Zoey set a loaf of white bread, a large bag of Lay's potato chips, and two bright pink plates on the table with a *ta-da* gesture. Charlotte smiled at her with something that felt almost like fondness. Zoey's short dark hair was standing up in spikes, and Charlotte wanted to reach over and smooth it down.

"You know, the corner market is mainly for tourists," Charlotte told her. "It's probably the most expensive place in town to buy groceries. There's a regular supermarket toward the center of the island, where most locals live."

"I'm limited to places I can walk right now. I don't mind," Zoey said. "As soon as my car gets here I'll drive around." She took a slice of bread and put it on her plate. She piled a small mountain of potato chips on it and placed another slice of bread on top. Then she flattened the sandwich with her hand, the chips shattering with a satisfying crunch. In response to Charlotte's curious look, she explained, "Potato chip sandwiches remind me of my mom."

Ah. That, Charlotte understood. Food memory was one of the few profoundly good things she brought with her from her own childhood. Sometimes Charlotte would still have chocolate milk over hot rice, something Charlotte and Pepper had eaten when they'd crept hungrily into the camp kitchen after dark during one of Minister McCauley's forced fasts. She could still remember how good it had tasted, like sweet soup.

Zoey obviously misinterpreted her pondering silence, because she said, "I don't really know how to cook. I mean, I know I'll figure it out, but there's just so much to think about. I'm always writing something down. You know what I realized this morning? I don't know where to get my hair cut here. I'm going to have to find a salon. I'm glad my condo was furnished. Because, how do you buy a couch? I have no idea. This grown-up thing isn't for sissies."

Truer words had never been spoken. Charlotte began to assemble her own sandwich. "What are you going to do when Lizbeth's condo is finished? Before school starts, I mean. Living here isn't cheap."

Zoey shrugged. "I inherited some money from my mom, along with her condo here. She died when I was seven. The money she got in the divorce settlement from my dad was held in trust until I turned eighteen last summer. It was enough for a car and for college, and a tiny income for a few years if I wanted to live on it. But I don't. I want to do something, I just don't know what." She looked down at her sandwich, then she looked back up at Charlotte with those dark eyes, obviously desperate for some compass. "Did you always know what you wanted to do? Where you wanted to be?"

Charlotte didn't think her life was a compass anyone should follow, but she answered honestly, "I was about twelve when I decided I wanted to travel and do henna. I went out on my own when I was sixteen. I've lived all over." She flattened her sandwich the way Zoey had done.

"What are you going to do now that you lost your job?" Zoey asked.

The question of the day. "I don't know. It's not going to be easy to find another space to do henna here, so I guess I'll have to find something else until I figure out my next steps." She took a bite of her sandwich, then put her hand over her mouth and said, "This isn't bad."

Zoey looked inordinately pleased that someone other than her liked something so odd, as if that kind of camaraderie, that sameness, was unfamiliar to her.

"So where is your car?" Charlotte asked while she chewed.

"A car-moving service is driving it here. I didn't like the idea of driving all the way from Oklahoma by myself."

"What about your dad? Didn't he want to come with you to help get you settled?"

Something, some small emotion, flittered across Zoey's face. She shook her head.

The white bread was sticking to the roof of Charlotte's mouth, so she got up and said, "I'm going to get a drink. Do you want a Coke?"

"Yes, thanks."

When she walked back outside with a beer for her and a Coke for Zoey, she found Zoey staring at Mac's door across the garden.

"Did I tell you I looked up the website for the restaurant where he works? Popcorn. Have you heard of it?"

"It's in the Mallow Island Resort Hotel. It's pretty famous around here," Charlotte said, handing Zoey the Coke and taking a seat.

"It's called Popcorn because they specialize in things made with cornmeal. The website calls it 'Gourmet Retro Southern Fusion.' He's *executive* chef."

Charlotte smiled. "You're a little obsessed."

"I know," Zoey said gamely. "But you guys are all I've got. He's really nice. I knew he would be."

Charlotte took a sip from the brown bottle of local marshmallow beer she'd discovered when she'd first moved to Mallow Island. She'd bought some the evening she and Benny spent drinking, and there were precious few bottles left. She was trying to savor her last sips, but it tasted more bitter than she remembered, probably because it made her think of her stolen money. She set the bottle on the table and started peeling off the label.

"*Charlotte,*" Zoey whispered a few moments later.

Charlotte looked over to her. Zoey was staring straight ahead.

"*Charlotte,*" she said again.

"Why are you whispering?"

"*Look,*" Zoey said, gesturing with her eyes.

Mac had opened his patio doors and was backing out like he always did, as if walking backward upon leaving was his own superstition. Either that, or he was trying to stop something from coming out after him, like a pet. That was unlikely. It was part of the legal agreement. Absolutely no pets. Not even birds. Roscoe Avanger didn't want anything endangering his precious bird population in the garden.

He was wearing black-and-white-checked pants and a white

chef's coat. He also had on those funny-looking clogs that kitchen staff often wore. In order to get by over the years, Charlotte had spent a fair amount of time waitressing and bartending. It paid the bills when her henna didn't support her, but she avoided it unless there was no other option. Teenaged Charlotte hadn't wanted to work in restaurants when she grew up, not after all that time at the camp where the kids were expected to be on dining room duty, serving the elders before they got to eat whatever was left over. Had it not been for school-supplied breakfasts and lunches, not a single kid at the camp would have ever had a full meal.

When Mac turned around after closing his doors, they saw that he was carrying a white platter. He walked toward them, his beautiful red hair and neat red beard catching glints of sunlight and making him seem effervescent, like ginger ale.

"Wait," Zoey said, reaching out to clutch Charlotte's arm. "Is he bringing us *food*?" She was acting like they were peasants being visited by a charitable prince. Charlotte had to laugh.

Mac hunched over the platter as he walked across the garden, protecting the food from the birds, who had flown from their hiding places in the brugmansia trees and were now swarming around him, chirping loudly.

"Hi, Mac," Zoey said when Mac stepped onto the patio. "You know Charlotte, right?"

Mac nodded. "We've waved and said hi over the years, but Lizbeth didn't exactly make it easy to stop and chat." The deep burr of his speech, like Frasier's, was distinctly Mallow Island, a local accent that always sounded to Charlotte like they were all just getting to the good part of a story.

"Well, Zoey has more than made up for that," Charlotte said. "I know a lot about you just from her. In fact, the only person she talks about more is Lucy."

"That's because I've never seen her," Zoey said plaintively. "It's like she only comes out when she thinks we're all asleep."

"Zoey believes someone is breaking into Lizbeth's condo at night," Charlotte explained to Mac.

"Why would someone do that?" he asked.

"Good question," they both said at the same time.

Mac regarded them curiously, but seemed at a loss as to how to respond. "Well, I just wanted to bring you something on my way out. Sort of a welcome gift. Rosemary cornmeal doughnuts with a lemon glaze, and cornbread tartlets with ricotta and heirloom tomatoes."

He set the platter on the table, and Charlotte and Zoey leaned forward to stare. The tartlets were small and perfectly round, with scalloped edges like the hems of Sunday dresses. Purple-tinged tomatoes were fanned on top, obviously cut by someone with seriously good knife skills. The doughnuts appeared to still be warm from the oven, the glaze dripping off them onto the platter. The green scent of rosemary and the sharp scent of lemon made Charlotte picture a long, sandy road. There was an old woman cooking in a summer kitchen somewhere down that road. *Home.* Charlotte blinked and the image was gone.

She turned to Zoey. "Puts our potato chip sandwiches to shame, doesn't it?"

"I'll never be able to cook like this," Zoey said, shaking her head.

"Ditto. So this is just something you whipped up on your way out?" Charlotte said, looking up at Mac with a smile.

"Yes," he replied.

She'd meant it as a joke, but he'd answered her sincerely, and she realized with embarrassment that he really *did* just whip this up. "Well, it smells amazing."

"Hey, Mac, do you have an opening at your restaurant?" Zoey asked. "Charlotte needs a job while she looks for another place to do her henna."

He looked as if something finally made sense to him. "I've always wanted to ask you what that was," he said, pointing to her bare legs. She watched as a blush crept up his neck into his beard. "I mean, it's beautiful work."

"Thanks. Most of it's fading now." She absently rubbed her thighs, where for months last winter she'd hidden Asher's initials in her practice work, hoping he would notice that she wanted him so much that he was etched on her very skin. Long ago, Charlotte and Pepper had read in the henna book they'd checked out of the library about how, in some Hindu weddings, a bride would have her groom's initials hidden in her henna for him to find on their wedding night. As girls, they'd been captivated by the thought of something so romantic and exotic and faraway. But if Asher had ever noticed his initials as they'd made love, he'd never said a thing.

"Are you really looking for a job?" Mac asked.

"Not a restaurant job, no. I had a booth in the Sugar Warehouse but had to leave because of the rent increase. I'll find something to get by. No worries."

He hesitated at the silence that followed; then he turned and left without another word.

"Bye, Mac! See, what did I tell you?" Zoey said as she took a doughnut. Charlotte did the same. As soon as she bit into it the lemon flavor burst in her mouth, immediately sweetened by the rosemary. The cornmeal didn't make the doughnut heavy or gritty,

but gave it a light earthiness. It was so perfect in its lack of preten-
sion, obviously designed not to impress but to comfort, to extend to
the eater a genuine piece of affection.

"You're right. Nice," she said, not entirely convinced that was a
good thing. Nice, in her experience, meant one of two things: It was
either hiding something darker just beneath the surface, or it made
you lower your defenses and believe that there was more of it in the
world than there actually was, which always led to disappointment.

Either way, she wasn't falling for it.

Chapter Nine

Zoey believed in things other people never would. She'd accepted that a long time ago. If there was one thing Pigeon had taught her over the years, it was that *invisible* did not always mean *imaginary*.

So when she found Lizbeth's door unlocked again for the fourth time in a row the next morning, she didn't bother telling Frasier or Charlotte. Nothing was taken, or even moved, as far as she could tell. But something was going on, and just because she was the only one who believed Lucy was behind it didn't mean that Lucy *wasn't* behind it.

Besides, the only other explanation was that someone was breaking in to actually sleep in here.

And that was even more improbable than an invisible bird.

Zoey stood in Lizbeth's dark bedroom doorway, adjusting her face mask and snapping her rubber gloves farther up her forearms. Enough boxes had been cleared in the living room that she thought she could safely enter the bedroom, which she was excited about despite the unwashed smell that emanated strongly from it. This was obviously the place Lizbeth had spent most of her time, which meant it was also likely to be where she kept what was most important to her. Roscoe Avanger's story? Evidence of her son, Oliver, having lived here? Whatever Lucy might be looking for? The possibilities were endless.

"Okay, I'm going in," she said to Charlotte.

"Good luck. Send me a postcard," Charlotte said, scrolling through the music on Zoey's phone before she got started on the boxes along the far wall near the galley kitchen. When Charlotte had shown up again this morning looking ready to work in her shorts, red cowboy boots, and a T-shirt that read MALLOW ISLAND BREWERY: DRINK YOUR SWEETS, Zoey had resisted the urge to greet her with a hug. She got the impression that Charlotte didn't like touching much. She was so guarded that Zoey would study her out of the corner of her eye so as not to spook her with too much interest. She wanted to know her story. She wished she could tell Charlotte her own story. But she'd only ever told her father about Pigeon, and he hadn't believed her. It was an odd feeling, when she really thought about it, not having anyone in the world who knew everything about you and loved you anyway.

Pigeon gave an angry coo from outside.

Well, no one she could see, anyway.

Her bird was seriously displeased about this job, but Zoey didn't care. She was still mad about Pigeon breaking her housewarming gift from Charlotte two days ago. She'd never before been given an actual, physical thing that said, *I'm glad you're here.* Charlotte had given Zoey another witch ball yesterday afternoon after they'd finished for the day, this time inviting her over to choose from the dozens hanging from her bedroom ceiling, which was the most magical thing Zoey had ever seen. She could have spent all night just lying on the floor, staring at them. She'd chosen a green one, which was now safely tucked in one of her dresser drawers because Pigeon had fixated on it when Zoey had taken it up to her studio. She obviously wanted to punish Zoey for as long as this job lasted.

Pigeon's biggest issue seemed to be that there was no place for her to perch in Lizbeth's place. The few times she'd tried, she'd brought down a veritable snowstorm of papers. So she spent her days on the patio, cooing with irritation and peevishly knocking over cleaning supplies, once causing Charlotte to say, "There's a lot of wind out there." The faster Zoey got done, the happier Pigeon would be. Pigeon had reacted the same way when Zoey had gotten her part-time job at Kello's used bookstore. Pigeon knew Zoey didn't need the money. Not that Kello, an old former academic turned Deadhead, paid her very much. More often than not, she'd come home with boxes of books instead of a paycheck. But that job, like this one, wasn't about money. What exactly Pigeon expected her to do with her time when she wasn't in school, especially after her best friend Ingrid moved away, had always been a mystery. Sometimes she seemed offended that Zoey didn't think her invisible presence was enough.

Zoey would always be glad Pigeon had come into her life after her mother had died, one day just swooping into her bedroom like a dream. For a long time, Pigeon's love was the only love Zoey had felt. At first she hadn't realized that no one else could sense Pigeon, and she'd talked endlessly about her new pet bird to her father. She had wanted to spend all her time with him after her mother's death, to hug him, to sit on his lap, to tell him stories about Pigeon. He would put up with it for a few minutes, then would push her away. He hadn't wanted her there, but she'd had nowhere else to go. Finding her another place to live had never been an option. What his family thought of him had always been too important to him. They were a well-to-do clan of Oklahoma judges and politicians, and Alrick had been something of a black sheep all his life, with a long list of failed businesses to his name. He'd found some success later in life with an import-export company in Charleston, where he'd met Zoey's mother at a gentleman's club. A few years later, beaming with success, he'd sold the business for a lot of money and moved back to Tulsa with his very young, beautiful bride and new baby. But whatever approval he'd hoped he would finally get from his brothers and sisters never came. Not with volatile Paloma there, always stirring the pot.

Pigeon had been overbearing from the start, but it had always been a welcome balance to her father's disinterest, and Zoey had never before wished for a separate existence from her. But something had shifted, just slightly, in her relationship with her bird since she'd arrived on Mallow Island. Coming here was the last break from the only world she'd ever known, and only Pigeon was left. She was a childhood relic like a stuffed animal or a security blanket, and Zoey didn't want to say goodbye to her. Where would she go? Would she ever mean as much to someone else as she did to Zoey? But nor did Zoey know how to fit her into this life she had to forge on her own.

Listening to Pigeon continue to fuss outside that morning, Zoey reached inside Lizbeth's bedroom and groped for a switch. When she found it, the dim overhead flicked on and illuminated the expected towers of boxes, but also a dirty nest of a bed, the sheets of which hadn't been washed in so long they formed stiff peaks, like the crests of waves frozen in midcrash. There was also a rickety bamboo desk supporting a humming computer and an old monitor roughly the size of a compact car. A large freestanding bookcase had fallen over in the middle of the room and had spilled books everywhere.

"I finally found some furniture!" She stepped inside and picked up one of the books. It was a copy of *Sweet Mallow*. She looked at it, then at the massive overturned bookcase, and it suddenly occurred to her. "Charlotte, I think I found where it happened."

"Where what happened?"

"Where Lizbeth died."

Charlotte immediately appeared at her side at the same time Pigeon zoomed in, her wings making a frantic whooshing sound.

Zoey pointed. "Frasier said a bookcase landed on her."

Charlotte paused for a few moments before taking action. "Right. We need to get all these books out first. Then we can scoot the bookcase to the living room for Frasier to deal with." She stomped into the bedroom, kicking some books with her boots. "He should have at least cleaned this part up. He should have *warned* you."

The outburst startled Zoey. She realized Charlotte must think that this discovery had upset her. "Hey, Charlotte, I'm okay. Really." Charlotte didn't look convinced. "Are *you* okay?"

"Yes. Yes, of course I am," Charlotte said, not looking at her as she started gathering books.

Zoey joined her and soon discovered that it was all the *same* book—hundreds and hundreds of copies of *Sweet Mallow*. She recognized them from her time at Kello's. Some had the original retro artwork cover, some had the cover of the movie poster, and others had the more modern cover that showed a photo of the back of a young African American man in a World War I army uniform, his head bowed, with an old man's hand resting gently on his shoulder as if to comfort him. All the copies were worn and some were wavy like they'd been dropped in water, but every single one of them had the same four specific passages highlighted, like Lizbeth had wanted to make sure the words were all in the same place:

History is known for sugar-coating. Sometimes it's the only thing that can make it palatable. So it can come as no surprise that even on Mallow Island, South Carolina, the past is not as sweet as the name suggests.

Second chances are not to be wasted. It is one of the most valuable lessons we can learn in life.

Stories aren't fiction. Stories are fabric. They're the white sheets we drape over our ghosts so we can see them.

How odd that pretending to be someone else has made me happier than I was when I was just being myself. It's almost as if, once I got over the guilt of loving my future more than I loved my past, my old life dropped away and became make-believe, and my present life became my second birth.

A lot of the books that had come through Kello's were marked the same way, and Zoey had always been fascinated by what spoke to other readers. Some customers didn't like when books were marked, like it was a crime against literature. But Zoey thought it was a far greater crime to forget passages like this, so beautiful they made you breathless.

Out of everything so far, the books were the hardest things for her to throw out of Lizbeth's condo. But they were all in such bad shape that they had to go into the recycling dumpster. Even Kello, with his questionable standards on what was sellable, wouldn't have taken them. Zoey did save one, the most cared-for one, which had been signed by Roscoe Avanger himself:

To Elizabeth Lime, Best Wishes, Roscoe Avanger.

He'd misspelled her name, but Zoey decided to keep it for Oliver.

After their last trip to the dumpster with the books, Charlotte said, "I don't mind tackling the bedroom if you want to stay out here in the living room."

It was obviously the last thing Charlotte wanted to do, so Zoey said, "That's okay. I'm curious. We keep all our best secrets in our bedrooms, don't we?"

"That we do." Charlotte sat down and opened another box. "Well, this is new," she said, tilting the box so Zoey could see. "Used birthday party hats. Think Roscoe Avanger has something written on them?"

Zoey smiled. Maybe it *should* have affected her more, seeing where Lizbeth died. But, curiosity aside, she thought there was a strange detachment in going through someone's personal belongings when she hadn't known them in life. It was like Lizbeth Lime wasn't even real, that she was just a story.

This was all just one big story.

Zoey tried to imagine what it would have been like if her own mother had left this much behind. When her mother and father had separated, Paloma had put all her belongings into a storage unit. She'd then, according to Alrick, proceeded to bilk him out of everything she could in the divorce. After she'd died Alrick claimed he hadn't known about the storage unit until it was too late, and all of Paloma's abandoned belongings had been sold at auction to strangers. Zoey could remember living in a fancy hotel room with her mother during the time her mother and father had been fighting over the divorce settlement. Paloma would often laugh and tell Zoey what a wonderful time they were going to have when they moved back to Mallow Island. She had signed the divorce papers the day she'd died. She had left seven-year-old Zoey in the hotel room, paying a housekeeper to check in on her, while she'd gone out for drinks to celebrate with her lawyer, a man Zoey remembered had often spent the night with Paloma. The policeman who had taken Zoey to her father after the car accident had packed a bag of Zoey's clothing. Zoey had later found a few of her mother's things mistakenly tangled in her own—a pair of lavender-colored leather gloves, a twisted and knotted gold bracelet, and a tube of saucy red lipstick, the color of which was called Bye Bye Birdie. The policeman had also placed in the bag a photo of her mother he'd obviously found somewhere in the hotel room, probably because he thought Zoey might want to have it with her in the hard days and months to come. It was a kindness she would always be grateful for, because otherwise Zoey would hardly remember what her mother had looked like.

About an hour later, Zoey was going through old fan mail addressed to Roscoe Avanger, which Lizbeth had obviously read so many times that the oil from her fingertips had made the pages as thin as rice paper. She looked up suddenly when Pigeon, who hadn't left the room since Zoey had discovered the bookcase, hopped across Lizbeth's desk and knocked over a box of flyers for a decades-old Girl Scout cookie sale.

"Pigeon!" she said angrily. "Go back outside and make some new friends!"

"What?" Charlotte said from the living room.

"Nothing," Zoey called back.

She set about picking up the flyers, and that's when she found it.

She thought it was an old bill at first, which stood out because she'd realized by this point that the only method to Lizbeth's madness was that each of her boxes contained similar things.

But it wasn't an old bill.

She hurried out to show Charlotte, all sorts of explanations playing around in her head. "I found a life insurance policy."

"Did she collect those, too?"

"No, it's the only one. What if *this* is what Lucy's looking for?" she said as she walked out.

"What are you talking about?" Charlotte called after her.

She walked around the garden to Frasier's door, trying to hide the papers in case Lucy was watching. He opened on the third knock and she held the papers up to his face. "Lizbeth had a life insurance policy," she said. "Not a big one, but Oliver is the beneficiary."

"It's probably expired," Frasier said, not in the least bit surprised. He took the papers from her and adjusted his square glasses to read.

"It's from last year. I don't think it's expired," she said. "Do you think she was afraid this was going to happen? That she knew she was going to die? Or maybe she was in danger?"

"Lizbeth gave as little thought to death as she did to life," he said, turning a page. Several dellawisps were taking advantage of the open door and were hopping into the office with an air of finding something to complain about, like they were tiny health and safety inspectors.

"Why would she have a life insurance policy, then?"

"She took out several policies over the years, when she could scrape together the money. Then she let them all expire. She did it for the only reason she ever did anything, to have more paper to put in her collection." He finished reading, then folded the papers. "As if she didn't have enough paper already."

"Oh," Zoey said awkwardly. "I see." She thought she'd finally found the reason Lucy was breaking in. She'd started to imagine that Lizbeth had been so afraid of her sister that she'd taken out the policy in case Lucy did something to her, and that Lizbeth's only hope for justice was for someone to find this and connect the dots before Lucy got to the policy and destroyed it.

It wasn't a particularly proud moment, how deflated she felt. All Lucy had done was keep to herself, and Zoey had created something nefarious out of it. Not only that, she'd been *excited* about being a part of a drama that was, even in Zoey's made-up version, extremely sad at its core.

She didn't move, and Frasier waited patiently for her to finally work through what she wanted to say. It was Lucy who was breaking into Lizbeth's place, Zoey was still sure of it. She'd smelled her cigarette smoke that night when she'd walked by her. But what if Lucy was doing it just to sit and grieve, surrounded by her sister's things? And maybe the reason she was doing it at night was because she thought she wasn't welcome. Maybe she was just waiting for an invitation.

"Is Lucy okay?" Zoey finally asked.

Frasier considered that seriously before he said, "That's a complicated question to answer, when it comes to Lucy. Why?"

"She knows she can come in and look around any time she wants, doesn't she? I wouldn't bother her."

"I don't think she'd like that." He started shooing the birds out of his office with a wave of the insurance policy. "Have you found anything else?"

"No. But I put a copy of *Sweet Mallow* Roscoe Avanger signed for Lizbeth in the box for Oliver." She stepped aside as the birds hopped out, puffy with indignation. "Listen, since Oliver isn't coming home, is there an address where I can send the things I've collected for him?"

"Zoey . . ."

"Would you at least ask him?" she persisted. She had her own small box of things of her mother's, and it meant everything to her. Surely his box would mean something to Oliver, too, one day. When Frasier hesitated, she asked, "What if *I* ask him?"

Frasier sighed and turned to write something on a Post-it note. He handed it to her, then closed the door.

When Zoey walked back to Lizbeth's condo, she waved the Post-it at Charlotte. "Guess what this is?"

"We're supposed to be taking paper out, not bringing it in," Charlotte said.

"It's Oliver Lime's phone number."

"Oh, so *that's* why we're doing this." Charlotte smiled at her. "There are easier ways to get a date than this, you know."

"I'm going to text him and ask if he wants me to mail him the box of things I've set aside for him." She stared at the number. "Do you think Lucy would like to join us for lunch one day?"

Surprised, Charlotte sat back on her crate. "My guess would be no. This is quite a turnaround. She's gone from prowler to guest of honor?"

"I just got to thinking, since Oliver's not coming home, Lucy doesn't have any family left at the Dellawisp. What if she's lonely? Like Lizbeth was."

Charlotte started going through the box in front of her again. "You have a good heart, Zoey."

Zoey smiled. "Thanks."

"A weird fascination with this family, but a good heart."

———

Later that afternoon, Roscoe Avanger poured himself some bourbon as he sat outside on his back porch. With a sigh, he took his first sip.

So it began, this cursed sameness.

He hated evenings, the way they stretched out like a long-winded speech. Starting at five, he allowed himself a drink. Then he walked around his property and greeted the neighbor's dog, a golden retriever named Goof, through the fence. Then he swam in his backyard pool. Then he showered. Then he watched television and ate what Rita left him for dinner, usually chicken bog, a dish of chicken, sausage, and rice he must have told her once that he liked, so now it was all she made. After that, there were hours and hours to slog through before he was reasonably tired and could go to bed. During those hours, he prowled through the rooms of his house, reacquainting himself with his lovely belongings. He sometimes went through his closet, trying on expensive suits he hadn't worn in decades to make sure they still fit.

The one place he studiously avoided was his office. Everything there was a shrine to *Sweet Mallow*, frippery the interior decorator had insisted would inspire him. He'd hired the decorator shortly after he'd bought this large old home on historic Julep Row, in the most affluent neighborhood on Mallow Island. He'd dreamed about living here as a boy when he would ride a stolen bicycle up and down the street until homeowners called the police. His grandfather, his only living relative since his mother died and his father left, would always take a switch to him when he got home. Roscoe would yell at him that he hated him, that he had no idea what it felt like to want to be someone else, that pretending to be the owner of a stolen bicycle and riding in a nice neighborhood was the only way to get away from the things that haunted him. If only they could all see him now. But very few people remembered that little boy. At one time he'd liked his office—the framed book covers, the original movie poster, the large photo of him at the Oscars above the case where he kept his Oscar for cowriting the screenplay for the movie. But as the years passed, he began to hate the room. It mocked him.

He didn't write for nearly three decades after *Sweet Mallow*, too busy basking in his own glory. He went on lecture tours, accepted awards, gave commencement speeches. But when those offers stopped rolling in, he focused on the one place he would always be a superstar: Mallow Island itself. He began to buy and renovate old properties, preserving the old Mallow Island of his youth, continuing to put a lasting mark on a town that both rejected him as a boy and gave him the success he had as a man. It gave him something to do when his fingers got twitchy, wanting to peck on a keyboard again. When he saw that old stable property for the first time, something awakened in him. He fell in love with the place and the birds, and he thought he finally had something else to share with the world. *Dancing with the Dellawisps* had been a tiny illustrated book, no longer than a novella, and he had published it himself. His hubris had convinced him that people would love anything he wrote, so why give a publisher a piece of the pie? But it turned out no one was as fascinated by the place as he was. He should have known. He wasn't put on this earth to tell his own story. It had been two more decades now since *Dancing with the Dellawisps,* and still not a single day went by that he didn't think of writing.

But he was a hermit now. He didn't write. He'd even stopped buying properties after the Dellawisp. He was an old man, and he was tired of being famous. He made sure that no one recognized him when he went out, but he was still a big fish in this small town, so it wasn't for their lack of trying. The Mallow Island trolley tour still rolled by his house every day, and tourists still tried to get photos of his house through the gate and wisps of Spanish moss. The island college extension still had *Sweet Mallow* as its only English reading requirement, but he no longer felt an obligation to give a speech there every year. Even his own housekeeper rarely saw him. Rita was always gone by five in the afternoon, and from that point on he had the house to himself, free to be unproductive without an audience. Rita handled everything he needed for day-to-day living. She did his grocery shopping, managed his household repairs, and left him notes on the refrigerator reminding him of doctors' appointments and missed calls. And there was always chicken bog left warming for him. She was like a fairy, flitting in and out of his life.

And if Rita was the fairy in the story of his life these past few years, then it stood to reason that Lizbeth Lime was the goblin.

Oh, Lizbeth.

Kindness wasn't something that came easily to him with most people. Certainly not with Lizbeth. She'd worked for him for nearly twenty years, doing who knows what. Something to do with the internet. As far as he knew, it had been her first and only job. He'd only offered it to her because her son Oliver obviously needed some stability. She'd never been put off by his arrogant dismissals when she would say what a great book her life would be. She'd said if he only knew what she had suffered at the hands of her sister, he would understand. She'd been like a child trying to get attention with a secret. But Lizbeth was like every person who had ever told him they had a story they wanted him to write for them—she'd wasted too much time thinking about doing it and now there was no time left. He'd once challenged her to put it all down on paper just so she would shut up about it. She said it was already written down, she just needed to find it. And that was how she'd spent her last years. She never did find whatever she was looking for, which didn't surprise him. Very little surprised him in his old age.

There wasn't a story in Lizbeth's condo, of that he was certain. But he felt he owed it to Lizbeth to at least look. He wasn't sure how he'd feel if there really was something. Probably not too terrible. Once you accumulate enough regrets in life, they cease to hurt you.

They are simply one more thing you collect, like age spots or ugly figurines. You barely even see them anymore.

As Roscoe put on his monogrammed pajamas and got into bed that evening, he finally let himself acknowledge what he wouldn't admit in the light of day, when it was much easier to still feel irritated by her.

He missed Lizbeth Lime.

He really missed that old bird.

GHOST STORY

Lizbeth

I read *Sweet Mallow* for the first time when Oliver's father, Duncan, told me it was his favorite book. That was before Oliver. It was the only time in my entire life when *everything* was good. Of course it wouldn't last, because Lucy then stole Duncan from me. She was awful to me, just awful, and no one *ever* believed me. Not even you, I'm sure. You probably think I'm making all this up. But Duncan was mine, my one true love. He was trying so hard to be clean, and she corrupted him with her addiction because she hated me. It resulted in both of them going to prison on those prescription-forgery charges. He died of an overdose as soon as he got out.

That was the end of that. The only thing I had left of him was *Sweet Mallow* and how much we both loved it.

Well, that, and Oliver.

But after Oliver was born, I didn't have much to do with him other than living in the same house with him and my mother. My mother just *loved* him. She played choo-choo train with his baby food on a spoon and potty trained him and took him to day care. She paid a lot more attention to him than she'd paid to *me* when I was that age. So I let them have their little lovefest and locked myself in my room all day and pretended to write. What I was really doing was stacking and organizing junk mail we received into boxes. I'd collected paper with writing on it since I was a child, but it got worse as I got older. I never truly understood why I did this, but it gave me comfort. Maybe I thought that if I just collected enough words, I could totally rewrite myself one day. When I wasn't collecting, I was reading *Sweet Mallow* over and over, lingering on passages that Duncan had liked best.

I'd always known that Roscoe Avanger lived on the island, but I never dreamed I would ever get to meet the author of my and Duncan's favorite book in the world. But then I *did.* Next to meeting Duncan, it was the best day of my life. Roscoe had been renovating the Dellawisp at the time and had gone to Sugar and Scribble Bakery for lunch. Before finally growing out his hair, he used to disguise his signature bald head with a hat and obscure his face with glasses because he hated when people bothered him in public when he was trying to do normal things. But I'd spent so much time staring at the author photo on his book that I recognized him right away. I ran up to him, bumping Oliver along in his stroller. Oliver didn't complain. He didn't complain about anything. Sometimes he was so quiet I forgot he was there. Oliver being there was the only bad thing about that day, but I'd had no choice but to have him with me because my mother had died of a heart attack in her sleep just months before, and had left me with him. That had never been the plan. She'd always said so. I wasn't ever supposed be responsible for Oliver.

Roscoe was annoyed by my intrusion and didn't mince words telling me to leave him alone. He knew it wouldn't matter how harsh he was. He was secure in the knowledge that when a reader falls in love with a book, they have no choice but to fall in love with the author, too. But he seemed to soften when he saw Oliver staring at him. He bent down to talk to Oliver, offering him some of the cheese Danish he was eating. Then he suddenly offered me a job. Just like that. I know he felt sorry for Oliver, even though he should have felt sorry for *me.* He had no idea the things I had to put up with in my life.

My job for him at first was just going through his fan mail, back when readers wrote actual letters to him. I would be in tears at some of them, how beautiful they were. I had finally found my true family in that daily pile of envelopes, a family of readers who wished books were their real lives, just like me. Their love of the book reminded me so much of Duncan. Roscoe told me to get rid of the letters once I went through them, but I kept them all in my boxes. Later, as Roscoe grew older and more cranky about the internet, I started moderating his official online fan club and social media groups.

I moved into the Dellawisp with Oliver not long after the renovations were complete. Roscoe gave me one of the condos for free, because he seemed to think the run-down house I had inherited from my mother was in too bad a shape for Oliver to live there. He didn't seem to care that I'd had to grow up in that awful house. Still, it was a generous thing to do, so in return I felt it was my duty to keep tabs on the Dellawisp residents just so Roscoe would know how awful they could be and that I was really the best there. Roscoe called me a snoop, but he did the same thing. There is no bigger snoop than a writer, even though sometimes he made me feel like the least interesting person in his world.

When Lucy finally got out of prison, I began to get calls from police and social workers when she was found sleeping on beaches and park benches on the island. I always hung up on these people, telling them I had no idea what they were talking about. But I knew exactly why she was back on the island. Oliver. Just like my mother, she probably thought she could be a better mother than me. My relationship with

Oliver was complicated. It wasn't that I liked having him around, it was just that I was . . . used to him by then, I suppose. And I hated the idea of Lucy thinking she could just show up and make him love her more than he loved me like she did with Duncan. Like she did with our father.

Probably because of how much I complained about the calls, Roscoe found Lucy and gave her a condo that he had just bought back after someone moved. He didn't make any money off of the Dellawisp. He has plenty of that. He just likes being able to choose the residents by how lonely or interesting he thinks they are, like they're all potential characters in his next book. But it was the exact thing I didn't want, her anywhere near Oliver.

I was shocked the first time I saw her. Oliver was, too, by the way he watched her with his big green eyes from behind a tree in the garden when she first moved in. Whether he was scared of her, or fascinated by her, I don't know. Prison had changed her. Deep lines were around her mouth and eyes, giving her an air of menace. And whereas once she'd been lush and curvy, now she looked like she'd been whittled down to nothing but gristle. She was no longer pretty and that made me happy, as if the less she was, the more I was—something true only in the universe of sisters. The day she moved in, I hissed to her that she should never, ever look at me or Oliver, that I didn't want to hear a word out of her, because if she did, I would have her thrown out faster than she could say *Duncan*. It took her a long time before she nodded, as if she was having trouble understanding my words.

Roscoe was immediately intrigued by Lucy, I could tell. But when he found out the truth, I knew he would think differently. The story is all there in my old diaries, which I could never find. Everything about Lucy stealing Duncan, and Oliver being born, and my mother's *brilliant* plan to have a second chance at raising a child.

And how not one of them *ever* stopped to think about how their actions would affect me.

Once Roscoe reads the diaries, he'll love my story.

Then he'll have to love me.

They will all finally have to love me.

Chapter Ten

There's an express envelope for you on the table in the foyer. I had to sign for it. The postmark is Mallow Island. Is it a graduation gift from your mother's old friend?" Garland said that evening as she walked into her bedroom. "Walked" being a generous word. She couldn't do more than take tiny bird steps in her skinny dress.

Oliver put down his phone and watched from his position against the bed pillows as Garland spritzed herself with a bottle of perfume on her dresser, something dark and Oriental, like opening a fragrant antique chest. She wasn't looking at him. He wondered what was wrong. Maybe it had something to do with the envelope. Frasier hadn't wasted any time sending the papers to sell his mother's condo back. He thought there would be a long legal process to go through first. Oliver wasn't sure if he was ready to deal with it yet. He felt untethered now that the single most powerful force in his life, his desire to distance himself from his mother, was gone. "It was presumptuous to give out your address without asking first," he finally said. "I'm sorry."

"Roy has his dealer bring his weed here. Do you really think I mind you having a graduation gift delivered?" She slapped his thigh as she passed him on her way back out. "Come on. Our Uber will be here soon."

"Have you heard from your dad?" he asked as he got up.

She rolled her eyes. "No. Don't *worry*, Oliver. Have you always been such a worrier?"

"Yes," he said simply.

They got back from the club near dawn, sticky with sweat and spilled drinks. Everyone floated up the staircase, but Oliver lingered in the foyer, watching them. Heather Two had on only one shoe. The back of Cooper's T-shirt was covered in glitter. It was like they were all survivors of some glamorous natural disaster. He waited for them to disappear into their rooms; then he took the express envelope off the table in the foyer where it was glowing in a menacing green color from the porch light shining through the stained-glass windows. He wanted to go through the papers away from prying eyes, and this might be his only chance given Garland's regimented schedule of I'm Going To Show Everyone How Wonderful I Am And We're Going To Have Fun This Week No Matter What, Damn It.

He went to the kitchen and filled a glass with water, then sat at the table to read by the dim night-light above the stove that the housekeeper always left on. She would be up soon. He felt awkward around her, always resisting the urge to ask her if she needed any help.

Several moments passed and he stared at the envelope, which was thin, as if it only contained a sheet or two. He thought there would be reams of paper to go through.

Just open it, he told himself. It wasn't like it contained a portal that would suck him back home.

He tore open the envelope and brought out what looked like a life insurance policy.

It *was* a life insurance policy.

His mother rarely did anything nice for anyone, and when she did she demanded a phenomenal level of worship in return, as if it was a great sacrifice on her part to actually think about a need that wasn't her own. So he knew this policy wasn't about him. She was always signing up for things just so she could collect more paperwork to put in her boxes. And he was only the beneficiary this time and not Roscoe Avanger because sometimes she would decide that she hated Roscoe and this was probably one of those days.

He had no reason to feel grateful to her, not even now. If he didn't need the money—and even this small five-thousand-dollar policy was a lot of money to him right now as he waited for that job at the Rondo—he would have torn it up.

He got out his phone to text Frasier that he'd received it. When his screen came to life, he noticed that he had a new text with a photo attachment from an unfamiliar number.

The text read:

> Hi Oliver, My name is Zoey Hennessey and I just moved into the studio at the Dellawisp. I guess Frasier's already told you that he gave me a summer job before I start college. I'm cleaning out your mother's place to find a story for Roscoe Avanger. Frasier said you don't want anything, but I couldn't throw these things away. I can send them to you if you'll give me an address. The birds are restless this evening. I took my sandals off on my balcony while I was writing this to you, and

several of them just swooped down and tried to take one!
What were they going to do with a single shoe? Frasier said
they like to steal things. Crazy birds. Do you miss them? Do
you miss your aunt Lucy? I can see her condo from here, and
I think she's in there, but I never see her come out.

Oliver's first thought was for Lucy. Lucy was still there. He'd
figured she would have left years ago. He'd always felt sorry for Lucy
in a way he could never bring himself to feel sorry for his mother.
Maybe because Lucy seemed to prefer self-punishment, while his
mother loved to blame everyone but herself.

He read through the text again, this time lingering on Zoey
Hennessey's name. When he was a small boy, he remembered a
pretty woman named Paloma Hennessey who had owned the studio
at the Dellawisp. She'd had a foreign accent. His mother had hated
her, had mumbled "Tramp" every time she'd been within earshot,
but Paloma had only laughed at this, completely unflappable, as if
it would take more than the likes of Lizbeth Lime to rattle her.
Paloma had moved away, but still visited Mallow Island from time
to time and brought her baby daughter with her. Zoey must be that
daughter.

Without thinking, he tapped the photo, and immediately wished
he hadn't. Zoey had snapped a picture of a box containing some of
his mother's belongings. In it was her lost necklace bearing Oliver's
late father's name, Duncan. His mother had been convinced that
Lucy had come in and stolen it. She'd frequently told Oliver that
Lucy had stolen Duncan from her because Lucy had hated seeing
Lizbeth happy. She'd said that Lucy's drug abuse had destroyed him
and he'd later died of a drug overdose because of her. Oliver had
no idea if this was true or not. His mother had always been strange

about her sister, and that was saying a lot. She thought Lucy had been the source of everything that had gone wrong in her life. It must have started at an early age, because the photo Zoey sent included several of his mother's old diaries from her youth, and when he zoomed in he saw written on one of the diaries, *This is the property of Lizbeth Azalea Lime. Do not look inside. This means you, Lucy Camellia Lime, you stupid cow!*

The sight of her manic handwriting made his stomach twist with nausea, not helped by the vats of alcohol he'd consumed that night.

He used to think he could stem the tide of his mother's compulsion to collect paper when he was a boy. He would sneak things out to the dumpster on his way to school, only to find it all back inside when he got home. The condos at the Dellawisp were stylish, because Roscoe Avanger was a stylish man of details, but they were also small. His mother had taken the single bedroom because she'd said she needed privacy to get her work done, so Oliver had carved out a place in the living room near the window. He'd made walls with her boxes and refused to let her stack things in his space, but it was a losing battle. Her stuff had eventually pushed him out the door.

Frasier should have known better than to think his mother had anything as organized as a story in there. Now, because of him, some girl was rifling through Oliver's past, thinking she knew him based on what she found. He'd always kept his life with his mother private from everyone he knew, particularly his peers.

He immediately deleted the photo. Then he texted Frasier.

Please inform Zoey Hennessey I don't want anything from my mother's place, and I especially don't want to see photos. Received the policy. Thanks for sending it.

He pressed Send and put his phone back in his pocket. He downed the glass of water, then took the envelope and walked up the staircase as dawn broke over the ocean in the distance. He stopped at the second-story landing and stared out the window.

He turned his head when a squeaking from down the hallway caught his attention. Curious, he walked toward the sound, which was coming from Cooper's room. The door was slightly ajar, and he peered in to see Cooper and Garland having sex. He couldn't see their faces, just Garland's narrow back and prominent ribs as she straddled him. Her hands were in her long hair as she moved.

He took a quick step back. It wasn't the act itself that worried him. He'd almost seen it coming. What worried him was that if Garland was through with him, what did that do to his chances of getting the job at the Rondo?

He tried to find some way this would turn out okay. Maybe she would feel guilty?

This was a new low. He was going to get the job out of pity?

He didn't care. He couldn't lose the Rondo. Everything would be fine once he started working there. Everything would finally fall into place. He'd known it as soon as he'd seen it. It had reminded him of something good, something he couldn't quite put his finger on. He was meant to be there.

"She always gets what she wants," Heather Two whispered behind him.

Oliver turned quickly to find her in a short pink robe, barefooted on the Aubusson rug.

"Garland never gave Cooper the time of day in high school, even though he panted after her."

Oliver steered her away from the door so they wouldn't be heard. He didn't want Garland to know that he knew. Not yet.

"But he has a lot of money now. He didn't have to wait until he was thirty to get control of his money, like Garland has to."

"She wants his money?" he asked softly, then wished he hadn't. He sounded naive.

"Of course she wants his money. She was okay as long as she was in school and her father gave her an allowance. But when she flunked out, he cut her off and told her she needed to get a job, which she refused to do. That's why she still lives here. She tried hooking up with Cooper after she flunked out, but Cooper had become a big man on campus. He wasn't the lapdog he was in high school. But she knew exactly what to do to get to him."

"What do you mean?"

"Cooper hates guys who are cuter than he is. That's why you're here. Garland's dad gave her an ultimatum before he left on vacation. When he got back, Garland had to have a job or she'd have to move out. Cooper and the place he just bought in LA are her safety net. Didn't you know?"

No, he didn't know. But he could hardly be angry about her using him to get what she wanted when he'd been doing the same thing. He rubbed his eyes tiredly. "You don't like her very much, do you?"

"It doesn't matter. I've known her my whole life. The more important question is do *you* like her?"

Oliver moved his hands from his eyes to see that Heather Two had stepped close to him, her chest grazing his. She put her arms around his neck slowly, not taking her bright blue eyes off him. He couldn't move. He just stood there as if watching the whole thing happen from outside his body as she put her lips to his. She'd just brushed her teeth. The taste almost made him gag and he pulled back.

He didn't understand these people. And he didn't know who he was when he was around them.

He turned without another word and walked back to the room he shared with Garland. He stripped, fell into bed, and was asleep before the squeaking down the hall ended with a muffled groan.

Zoey heard Frasier's voice coming from Lizbeth's living room later that morning. Charlotte greeted him, then asked him when he was removing the bookcase. Her words were clipped with censure. She called it a deathcase.

A moment later, Frasier knocked on Lizbeth's bedroom door. Pigeon, who had been hopping around the floor pecking and tearing at stray pieces of paper while Zoey blindly followed her, trying to make her stop, flew up. Frasier put his hand to his wiry white hair as if he'd felt her fly out of the room.

Zoey's brows knit. No one but her had ever felt Pigeon before.

"I was okay, finding the bookcase yesterday," Zoey said before he could say anything. Then, in a lower voice, "I think Charlotte was more upset about it than I was."

"She's right, though. I should have had it removed before I asked you to do this. Sometimes I find myself with an astounding lack of long-term thinking when it comes to people I care about. Charlotte is just looking out for you." He walked in and sat at the computer desk, his eyes going around the room. "I haven't seen these walls in a long time. Hello, walls."

He didn't say anything else. He just sat there, looking around. Zoey, still kneeling, moved her mask to her head and pointed behind him. "Did you know Lizbeth's computer is still on? I didn't want to turn it off in case Roscoe wanted to go through it to see if she had any kind of document on it. I mean, I didn't want to turn it off in case it wouldn't turn back on again. It's pretty old. Lizbeth was logged on to a message board for fans of *Sweet Mallow,* and the board is still active. Should I write to them? The fans, I mean? To tell them about Lizbeth?"

Frasier swiveled to the computer and pressed the space bar on the keyboard. The monitor sprang to life. He gave the message board only the briefest of glances before turning back around. "If you'd like."

"I figure Roscoe wouldn't want the board to descend into chaos."

"It meant much more to Lizbeth than it ever meant to him."

"He doesn't care what his readers are saying?" she asked, surprised.

"*Sweet Mallow* took on a life of its own after it was published. Roscoe doesn't even think of it as his book anymore. He always wanted to move past it."

"Mac told me he wrote another book, *Dancing with the Della-wisps,*" she said. "And that you illustrated it."

Frasier nodded slowly, almost as if he considered her question suspicious. "Roscoe and I have known each other all our lives."

"It must have been a great experience, working with him."

"It was a long time ago," he said.

"What is he like?"

"Old, like me. And cranky. Resting on your laurels isn't as comfortable as it sounds. In fact, if you asked him, he would probably say it was more like sitting on thorns."

Zoey hesitated, then figured there wouldn't be any harm in asking. "Do you have an extra copy of *Dancing with the Dellawisps* I could read?"

"No. I gave the damn things away years ago. And good riddance," he said. When he saw that she'd raised her brows, he added in a gentler tone, "I'm sorry, Zoey. If I still had one, I would give it to you."

"Lizbeth had hundreds of copies of *Sweet Mallow*. But not a single copy of *Dancing with the Dellawisps*. I wonder why?"

"Because she hated the dellawisps. I enjoy drawing them, but Roscoe should have known that most people wouldn't want to read about them. They're like spoiled toddlers. Who wants to read about spoiled toddlers?"

"I would," Zoey said. "I think they're beautiful, and unusual."

"Me, too." He smiled. "There are birds, and then there are *other* birds. Maybe they don't sing. Maybe they don't fly. Maybe they don't fit in. I don't know about you, but I'd much rather be an other bird than just the same old thing." He took his phone out of his work shirt pocket and called something up. "Now, for the reason I'm here. Oliver sent me a text this morning." He handed the phone to her.

She read the text, wondering why Oliver hadn't responded to her. She'd been checking her phone all morning. She handed his phone back to him.

"Don't take it personally," Frasier said. "He's under a lot of stress. He just graduated from college."

"Really?" Zoey asked. "Where?"

"California. He was whip-smart as a boy, interested in everything. He used to spend a lot of time with me in the garden. His favorite thing to do was search the brugmansia trees for things the birds had stolen, like he was sure one day he would find great treasure."

"So you've known him all his life?" she asked, and he nodded. "How long have you worked here?"

"Since Roscoe bought it."

Something suddenly occurred to her, and it felt like a sharp ray of light through a slit in a dark curtain. She sat back on her heels, the enormity of it almost too much. "Then you knew my mother!"

"Yes," he said, standing as if she'd said something alarming. "Not well, and not long. But, yes."

"What was she like?"

He began to back out of the room. "She was dramatic. And very beautiful. I was sorry to hear when she died."

"How did you find out?" she asked as he eased closer to the door.

"Your father told me after it happened. Eleven, almost twelve, years ago now. He said the studio was being kept for you for when you moved out."

Her father had told her as much, never saying outright that she would have to leave when she graduated, but the implication was there. She knew from her stepmother Tina that they had hoped Zoey would want to move out last year when she'd turned eighteen, to spend her senior year of high school here. Maybe she should have, but she had only just come into her money and she didn't know anything about what it would take to manage it or how to move yet. It had taken her a whole year to figure it out.

She'd seen on Tina's Facebook page that they were all planning a vacation in Florida now that Zoey's younger twin stepsiblings were out of school for the summer. Tina did this not by announcing that they were going, that would be far too obvious, but by asking, *Does anyone have resort suggestions for a Florida stay?*

Florida was close, close enough to stop by and see Zoey if they wanted to.

But they wouldn't.

"Do you remember *me*?" she asked Frasier.

"I do. And I remember that Paloma loved you very much."

"I've been looking for her here, any trace of her," Zoey said help-lessly. "It's like she never existed."

"You're here, Zoey. She'll always exist as long as you're in the world."

She felt tears come to her eyes, which surprised her. She wasn't a crier. There had been no point. Her family would never have responded to tears in any way she would have wanted them to. She supposed it was because this was the first time anyone had ever said anything good about her mother. "Why didn't you say anything when I moved in?"

"Because, Zoey, there are some stories that shouldn't be told," he said as he left.

Zoey appreciated that he seemed to want to spare her feelings, that he didn't want to reveal a secret he thought might upset her. But he really needn't have bothered.

Her father had told her a long time ago that her mother had been a prostitute when he'd met her.

Chapter Eleven

Charlotte had never given much thought to what the other condos at the Dellawisp looked like. When she followed Zoey up the curling metal staircase for lunch later that day, she didn't know what to expect. Certainly not this sea of pink and white. She stopped in her tracks. The studio was undeniably stylish, like something out of a magazine, but utterly devoid of personality. She never would have guessed that this was where Zoey spent most of her time. Zoey, with all her energy and imagination and plots. The only real teenager touches were the clothes on the floor and the books, some of them piled several feet high, scattered around. The rest of the space was dominated by an obscenely large white sleigh bed against the far right wall and a go-go-boot-white leather couch against the far left wall.

"Well," Charlotte said. "This is something."

"I know," Zoey said with a laugh as she walked to a pink refrigerator, on which was an empty wicker birdcage. She opened the freezer and brought out two boxes of chicken sandwiches. "I think my mother must have redecorated just before she died. The dresser still had the price tag on it."

Charlotte approached the refrigerator to look at three photos tacked there with magnets. "Is this her?" she asked, indicating the photo of a woman with stunningly symmetric features. She was beautiful, the kind of beautiful that men would move mountains for, but there was also something hard and unpredictable about her as she stared at the camera, like you didn't want to get on her bad side.

"Yes," Zoey said. "I think it was taken just after she arrived in America. She immigrated from Cuba."

"You look like her."

"No, she was beautiful."

"So are you."

"Not like her." Zoey opened the boxes and put the sandwiches in the microwave. "I still can't believe Frasier knew her and didn't say anything."

She'd been going on about that all morning. "Frasier probably has more secrets than the rest of us combined."

"He certainly seems good at keeping them," Zoey said, punching the microwave buttons.

"Who is this?" Charlotte asked, pointing to the photo of an old man in a tie-dyed T-shirt. What was left of his hair was in a salt-and-pepper ponytail. "Your dad?"

"No. That's Kello. He owns the bookstore where I used to work. I wanted a photo of him to take with me, but he hates having his photo taken. He made me promise not to post it online. He's a little paranoid about technology."

"I don't like having my photo online, either. And this?" Charlotte indicated the last photo. It was of Zoey and another, heavier girl sitting in a restaurant booth with two ice cream sundaes in front of them. They looked young, about twelve, and had smears of ice cream on their noses and were laughing about it.

"That is, was, my best friend, Ingrid."

"Was?"

"She moved away about a year after that photo was taken. Those are the three people who've meant the most to me, so I like looking at them."

"What about other friends?" Charlotte asked.

Zoey shook her head. "I sort of did my own thing after Ingrid left."

"A boyfriend?" Charlotte waggled her brows.

Zoey snorted, which Charlotte took as a no. The microwave dinged and Zoey played hot potato with the sandwiches, still in their plastic bags, before tossing them onto plates. "I don't remember seeing any photos in your place."

"There's no one from my past I want to remember." But then she thought of the photo of Charlotte and Pepper under her bed. "But I had a best friend once, too. She was my whole world."

"Yes!" Zoey said. "That's how it was with me and Ingrid. I used to spend more time at her house than I did my own. When my father and stepmother and my stepmother's kids went on summer trips, I even asked to stay with Ingrid. We said we were going to keep in touch, and I don't know why we didn't. Sometimes I'll look for her online, but I wonder if she changed her name. Maybe her mother remarried and she was adopted." Zoey set the plates on the coffee table in front of the leather couch. "Did you lose touch, too?"

"In a manner of speaking," Charlotte said. "She died when we were sixteen."

"Oh. I'm sorry." Zoey sat on the couch heavily. "That's when you said you went out on your own. Sixteen."

Charlotte nodded, but was saved from any more questions by a voice calling from the garden. "Hello?"

They exchanged glances, then walked to the balcony to see Mac standing at the base of the staircase. He was looking up at them like they were maidens in a turret.

"Do you mind if I come up?" he asked.

"Of course!" Zoey said. "We're having chicken sandwiches. Do you want one?"

"No, thank you," he said as he navigated the twirly staircase with care. "I just wanted to give something to Charlotte."

When he reached the balcony, Charlotte took the piece of folded notebook paper he held out to her.

"It's contact information at Popcorn, if you change your mind about a restaurant job," Mac said. His meaty, freckled hand was grasping the balcony railing so tightly his knuckles were white. He obviously didn't like heights. "Also, there's the name and number of a friend of mine named Flo who runs the Mallow Island tour around the corner. I happen to know she's looking for help at their ticket desk right now. I asked around, but I couldn't find anyone who had space for a henna table, but that could change. I know the owner of the art gallery here on Trade, and he gets great foot traffic. I think it would be a good match—his traditional meets your edgy. I'll see if I can convince him to let you rent out there."

Charlotte held the paper back out to him with a knot of suspicion. "Thanks, but I've got it under control." And if *under control* meant ignoring her jobless situation entirely and spending the past five days with Zoey instead, then yes, it was completely true.

"Keep it anyway. Just in case," Mac said, and then he walked gingerly back down.

Charlotte's eyes followed him back to his condo. She didn't quite know what to think of him.

Zoey, watching Charlotte, said, "I think he likes you."

"Come on," Charlotte said, walking down the stairs. "I want to check out this gallery." Whatever his motives, she wasn't going to look a gift horse in the mouth. If Mac could help her find a place to work on the island so she could stay and just be still and settled for a little while longer, she'd find a way to pay him back so that they'd be square.

Zoey grabbed their sandwiches and they ate as they walked down the alley to the street. The Mallow Island Gallery was on the far corner, and was one of those touristy places that sold soft-focus, romantic prints of beaches that usually hung in guest bathrooms. In the Sugar Warehouse, this kind of sweet and popular, but very cheap, art was looked down upon. But Charlotte secretly gave kudos to the owner for finding this niche. It had no competition here on Trade Street, being one of only a handful of storefronts that didn't sell food or sweets.

They tried the door, but it was locked. There was a note on the glass saying the owner had gone for a swim and would be back in an hour.

"Gone for a swim? Do you think that's a daily occurrence?" Zoey cupped her hands around her eyes and looked inside.

"I wouldn't be surprised," Charlotte said. Tourists were always in a hurry to get somewhere, but locals on Mallow Island seemed to move at their own speed, which was about five times slower than actual time.

Zoey turned from the gallery window. She saw a bright red trolley bus parked across the street and said, "There's the place Mac said was looking for someone for the ticket desk." She was crossing the street before Charlotte could tell her that she wasn't interested in ticket-taking, and she was already inside the pistachio-colored building by the time Charlotte caught up with her.

It was a weirdly wonderful place, full of eclectic hand-painted furniture. A foosball table was in a corner and a set of checkers was on a coffee table, ostensibly so people could play while they waited for the next trolley. The ticket counter looked like it had been re-purposed from an Old West saloon. An elderly woman with orange lipstick was standing behind it wearing a T-shirt that read GOOD GOLLY, MISS TROLLEY.

"Have you ever taken the tour?" Zoey asked as she took a bro-chure off the counter.

"No."

"Me, either! Want to take it with me?"

Charlotte hesitated. Helping Zoey out with Lizbeth's condo was one thing. Charlotte was basically doing it only as a way of distract-ing herself. Going out on adventures with Zoey was a whole new dynamic, and she didn't know what to make of it. She'd never con-sidered herself a particularly good friend. She'd had very few female acquaintances since leaving the camp. She'd often wondered, if she had been better and braver, what would have happened ten years ago. Her best friend had saved her, but Charlotte hadn't been able to do the same for her.

Zoey was looking at her with anticipation, and Charlotte finally smiled. An afternoon was such a small thing to ask. "Of course I will."

They bought their tickets and went outside because the next tour was about to leave. "If you've never taken the trolley, then you obvi-ously didn't come here as a tourist first," Zoey said as they climbed on board.

"Not really. Though South Carolina was on a list of places I wanted to travel to. I looked at condos in Charleston, but couldn't find anything I liked. I heard some people talk about the Sugar Warehouse here, so I thought I would check it out. When I drove in, it felt like entering a movie set. I loved it."

Zoey took her seat and started reading the tour brochure. "Maybe it's because the movie based on *Sweet Mallow* was filmed here."

"Maybe," Charlotte said, sitting behind her on the vinyl seat, which was hot from the sun and slightly sticky from its previous occupant's sunscreen. "I never saw the movie."

"Did you ever read the book?" Zoey asked, turning to her.

Charlotte shook her head. "I never got around to it. Maybe I should have kept one of Lizbeth's copies."

"You should definitely read it. I'll let you borrow my copy, if you want. It's one of those books that make you want to become a writer."

"You want to be a writer?"

"Me? No," Zoey said with a laugh. "I just love to read. English was my favorite class. My senior advisor said I should teach."

Charlotte considered her for a moment. "I can see you as a teacher."

"Really?"

"You're good at sweeping people up in your enthusiasm." Tourists were still filing onto the trolley, so Charlotte said, "Tell me about the book. Make me love it as much as you do."

Zoey sat on her knees on the seat so she could fully face her. "Okay. Part of the book is the real history of the island, back when it was called Summey's Landing and there was a rice plantation here. Then how an Englishman bought the burnt island after the Civil War and discovered the mallow plant growing here in the marshes.

He was the one who opened all these sweet shops and renamed the place Mallow Island. But when the Great Depression hit, most people tied to the candy trade left, leaving this unique community descended from emancipated slaves, Civil War objectors, and European candymakers. The fictional part of the book is about two men who meet overseas during World War One. They look so much alike they could have been twins. When one of them dies, a man named Henry Sparrow, the other man, Teb Wayne, takes Henry's identity and returns to Henry's home here on Mallow Island. Henry had told Teb all these stories about his life, so Teb was sure he'd be able to carry off the ruse. But it turned out that almost everything Henry told him was fiction, and it was harder to impersonate him than Teb thought it would be. But Teb is charmed by the island, and grows to love Henry's blind grandfather, Silas Sparrow. There's a lot about the Old South and race relations and the ghosts that haunt the town. Then police from Teb's hometown in Ohio show up. They'd been looking for him because of some crimes he'd committed before going to war. Teb was an orphan who went to war to escape poverty, and he had a hard childhood. Old Silas Sparrow gives a famous speech to the town, and everyone on the island rallies around Teb—young, old, rich, poor, black, white—and they convince the police that Teb really is Henry. The beauty of the speech is that you suddenly understand that old Silas has known that Teb wasn't his grandson all along. Henry's ghost had told him. The ghost had also said that Teb had stayed with Henry as he'd died during the war, and that had meant everything to him."

"A ghost, huh?" Charlotte said. "There's a twist."

"You don't believe in ghosts?" Zoey asked, surprised. "What about your witch balls?"

"That's just a story. Real life is scary enough."

"You don't strike me as someone who's afraid of anything."

Charlotte had heard that for years. And she'd carefully cultivated that image, traveling alone across the country on her scooter. She would never tell anyone the truth. That she was scared. All the time. Of everything and everyone. Especially of herself. "I'm not that hard."

"I don't think you're hard," Zoey said. "You're just . . . guarded."

"Do you believe in ghosts?"

Zoey thought about it for a moment. "I've never seen one. But that doesn't mean they're not real. There are a lot of things we can't see that are real."

"Such as?"

Zoey shooed something away above her head. "Stories. Scent. Love. Lots of things."

She turned back around to face the front when the old woman from the ticket counter hopped on the trolley and introduced herself as Flo.

"Have you ever wondered how the beloved white confection we know as *marshmallow* got its name?" Flo asked. "It's actually named after a leafy green plant. Confectioners—including the very ones who came to this island—used to use the root of the marshmallow plant as a thickener to make it. These days, modern marshmallows are mass-produced using gelatin and don't actually contain any part of the marshmallow plant. But the name stuck. Now you can go home and impress your family and friends with this little bit of trivia. You're welcome."

Everyone on the trolley laughed. Even Charlotte.

The man at the wheel turned at the end of Trade Street and drove down the coastal highway. Flo pointed out the tidal marshland where the marshmallow plant with its tall reeds could still be found growing, so densely it almost obscured the water and gave the impression of a great field of overgrown land. They were soon passing the Mallow Island Resort Hotel, which was a large Greek Revival–style house set back on what looked like miles of tended gardens. Flo informed them that it was once the stately home of Edward Pelletier, referred to by islanders simply as the English-man, who had bought the island after the Civil War, discovered the marshmallow plant growing here, and spearheaded the island's short-lived marshmallow-candy boom.

Zoey turned to Charlotte and mouthed, *Mac works there!*

Charlotte smiled and nodded.

The trolley then turned and drove through the center of the is-land, a lost-in-time place of locals. The buildings were all low and old, as if ducking to avoid high wind. Flo pointed out places where the movie adaptation of *Sweet Mallow* was filmed, including the courthouse steps where Silas Sparrow gave his famous speech. The trolley finally meandered down a long residential street of an ex-clusive neighborhood with large old homes in bright candy colors like those on Trade Street, homes built by the Englishman for the candymakers he'd brought over from England. There, the trolley stopped in front of the home of Roscoe Avanger himself. The bus almost tilted as everyone on board craned over, trying to make out his house past the gate and pecan trees. Until this tour, Charlotte hadn't realized just how important the book and the writer were to the island. He had preserved it all with a story, like putting it under glass. How much of this place would still exist, would still be remembered, if he hadn't shared it with the world?

On the hot drive back, she watched Zoey stare out the open window, wind lifting her dark hair. She saw something faraway and sad feather across Zoey's face, which was surprising. She'd never thought of Zoey as anything but happy and bright. It occurred to Charlotte that there was more to Zoey's story than she wanted to reveal, the story of a hard, dead mother and a father who didn't help her move.

She tapped her on the shoulder. "You okay?"

Zoey nodded. "I was just thinking that I understand why my mother loved this place."

As the trolley pulled back in front of the building on Trade Street about an hour after it had left, Charlotte thought she understood why she loved this place so much, too, why it spoke so strongly to her, and probably Zoey, and countless others. Mallow Island had reinvented itself over and over. And just like the candy itself, no one here had to be made up of what they used to.

Zoey waited outside while Charlotte went in the ticket office to talk to Flo.

And based on Mac's recommendation alone, Charlotte was offered a job on the spot.

———•••———

The air was swollen with moisture as Mac drove home from work that night. He took the coastal highway and could see the storm moving toward the island. By the time he got home, the first fat drops had started to fall. He crossed the dark parking lot and hurried through the garden gate as the rain got heavier. He unlocked his door, almost kicking the small white box with a note taped to it sitting on the patio. He picked it up and went inside.

He set his keys on the coffee table and shook the rain out of his hair. Holding the box in one hand, he opened the note with the other.

*I got that job at the trolley tours today. As a thank-you, here's an
ornament called a witch ball. I collect them. I hope you like it.
Charlotte*

She had drawn intricate patterns around the edges of the paper. Heart-shaped petals formed into flowers, and paisley curlicues
formed into leaves, all of which connected to look like lace. It was
similar to the designs he'd seen decorating Charlotte's skin over the
years. He opened the box and lifted out a glass ball. He held it up
and saw tiny glass threads inside that reminded him of strings of
batter falling from a spoon.

He stared, mesmerized as he twirled it back and forth, until Fig
meowed from the couch.

He snapped out of it, embarrassed. He put the ball, the box, and
the note all on the coffee table quickly. "I'm not smiling, *you're* smiling," he said as he headed for the shower.

Fig jumped down and followed him, meowing again.

"No one likes a know-it-all, Fig."

GHOST STORY

Camille

I don't want him to be lonely. He needs someone. Even I got married.
Even I had kids. Not my own, mind. And I only married because I
needed someplace to live. But sometimes it doesn't matter how you
get there, it only matters that you do.

My mama died of lady cancer when I was fifteen, then my brother
John got a wife who soon filled our little house with babies. I had to get
out of there, and I set my sights on an old man who lived at the end of
the road. He was alone because he never married, and he was drunk
most of the time. But sad drunk, not mean drunk. I wouldn't have put
up with a mean drunk. His house was a mess and, as children, we
used to throw our candy wrappers into his yard because we honestly
thought that was where all the neighborhood trash was supposed to
go. The day after my sister-in-law gave birth for the fifth time in seven
years, and to twins, no less, I marched down the road to his door and
knocked. He answered, all stooped over, and I said, "I'm Camille
and I'm twenty-two and I work hard and I cook good. You got a house
and I need a place to live. If you marry me, I'll take care of you." He

was probably too drunk to really understand, but he seemed to think it was a good idea. So we got married. I cleaned up his place, which was just a tar paper house, but it looked pretty nice once I got at it. He was still a drunk, but my cooking and cleaning kept him alive for almost ten more years, and he died just short of his ninetieth birthday.

He was a nice man, all in all. He'd worked for the railroad when he was younger, until his back gave out. He had a photo in a frame of himself with another man, both in overalls with the tracks behind them, and it was the only thing he ever took care of. At first he said the man was his brother. But then he'd get drunk and he'd cry, "I loved that man!" He'd look at me with tears in his eyes and say deeply, as if he really wanted me to understand, "I *loved* him." He liked the men, my husband. Or, probably, just that one man. I never told anyone. At that time, in a neighborhood like ours, you didn't have the luxury of loving anyone you pleased. People would kill you because you thought you had that right.

His name was Lowry, my husband. I had him buried with that photo. I thought he'd like that.

When he died, I started working at the touristy restaurant they called Sea Food Paradise. When it burnt down, people said the live crabs escaped from the tanks and walked with flames on their shells all the way to the ocean. Days after it happened, there came like always the truck with the weekly delivery of cornmeal. Because, for those of you who don't know it, around here you have to have hush puppies with your seafood. That's just the way it is. I made so many of those things I'd wake up in the middle of the night and find myself in my kitchen making them in my sleep. Anyway, there was no place to deliver it, and since it was paid for and couldn't be taken back, the owner sent that damn truck to me. I guess he thought it was some kind of present to keep me happy until he rebuilt, which he did, eventually.

He called it the *New* Sea Food Paradise, as if it didn't serve exactly the same thing. But in the meantime I was stuck with six big paper bags of cornmeal, almost as tall as me, making my back porch sag with the weight of them.

That's when it really began. When I started caring for the neighborhood kids. I needed to get rid of all that cornmeal before the weevils and the meal moths got to it, so I got to making a lot of corn bread. It was summer and those kids were hungry. They started coming to my door and I'd give them plates of it. I could tell the children who were going to be okay. They may not have had anything, but they still had a parent, usually a mother, who loved them. Those were the ones who went home after they had their Cammie snack. But then there were the children I knew weren't okay. Usually skinny boys with big eyes wild with fear, like horses. They'd stay on my porch all day. Some of them showed up at night, quivering like bony branches, and I'd take them in and let them sleep on the couch. Most of them didn't stay long in the neighborhood, a few years at most, before their families got kicked out for not paying rent, or when the little houses, deteriorating with salt and sand, were condemned. Up the road a ways, some Habitat for Humanity houses were built, and that changed things some in the neighborhood. But here at my end of the street, there was still this unimaginable poor. Most folks in America can't imagine a world where you don't have *something.* But I saw it every day, those kids who didn't have a single thing. So, for all my life of not wanting kids, I ended up with hundreds. I fed them, and I let them know that this was something they had. They had my food. And food is love. They were all colors, because this is a colorful island, but they all had one thing in common. They were skinny, skinny, skinny.

Until my Macbaby came along, as big as a Christmas turkey.

He needs that. He needs to cook for someone who loves him. He needs to take care of something other than that cat. She's a sweet thing, don't get me wrong. She knows I'm here. Sometimes I sit with her on the couch. But a cat can't love you like a person. A cat can't make you whole.

And neither, in case you're wondering, can a ghost.

Chapter Twelve

The next morning, Zoey sat on the couch as she scrolled through Instagram. There were a few people from high school who were posting photos of things they'd already bought for their dorm rooms. Every photo included pillows. For a reason she had yet to suss out, moving into a dorm room involved bringing a mountain of pillows with you. Zoey had her college list, which she'd been adding to all year with each new correspondence from school and each new article she read about what she'd need. She would have to start buying stuff soon. She had a countdown on her phone, marking how much time she had before she moved into her dorm. She already planned to come back here as often as possible. Every weekend, if she could. When asked about home, she could imagine herself saying, "Oh, I live on Mallow Island." Not Tulsa.

Zoey paused in her scroll. Her stepmother had posted photos of Zoey's old bedroom—her burgeoning new craft room, Wonderland. The carpet had been torn out and pale hardwood flooring had been installed. The walls had been painted a soft aqua, and above the windows overlooking the garage LIVE YOUR BEST LIFE had been stenciled in fine gold lettering. One of the photos showed Tina on a stepladder at the windows, a tiny brush in her hand. She was in full makeup and her hair was piled high on her head. She was wearing capri overalls and a crisp white button-down shirt with blue pin-stripes. She knew exactly the kind of person she wanted to portray on social media. And Zoey would give her this—in real life she was just as concerned with aesthetics as she was online. She liked things to be pretty. She shared that trait with Zoey's father. But unlike him, she knew how to actually create pretty things, and not just collect them. She'd taken the large but oddly decorated home Alrick had bought when he and Paloma and baby Zoey had moved to Tulsa, a home that had been full of dark antiques Alrick had bought because he'd thought they made him seem important, and she'd turned it into a true showplace. Tina probably really did do that stencil herself. But certainly not in those clothes. Those were bought just for the photo.

Her bedroom looked so different. Zoey studied it carefully, re-alizing that what bothered her the most was that it looked *better.* She remembered her white walls and the scuffed blue bedroom set she'd had since she was seven and the dark curtains that were always drawn because the way the sun angled into the room made it the hottest on the second floor. Tina had wanted to paint the walls and take out the carpeting while it had been Zoey's room. And Zoey had known how much she'd wanted it, which was the very reason she'd never let her touch it.

Zoey wondered if her family imagined her living someplace just as depressing now. They probably did. They probably assumed that she had taken her quiet, unpretty, bookish life with her and was even now holed up in a dark room, reading—no friends, no social life.

Zoey lifted her phone to take some photos of her studio to show them just how magical it was, but then stopped. Some of her clothes were still in boxes, there were books everywhere, and the sink had dishes she hadn't put in the dishwasher yet because she kept forgetting to buy dishwasher pods.

There was a knock on her balcony doors and she gave a start. She looked up to find Charlotte standing there, that peculiar pink Mallow Island morning sunlight behind her. Instead of taking a photo of the studio, Zoey snapped a photo of her. She imagined posting it with the caption *My creative friend Charlotte. She does henna, drives a scooter, and collects witch balls.* She wouldn't, of course, because she remembered Charlotte saying she didn't want her photo online. But Zoey liked the idea of having it on her phone, maybe to show people at college if they asked about her life on Mallow Island.

"I saw that your doors were open," Charlotte said. She was wearing her official GOOD GOLLY, MISS TROLLEY T-shirt. "I just wanted to say bye."

Zoey lowered her phone. She had almost forgotten that this was Charlotte's first day at the trolley tours. Her heart sank slightly at the reminder, but she said, "Good luck. Thanks for all your help this week with Lizbeth's place."

"I should be the one thanking you."

"Me? Why?"

Charlotte looked embarrassed. "It was just something I needed. I didn't think I was going to miss it, but I am. Not the smell. I'm definitely not going to miss the smell."

Zoey got up to join Charlotte on the balcony, which was still wet from last night's storm. Below them in the garden, the della-wisps were engaging in their morning ritual of arguing loudly about absolutely nothing. Pigeon had wanted out very early to join them.

"I think I'll have it finished today. Frasier said eventually there'll be a crew coming in to tear out the drywall and gut the kitchen and bathroom."

"Then, unless Lizbeth hid something in the walls, I don't think Roscoe Avanger is going to get the story he wants."

Zoey sighed as she looked out over the garden. "It was fun to think about."

"Maybe some stories aren't meant to be told," Charlotte said.

That had been exactly what Frasier had said. But Zoey was uneasy with the thought of untold stories. What happens to them? Where do they go? If you never share your stories with at least one other person, does that mean they weren't real, that they never really existed?

Mac's door opened and they both watched him walk out backward. When he turned, he immediately lifted a hand to wave to them, as if he'd seen them before he'd come out. His red hair, which was usually combed and gelled, was falling over his forehead sleepily. He walked to the base of Zoey's staircase. "I'm glad I caught you before you left, Charlotte. Thank you for the witch ball."

"You don't have to thank me," Charlotte called down to him. "It's the least I could do."

"She gave you a witch ball, too?" Zoey asked. "Aren't they beautiful?"

"They are. But I need to confess that it broke last night. I don't know how it happened. I walked away and *bam*." He lifted his hands, palms up, and flexed his fingers like he was releasing magic sparks. "It just shattered."

"Don't worry. I have another," Charlotte said, walking down the steps. "Wait here and I'll get it."

"No, you don't have to do that," he said, clearly flustered. "I just didn't want you to think I didn't like it." Mac had such an easy confidence, one that matched his larger-than-life size, around everyone Zoey had ever seen him interact with. Everyone, that is, except Charlotte. With her, Mac reminded Zoey of an elephant encountering a bumblebee. Charlotte seemed such an unknown entity to him that his reaction to her was sometimes a curious *What is this thing?* and sometimes a panicked *WHAT IS THIS THING!* And in true bumblebee fashion, Charlotte seemed to have no idea as she buzzed along, trying to mind her own business.

Charlotte waved away his concern. "I insist. I owe you." She headed to her condo, unlocked it, and disappeared inside.

Zoey, who had followed Charlotte down the steps, looked at Mac strangely. She saw now that the reason his hair was weighted down around his forehead and ears was because it had some sort of powder in it. "You have," she pointed to his head, "something in your hair."

A flash of alarm passed over his features before he caught it and smiled. "It's just cornmeal. Chef's hazard."

Although she desperately wanted to know how that much ended up in his hair, as if he'd plunged headfirst into a vat of it, she resisted. What did she know about cooking? "When Charlotte and I took the trolley tour yesterday, we drove by the Mallow Island Resort Hotel. It's a beautiful place."

"They offer walking tours called Butterfly Walks in the front garden. You should take one," he said as Charlotte came back out.

"Do you want to go with me, Charlotte?" she asked. "Or maybe we could even eat at Popcorn one day!"

"I could make that happen," Mac said. "Just give me a date. My treat."

Charlotte handed him a beautiful purple ball. "That's okay. You've done enough for me."

"I'd love to cook for you. Both. I'd love to cook for you *both*," he clarified, and his neck began to redden. "What about Thursday night?"

"Yes!" Zoey said before Charlotte could refuse.

With a nod, Mac walked away.

"He's a James Beard Award winner," Zoey said. "It's on the website. I don't know what that means, but I think it's important."

"Well, I'm no James Beard Award winner, but I'll make tacos for dinner for us when I get home, okay?"

"Okay." Zoey paused, then she said, because she felt it needed saying, "You know that invitation wasn't really for me, don't you?"

"He's nice," Charlotte said, taking an elastic hair band out of her jeans pocket. "I'm definitely no expert, but isn't that what nice men do?"

"If he asked you to dinner, only you, what would you say?"

Charlotte put the band between her lips as she brought her long blond hair up into a ponytail. "I would say I don't like eating out alone," she said around the band.

"You know what I mean."

"You're making something out of nothing." She tied up her hair. "Now, I've got to go. It's not a great start if I'm late on my first day when I live zero-point-two seconds away."

When Charlotte left with a squeak of the garden gate, Zoey thought about going back up to her studio just so she could put off going to Lizbeth's. The sooner she got started, the sooner she would finish, and she didn't want to be finished, to go back to waiting for things to happen.

One week. That was all it had taken. There was a perverse part of her that wished Lizbeth's place had been bigger so it would have taken all summer to go through.

But the allure of those last boxes ultimately got the better of her.

"Come on, Pigeon," she called to the garden. "This is the day you've been waiting for."

A few hours later, after looking through four consecutive boxes of brochures from television offers that Lizbeth had obviously sent off for just to collect—information about retractable awnings and gutter systems and erectile-dysfunction supplements—Zoey suddenly had a feeling that she should be annoyed. She stopped and looked up, automatically frowning. But there was nothing to be annoyed about.

That's when she realized Pigeon wasn't with her.

The more that had been cleared from Lizbeth's place over the past week, the more time Pigeon had spent inside with them. She would pace across the floor while Zoey tried to ignore her coos, claiming she had no idea why stray pieces of paper in corners seemed to rip on their own when Charlotte's back was turned.

"Pigeon?" she said. The space was so empty now that her voice echoed off the dirty walls.

Nothing.

She took off her mask and gloves and got up. She walked out into the summer sunshine, which was still catching glints of raindrops lingering on the garden foliage. She put her hands to her lower back and stretched. The dellawisps were pecking around on the ground, and Zoey figured Pigeon was with them. She didn't know if she felt offended that Pigeon had finally decided to leave her alone, or relieved. She'd told Pigeon to make friends with the other birds, after all. But Pigeon never did what she was told. And Zoey didn't like the thought of Pigeon letting go of *her* so easily, as if Zoey were the only one who could say goodbye.

While she was standing there watching the birds, trying to determine exactly where Pigeon was, she caught a movement across the garden.

Had she imagined it, or had the sheer curtains covering Lucy Lime's patio doors just moved?

Was Lucy watching her?

Lizbeth's condo had been unlocked again this morning. By now it made Zoey smile, imagining Lucy coming in to sit and talk to Lizbeth. The stone floor had even still been wet in places, as if Lucy had tracked in rain during last night's storm.

Zoey lifted her hand slowly and waved. It had been days since she'd resolved to ask Lucy to lunch. And now it was the last day any of them would get to spend in Lizbeth's place, the last day it would really *be* Lizbeth's place.

So why not ask her now? The worst thing that could happen was that Lucy would say no.

She walked around the garden and onto Lucy's unswept patio. She could smell the cigarette smoke from here, as if it were leaching through unseen cracks. She tried to look approachable, though she was suddenly self-conscious because she realized she didn't know what approachable looked like. She hunched her shoulders a little and shifted her weight onto one foot. She put her hand on her hip, then dropped it. Oh for heaven's sake, what was the matter with her? She reached out and knocked. Then she knocked again. Somewhere around minute three, she knew Lucy wasn't going to answer. Still, she called, "Lucy? My name is Zoey. I live in the studio. I just wondered if you wanted to have lunch with me."

Nothing.

"I'll be finished cleaning out your sister's place today. Frasier said repairs will be starting soon. I just . . . I thought you'd like to know."

Wait, was there sound coming from inside? Was Lucy coming to the door?

Zoey held herself very still.

Nothing.

Zoey finally turned and left. It was a first step. She'd only been here a little over a week, and already she and Charlotte were friends, and Mac had invited them to his restaurant. Maybe Lucy would soon come into the fold, making their little Dellawisp circle complete.

She wasn't going to give up on her just yet.

The last box, hundreds of free South Carolina tourism brochures Lizbeth had apparently liberated from local gas stations, was done.

Well, that was it.

Zoey stood and looked around the empty space. The infamous bookcase was still in the middle of the living room where she and Charlotte had moved it, but it was going to be removed soon, along with Lizbeth's bedroom furniture. Frasier had taken the computer, but he said there wasn't anything on it of interest to Roscoe.

Zoey picked up the box bound for the recycling dumpster and whispered, "Bye, Lizbeth."

She turned, an edge of the box hitting the grimy window frame as she did so. The impact caused a small piece of paper to flutter out of nowhere from below the window. Zoey set the box down and picked it up. It was an old photo of two girls in bathing suits, standing in a trashy yard of dead grass. One was blond and pretty, about ten years old, striking a pose that was almost uncomfortably sexy for a girl that age. The other was about four, dark-haired and square-shaped, caught in midwail and holding her shoulder as if the other had just hit her.

On the back was written *Lucy and Lizbeth*.

Excitement lit Zoey up like a sparkler. Out of all the paper she'd gone through, this was the only personal thing she'd found, besides the diaries. Where on earth had it come from? It had obviously been dislodged from somewhere. She knelt by the window and looked around it. She found several tiny stick figures drawn on the baseboard, so small she had mistaken them for the splotchy dirt that had permanently stained all of Lizbeth's walls. It appeared as if a child had once spent a lot of time in this area. She felt along the edges of the window and discovered a gap where the frame met the wall, and from that gap she carefully plucked out several more photos.

She sat cross-legged on the floor and went through them slowly. The photo of Lucy and Lizbeth was the only older photo. The rest were fairly recent school photos of the same boy, an almost preternaturally pretty child with curly brown hair and green eyes that shone cleverly, like he was part avian. His smile was as charming as a piece of candy, which automatically made Zoey smile back at him. The school photos stopped sometime in his early teens, when he had grown gangly and awkward and his smile had turned into just a reluctant lift at the corners, as if he was trying not to laugh at something he actually found funny.

She turned over the photo of him at his youngest, and found the words *Oliver Lime. First Grade.*

These weren't Lizbeth's photos, she realized. These were *Oliver's*.

And this was where he'd lived. She looked around, trying to imagine him carving out space in all the clutter. She'd never before considered where he'd actually slept. There was only one bedroom, and that was all Lizbeth's.

She wondered why he'd hidden the photos. Was it because he didn't want his mother to have them? Or was it because his mother didn't want *him* to have them?

She stood and picked up the box again.

With one last look, the photos safely in her pocket, she closed the door behind her

---

Pigeon finally flew in and landed noisily in her birdcage just as Zoey emerged from her bathroom after a shower.

"Where have you been?" Zoey asked as she got something to drink.

Pigeon cooed as if to say it was none of her business.

"Fine, don't tell me," she said, going to the white leather couch. She'd left Oliver's photos on the coffee table, so she spread them out to stare at them again as she opened her Snapple bottle and took a sip. It was something of a surprise that Oliver didn't look more messy and Harry Potterish, having grown up in a corner of a packed living room with little sunlight. Instead, he looked vibrant and popular. In one photo he was even wearing braces. *Someone* had been caring for him. She wondered who. Frasier? Lucy?

She warred with herself for several minutes before she decided to take a photo of each and text them to Oliver. If he didn't want them, he could just delete them and report her to Frasier again. But there had to have been a reason he'd kept these in his corner.

Once all the photos were sent, she checked the time on her phone. It would be hours before Charlotte got home. She sat back on the couch and wiped away the condensation on her Snapple bottle with the hem of her shirt. She looked around her studio listlessly. After a few moments, a frown began to form and she sat up. Where exactly had her mother planned for Zoey to sleep after they moved back to Mallow Island? There was only one bed, just like at Lizbeth's.

Zoey had seen enough mothering to understand when it was done right. She'd watched her best friend Ingrid's single mother hold down a full-time job on weekdays and a part-time job on the weekends, and yet it had still seemed like she'd been home with her two kids all the time. That was how present she'd been for them. She'd never been late signing permission slips, because she'd been the one who'd remembered to do it. Her children's clothing had been cheap, but never snug, because she'd been the one who had noticed when her children were growing. It had never been up to the children to ask for these things, like Zoey had had to do. Even Zoey's stepmother Tina, though clearly and unabashedly concerned with how other people saw her, still paid attention to her twins when no one was looking. So Zoey understood that mothering was in the details you never saw. And the lack of it was the things you always noticed.

And she saw now, for the first time, that whatever her mother had been planning for this move, it was without taking Zoey's needs into consideration. Paloma had been a young mother, yes, but young or not, if you took the time to have a place redecorated before you and your daughter moved in, wouldn't you at least think about where you were going to put her?

Zoey had spent so much time blindly defending her mother to her father, who was equally as determined to speak ill of her, that she'd never let herself think of Paloma as anything other than a good mother. It was the natural result of losing her so early. She got to make up what she wanted to fill in the gaps. Zoey thought about what Charlotte and Frasier had said about some stories not needing to be told. Zoey had only thought about the loss of the story itself.

But now she wondered if finding out the truth behind some stories would constitute an even greater loss, because it meant losing something you were happy believing.

There would always be stories Zoey would never know about her mother, questions she would never have the answers to.

But maybe, just maybe, that would be okay.

Her phone suddenly dinged.

Zoey, this is Oliver Lime. Frasier told you that I don't want anything from my mother's place, but I guess you need to hear it from me personally. Please stop sending me photos.

Oliver! He'd texted her! She wrote back immediately.

I understand, I really do. And I'm sorry. It's just the only thing of yours I found and I thought you might want the option of keeping them. I finished cleaning out your mother's condo a few hours ago. Do you think your aunt would want anything out of the box of things I saved?

She stood and walked to the balcony as she waited for him to respond. There were three dots indicating he was writing back, but then they disappeared.

She looked out over the garden before she added:

There's a fat dellawisp hopping around the garden path right now. It has a long red ribbon in its beak. The others are chasing it like it's a worm. The bird with the ribbon is very annoyed about this.

Nothing. She waited a few more minutes, and was about to put her phone away when his response appeared.

> I haven't seen Lucy since I left for college. And she barely said more than a handful of words to me while I lived there. In fact, the only thing I ever remember her saying is, "Are you all right?" when I fell in front of her patio once and she opened her doors to kneel by me. She kept looking over to my mother's condo, as if afraid she'd see her. So I have no idea what she would want. My guess is nothing. I kept that photo of them as girls and hid it because the only thing I ever remember my mother voluntarily throwing out was evidence of her family. She wanted nothing that reminded her of Lucy. Before you ask, I don't know why. At this point, you probably know my mother better than I ever did.

She knew the feeling. She didn't want to lose him while she knew he was there, so she quickly typed:

> Frasier said you just graduated. Congratulations, that's a big deal! I start in the fall.

> What college?

> The College of Charleston. But I don't know what I want to do. What did you major in?

> I have to go. I can't write right now.

Zoey started to lower her phone, but then Oliver added:

> But it's okay if you want to text me later.

Smiling, she went back to the coffee table to look at photos again. Her eyes fell on the photo of Lucy and Lizbeth, and she suddenly had an idea. She and Oliver both had digital copies now ... what would be the harm?

She went in search of an envelope, looking in drawers and shaking out random books. But there wasn't one to be found. It was something that was just around her old house in Tulsa because someone else had thought to buy it. She cursed with impatience and put envelopes on her grocery list on the refrigerator. Then she made a makeshift pouch out of aluminum foil. She put the photos in it, along with a note saying she thought Lucy would like to have them.

She walked down the steps and over to Lucy's patio. There, she wiggled the pouch partially into the seam where the patio doors met the frame, knocked, and returned to her balcony.

It was still there when Charlotte got home.

It was still there when they had dinner.

And it was still there when Zoey walked back up to her studio.

She sat on her balcony as long as she could, well into the night, waiting for Lucy to come out and take it. She finally had to give up and go to bed.

But when she woke the next morning, it was gone.

Chapter Thirteen

When Mac started working in the Mallow Island Resort Hotel, the restaurant had been a posh place called the Marsh. He'd made sous-chef while working at the Marsh. Camille, who had been nearly one hundred years old at the time, had come to dinner to celebrate. It was one of his best memories, cooking for her that night and making it a celebration of *her*, because all that he'd become was due to her.

Later, when the restaurant changed hands, the new owners decided to take the restaurant in the same eco-direction as the hotel, focusing on sustainability. Despite Mac's lack of formal training, he'd applied for executive chef and pitched his idea of paying homage to Camille with dishes created around cornmeal. The new owners were impressed with his respect for locally sourced food and his extensive knowledge of Low Country cuisine, so they decided to take a chance on him.

And Popcorn was born.

Work never started slow. From the moment Mac entered, there were meetings and questions about order shipments that didn't come in and holes in the menu to fill. It was hard work, mentally and physically, with long, chaotic hours. Burnout was so typical in kitchens he'd worked in in the past that there were secret bets on the line on all new hires. Popcorn had a reputation for being different, though. Because for any new hire, Mac listened for the stories. There was always a story that made him sure of who would work well on his team. The story of the grandmother who could stretch eggs a hundred different ways, so that even if it was all the family had to eat for a month, it still felt new. Or the story of a father who taught his kids to fish, but to release what they didn't need for that night's dinner around a campfire, which was sometimes their only way to cook because there wasn't a home to go back to.

He was proud of his kitchen, and he liked everyone who worked there. He met them where they were and encouraged creativity. He'd earned his place in the hierarchy, and they all respected him. But as he walked in that day, he wondered how they would react to the news that he was going to have guests.

After putting out a few small fires as soon as he arrived, he went upstairs to his small, windowless office. He'd no sooner turned on his laptop than Christine knocked on the door and showed him the two menus he'd asked to be printed out for Charlotte and Zoey.

Mac was hardly surprised when Javier, his sous-chef, poked his head in seconds later. Javier had a sixth sense for gossip.

"What is going on?" Javier asked in his charming Spanish accent.

"I have guests tonight." Mac handed the menus back to Christine. "That looks great, Christine. Thank you."

Javier plucked the menus from Christine's hands as she passed him in the doorway. "Two *female* guests," he said, reading their names on the menus.

"Give me those," Christine said, snatching them back. She was one of the few women here who didn't give him any latitude. It annoyed Javier, like a magician whose card trick had been figured out. "I don't know why Mac puts up with you."

"My sparkling personality, of course," Javier said as she left. He came in and sat on the edge of Mac's desk. "So, what is the story with these guests?"

"No story," Mac said, calling up his email.

"There is always a story, my friend. You taught me that." Javier's own story had been about his mother's flan, which she'd only made on birthdays and Javier said tasted like unconditional love.

"One of them is a teenager. She just moved into the Dellawisp."

"And the other one?" said Javier suggestively.

"She's lived there a couple of years." Mac paused. "She's not a teenager."

"Ah. So the picture, it becomes clearer to me."

"Shouldn't you be working?" Mac asked, even though Javier leaving would mean this would soon be all over the kitchen. But there was no use trying to stop it.

Javier left with a wink and said, "Benedict would approve."

Mac rolled his eyes. *Benedict would approve* was a chorus that erupted on the line after a particularly lascivious tale was shared. Benedict was the ghost that supposedly haunted the kitchen at Popcorn, and he had become their patron saint of bedroom antics.

The real Benedict, by all accounts, had been a young, painfully shy candymaker brought over from London by the Englishman during the island's post-Reconstruction marshmallow boom. He'd been so talented that the Englishman took him in as his wife's personal candymaker. Rumor had it that Benedict then fell in love with the Englishman's beautiful, full-bodied wife, and she with his sweet treats. They disappeared from the island together and many believe they ended up on the southern coast of France based on the modest success of a marshmallow maker there around that time who had a large, beautiful wife and, eventually, eight large, beautiful children.

The myth of Benedict lived on at Popcorn, perpetuated mostly by randy young prep cooks and dishwashers, but also, curiously, by the occasional strange occurrence. Like the time one of the waitresses found a single rose in her locked locker and thought it was from a saucier she had a crush on. That started a conversation, and the two were married just last year in the hotel's front garden. The saucier eventually admitted that he hadn't left the rose, and no one ever came forward to claim responsibility. Then there were the footsteps that often appeared in spilled flour overnight. And, most curiously, the heart-shaped chocolates that randomly turned up around the restaurant, known as Benedict's Calling Card.

After finally getting through his email, Mac used his desk as an anchor to get to his feet, dislodging some papers and knocking them to the floor. He bent to pick them up, and was about to put them back when he stilled.

There, on his desk where the papers had been, was a single piece of heart-shaped chocolate.

He was startled enough that his first thought was *Benedict?*

Then he shook his head. He had no idea how Javier had managed to have chocolate on him at just the right time but, knowing him, he'd been waiting for just such an opportunity for a while.

Mac threw away the chocolate as he left for the kitchen.

There was a lot to get right this evening.

———————

Ever since she'd arrived on the island, Zoey's style could best be described as This Was The First Thing I Found. So she had to go through clothes she hadn't even unpacked yet to find something she thought was appropriate to wear to Popcorn. She finally found the yellow dress she'd bought for her high school graduation ceremony last month. Her father and Tina hadn't attended because of some fundraiser, but good old Kello from the bookstore had been there, and he'd said Zoey looked like sunshine in it. She'd never been very good at picking out clothes. Anyone who didn't know her family had money probably assumed Zoey couldn't afford fashionable things by the way she had dressed in high school. When she'd first started working at Kello's bookstore, before she'd gotten her car, Kello had insisted on dropping her off at her house after they closed for the night because he'd worried about her taking the bus home after dark. He'd been surprised when he'd first seen her house. She'd been embarrassed about not seeming to live up to the standard of such a place, and she'd tried to explain about not yet having access to the trust from her mother. Kello had looked at her in the dim light of his old white VW Beetle and said something she would never forget: "If the people around you don't love you just as you are, *find new people.* They're out there."

She paired the dress with her gladiator sandals and was out the door without Pigeon once getting in her way, fussing about where she might be going.

Something was up with that bird.

Charlotte wasn't home from work yet, so Zoey sat on Charlotte's patio to wait for her. Her eyes kept going to Lucy's condo, wondering if she liked the photos Zoey had left for her. She hoped that Lucy had actually gotten them, and not the dellawisps, who were at that moment working together to drag what appeared to be a tourist's lost pink fanny pack across the garden toward one of the brugmansia trees.

"Hey, you look nice," Charlotte said as she stepped onto her patio and took her keys out of her jeans pocket. "I'll take a quick shower and then we can get an Uber."

"We're not going to take your scooter?" Zoey asked as she followed Charlotte inside, where the dusty and dinged scooter was parked by the couch. Zoey walked to it and patted it like a good dog.

"You want to?"

Zoey looked sheepish. She'd spent way too much time thinking about it. "I was kind of looking forward to it."

"Okay," Charlotte said with a shrug. "But it's not as fun as you think it is. It might be a glamorous way to get around Rome, but not an American highway. The truth is, I don't even like it that much."

"Then why do you drive it instead of a car?"

"Dreams from when I was a teenager. And it's easier to leave and take only what I need on a scooter," she said as she headed to her bedroom.

That explained a lot of things. Charlotte's place was almost aggressively anti-clutter. There wasn't a single thing here except the witch balls in her bedroom that gave Zoey the impression that it was important to Charlotte, or that it had been carried here from someplace else. Her home didn't tell many stories, much like Charlotte herself.

When Charlotte emerged about twenty minutes later, she was wearing a short madras dress and denim sneakers, and her hair was in a long, skinny braid. She handed Zoey a helmet and said, "Don't say I didn't warn you."

But aside from the heat of the helmet and having to hold her dress down, obviously the reason Charlotte favored bicycle shorts under her skirts, Zoey loved the ride. The young man at the valet stand obviously shared Zoey's enthusiasm. When Charlotte pulled in front of the hotel and Zoey got off, her body still humming from the motor and her hair plastered to her head, he said, "Cool," and gave her a fist bump.

It had a grand front garden and imposing Greek Revival architecture, so Zoey was surprised when the outside of the Mallow Island Resort Hotel gave way to a relaxed atmosphere inside. The large staircase in the lobby probably led to some guest rooms, but the bulk of the accommodations appeared to be colorful bungalows in the smaller back garden, which could be seen dotting the landscape all the way to the water.

She wanted to look around, but the AC felt glorious when they walked in. They just stood there for a moment, reveling in it. Then Charlotte nudged her and indicated that she'd found Popcorn's entrance, to the left of the doors.

There was a party of six already waiting, so Charlotte took a seat on a leather banquette by the hostess stand and began to rebraid her hair, which had become loose in the wind.

"There's Mac," Zoey said, pointing to a framed magazine article on the wall behind the banquette. Charlotte craned her head to look.

Zoey stepped closer. In the photo Mac was standing in his kitchen wearing his chef's whites and a tall white hat that looked like a stovepipe. His burly arms were crossed confidently over his chest, and around his neck was a large medal. The headline read: LOCAL CHEF WINS PRESTIGIOUS JAMES BEARD AWARD.

"Charlotte, listen to this. 'Chef Mac Garrett was born on Mallow Island. He credits his love of food and the inspiration for Popcorn to Camille Hyatt, the woman who raised him and taught him to cook. Mrs. Hyatt worked for fifty years at the beloved Mallow Island seafood shack, the New Sea Food Paradise, once said to have been a favorite of Roscoe Avanger's.'"

"Roscoe Avanger again," Charlotte said. "He's everywhere and nowhere."

Zoey continued to read. Soon she said, "And listen to this. 'There are several ghosts said to haunt the property of the Mallow Island Resort Hotel, some from its tragic plantation days before the original house burned. People claim to hear voices near the adjoining nature preserve, speaking in Gullah. And in the newer, post–Civil War house built by the Englishman, Popcorn's kitchen is supposedly haunted by Benedict, a candymaker brought over from England, said to have been in love with the Englishman's wife.'"

"Ghosts, too. I should have known."

After the party of six was seated, Charlotte gave their names and they were led to a round table near the windows overlooking the front of the hotel. Zoey tried to take everything in at once. The bar was made with reclaimed wood and pressed tin. The walls were covered with framed photos of old Southern grain mills. And several antique cornmeal grinders were on display.

"Chef Garrett has chosen your menu tonight," the hostess said, once they were seated. She handed Charlotte and Zoey small single-page menus, different from the heavier-stock menus others were holding.

Printed on the page in elegant script was:

Dinner for Charlotte and Zoey

FIRST COURSE
Sweet potato soup, sorghum marshmallow

SECOND COURSE
Chilled cornmeal crab cake, mustard cream, curly endive

MAIN COURSE
Crispy pork belly, Coca-Cola glaze, polenta

DESSERT

"Cornbread in a glass of milk"
Whipped milk ice cream with crispy brown butter cornbread pieces

It seemed an absurd amount of food to Zoey. She hadn't expected this, and as soon as their server filled their water goblets and walked away, she leaned forward and whispered, "What if I can't eat it all?"

"Each course is a tiny portion, don't worry. They're like little works of art," Charlotte said. "I used to work for a place like this in San Antonio, years ago."

Zoey tucked away that interesting fact for later. *She used to live in San Antonio.* Right now, Zoey had bigger concerns. "But what if I can't finish and I hurt Mac's feelings? I mean, our names are on the menus." She waved her menu for emphasis.

Charlotte lifted her water goblet and took a sip. "Some restaurants will print out commemorative menus for special occasions, like for birthdays and anniversaries."

Zoey sat back and grinned.

At her silence, Charlotte said, "What?"

"He thinks you're a *special occasion*."

"I can't take you anywhere." Charlotte tried to hide her smile as she took another sip of water. She didn't want to let it show, like she didn't like for anything to show, but Zoey could tell the thought pleased her. And that tiny crack let Zoey see inside to the only part of Charlotte's story she figured she really needed to know:

We all want to think we're worth the trouble.

The first course arrived quickly. When the bowl was set in front of her, Zoey looked down to find it empty save for three dollops of creamy white marshmallow. The waitress proceeded to pour sweet potato soup onto the marshmallow from a small white pitcher.

Zoey looked to Charlotte as if to ask if this was normal. She'd never had soup poured for her before, and she worried that it was because the waitress didn't trust her to do it herself. But Charlotte gave her a reassuring nod. Zoey picked up her spoon and tasted it, and she was immediately and startlingly transported to a perfect autumn childhood day, the kind of day when sunlight is short but it's still warm enough to play outside.

For the second course, the chilled crab cake was only the size of a silver dollar and the mustard cream and the green endive were just splashes of color on the plate. The visual experience was like dreaming of faraway summer while staring at Christmas lights through a frosty window.

The third course brought to mind the first hot day of spring, when it's too warm to eat in the house so you sit outside with a dinner plate of Easter ham and corn on your lap and a bottle of Coca-Cola sweating beside you. Zoey could feel the excitement of summer coming, and she couldn't wait for it.

And then summer arrived with the final course. And, like summer always is, it was worth the wait. The tiny container looked like a miniature milk glass, and the whipped milk in it reminded her of cold, sweet soft-serve ice cream on a day when the pavement burns through flip-flops and even shade trees are too hot to sit under. The savory bits of crispy cornbread mixed in gave the dessert a satisfying campfire crunch.

Zoey set her spoon down after she finished, blinking like the lights had just gone up in a theater.

"I feel like I've been listening to a story Mac was telling," she said in a daze. "He must *really* like you."

Staring into her empty glass, Charlotte didn't respond, but she seemed to be taking it under thoughtful consideration.

Because it was clear that this wasn't the kind of meal someone prepared for just anyone.

⸺ ⋆ ⸺

Full and cheery, two things she wasn't used to feeling separately, let alone together, Charlotte said good night to Zoey as she pushed her scooter onto her dark patio.

"Hey, Charlotte," Zoey called when she reached her balcony.

Charlotte turned to look up at her. Zoey's yellow dress was billowing in the island wind. She looked like she'd flown there on golden wings.

"I think you're a special occasion, too."

Charlotte laughed. "Go to bed."

Zoey unlocked the balcony doors and waved her commemorative menu at Charlotte before she went inside. She was going to stick it to her refrigerator, she'd said, because she wanted to always remember this evening. Without Zoey seeing, Charlotte had taken her menu, too. It was hidden in her backpack.

As soon as Zoey was safely inside, Charlotte brought out her house key and stepped to her doors.

There she paused, her smile fading.

She slowly reached out and put her palm flat against one of the glass panes, and pushed.

The door opened on its own.

She clearly remembered locking her doors before she left. Zoey had been with her and Charlotte had asked her to push the scooter to the alley while she'd turned the key.

She made herself step inside. She reached for the switch, and her living room burst into light. She felt it in the air, making her skin prickle.

Someone had been in here.

She stepped quickly and lightly across the living room and peered into the kitchen; then she went to her bedroom and looked under the bed and in the closet.

She'd left her scooter on the patio with the doors open in case she'd needed a quick escape, but now she dragged her scooter inside. She locked the doors and secured the dead bolt. Jelly-legged, she went to the couch and sat. She dropped her helmet and backpack to the floor and put her head to her knees, taking deep breaths.

She hated how close to the surface her fear still was after all these years, simmering like a watched pot. What were the chances it was someone from her old life? Wasn't the more logical explanation that it was Benny, thinking there was more money to steal? Or even Lucy made more sense. She tried to calm down by reminding herself that in her early days after running away, she had lived in a few dodgy places that had been broken into. And nothing had been taken because, like now, she didn't keep anything worth stealing. Benny had lucked out with the money she'd had on her that night.

She lasted two hours, two hours of pacing in the dark, periodically going to the patio doors to look out. Every noise sounded like someone trying to get in. More than once she'd grabbed her keys and helmet and went for her scooter, determined to push it out and drive to the all-night café called I Hate Mondays near the library at the center of the island. But she couldn't make herself go out. Teenaged Charlotte had been *fearless*. Why couldn't she call upon that right now?

The next time she looked outside, she noticed Mac's lights were now on across the garden. Without another thought, she slipped out and walked around the garden to his patio.

It only took a few seconds for Mac to pull back the curtain after she knocked. Seeing her, he immediately opened the door and stepped out. His hair was damp and he smelled like soap, like something fresh and green. He was wearing striped cotton pajama bottoms and a black T-shirt, but no socks. For some reason she felt comforted by the normalcy of his pale, freckled feet. She stared at them until he said, "Charlotte? What's wrong?"

She finally looked up at him. She was short, so she was used to most people being taller. But with Mac it wasn't just height, it was breadth, and she wanted to step forward and bury herself in his chest. "When Zoey and I got home, I discovered someone had been in my condo."

"What?" he said, looking across the garden. "You were robbed?"

"No. But my door was ajar, and I know I locked it before I left."

"What did the police say?"

"I didn't call the police," she said. "Nothing was taken this time."

Pause. "What do you mean, this time?"

She'd walked right into that one. What had she been thinking? This had been a bad idea. She wondered if he would notice if she started backing away gradually. Maybe he would think he'd imagined her as she slowly faded into the night.

"Charlotte?"

"The night Lizbeth died, some money went missing from my condo."

He looked confused. "Lizbeth robbed you before she died?"

"No," she said, rubbing her forehead.

He lowered his voice. "Lucy?"

"No. At least, I don't think so. But I'm sure Zoey would think that, which is one of the reasons I didn't tell her. I'm sorry. I just got spooked and I wanted to tell someone."

A few uncomfortable moments passed before Mac said, "Would you like to come in?"

His hesitation made it clear that he was only asking to be polite. She tried to force a smile, but the muscles in her cheeks felt tight with embarrassment. After that meal tonight, she'd thought . . . "No, that's okay," she said. "I'm going to go now."

"I don't mind, really." He turned and opened his door, standing back to let her enter. "Come in. I'll show you."

She waited the length of a few heartbeats before she walked by him and inside.

There was even more comforting normalcy here. Area rugs over-lapped and zigzagged across the stone floor. A half-filled glass of am-ber liquid was on the coffee table. On the far wall was a huge television on mute, with several Medusa-like cords connecting to boxes below. Something moved on the brown sectional, and she turned to it.

"You have a cat," she said, surprised. It was an odd-looking cat with no hair on its back and strange ears, but with beautiful green eyes focused on Charlotte. As soon as it saw that it had Charlotte's attention, it meowed several times with a soft, creaky voice, as if there was a lot it needed to tell her.

"I'd appreciate it if you didn't tell Frasier. She's absolutely no danger to those birds. She was a stray and badly burned behind Popcorn a few years ago. When she's not talking, she sleeps, mostly."

"What's her name?"

"Fig," Mac said. "Short for Figaro. Because she talks so much she's downright operatic."

"She's lovely." Her tragic beauty made Charlotte want to cry. "Of course I won't say anything. I'm sorry. I've put you in an uncomfort-able position. Thank you for that remarkable dinner tonight, and thank you for getting me the trolley job. You've done enough for me already. I shouldn't have bothered you." She turned to go, but Mac caught her by the arm.

"Didn't Zoey say she thought someone was coming into Lizbeth's place at night?"

Charlotte nodded.

"Then you should stay the night here. The couch is yours. Tomorrow we'll tell Frasier that the gate needs a keypad, or at least a lock."

"I don't know what's the matter with me. I'm not usually like this." Which wasn't true. She was exactly like this, deep down. More cracks were showing.

"Only two letters separate 'usual' and '*un*usual.' They're more similar than not. Especially on this island." He smiled as he dropped his hand from her arm. "The woman who raised me used to say that."

"Camille?" she asked, and he looked surprised that she knew. "She was mentioned in that framed article about you at Popcorn."

He pointed to a photo on the wall behind her. "That's her."

Charlotte turned. Mac was in a high school cap and gown, standing beside an elderly Black woman in a dress suit and hat. He was stooped down, and both his arms were around her like he was afraid she would slip away from him like water. Something about the old woman seemed familiar. It radiated so strongly that Charlotte could feel an actual warmth coming from the photo. *Home.* "How did you come to be raised by her?"

"My mother left one day when I was eight, and never came back." He shrugged. "She was always restless. Someplace else was always better than where she was. I was used to her disappearing for days at a time. She would leave me with a ton of food. But this time, weeks passed. We'd just moved into a new neighborhood, so I didn't know anyone and I didn't know what to do. But every morning I would see an old woman down the road hand out plates of food to kids, so I started showing up. It was Camille. She took me in when it became clear my mother wasn't coming back, though I don't think I gave her much choice. I attached myself to her like a barnacle."

She would never have suspected that Mac had survived a dysfunctional childhood. He seemed so composed. Solid. Put-together. "Where's your mother now?" Charlotte asked.

"I don't know. Probably dead."

Charlotte paused before asking, "What would you do if she showed up?"

"She won't," he said.

"How do you know?"

"Because she's always known where to find me." He went to the living room closet and lifted a throw from a high shelf. He handed it to her and said, "We'll talk to Frasier first thing in the morning, okay?"

She nodded.

"Feel free to watch television. And help yourself to whatever's in the fridge."

She nodded again.

He said good night and walked to his bedroom, closing the door behind him. Charlotte stood there clutching the throw as Fig stared at her, blinking slowly.

Why had she let Zoey get into her head? Zoey was a teenager. It was obvious Mac *wasn't* attracted to her. Which was good, she told herself. It was one less thing to worry about, one less connection to untangle before she eventually left again. She should feel relieved.

So why did she feel so bereft?

She turned back to the photo of Camille.

How on earth could she miss something that hadn't been there in the first place?

Mac rested his forehead against his closed bedroom door, then he turned the lock quietly so Charlotte wouldn't hear. She was here in his condo, a beautiful, wide-eyed fairy asking for help, and the best he could do was to leave her alone in his living room with his cat because he couldn't fall asleep anywhere near her.

It was an easy enough thing to say he rarely thought of his mother. He didn't remember her much as a person. She'd had red hair and a crooked front tooth. She'd smoked Salem cigarettes. And she'd always used the phrase "How's it hanging?" when greeting people on the street, her eyes darting around, looking for that next new opportunity. But he didn't know her. He didn't understand her. All he knew was what she should have been. And that concept alone defined her and, to a certain extent, him. She should have cared for him. She should have stayed. And because she didn't, and because he didn't know why, he would always wonder if it was because he hadn't held on to her strong enough.

He remembered asking Camille once, after living with her for about a year, if she was ever going to leave him. She'd said, "I'm yours and you're mine, Macbaby. Nothing's going to change that. But this is an earthly world, and no one gets to stay forever."

And yet Mac was still holding on to her. He didn't want to say goodbye. She had been the source of all that was good in his life. Had she known that? Was part of his holding on proving to her how much he loved her, because he hadn't said it enough? Or was it because he secretly believed no one could ever love *him* but her? He didn't know.

He just knew that her presence now didn't come without a price. It made him even more scared of rejection, because who would ever believe in a loneliness so overwhelming that you called upon a ghost to alleviate it?

Eventually he pushed himself away from the door and took a sheet from the stack on the chair in the corner. He spread it over his bed and crawled under the covers.

And when he woke in the morning, he was again covered in cornmeal.

GHOST STORY

Camille

It doesn't surprise me that he's embarrassed to tell anyone that he misses me so much that he makes this happen. He's always been afraid of people making fun of him.

Kids used to tease him when he was a boy because he was such a big, dirty thing, always covered in food. His mama had left him alone with all the kid food her food stamps would buy, and he was always sticky with that orange powder from instant macaroni and cheese, which he'd just pour into his mouth because they didn't have a stove to cook it on. I finally got him to come to me just before school was back in session. I'd cooked that morning before it got too hot. I went to my screen door and yelled "Cammie snacks!" and heard the stomping of little bare feet on my porch. I came out and handed the neighborhood kids the paper plates, and I saw him standing in the middle of the road in front of my house. The children told him to go away, that he didn't need any food, but I told them to hush and motioned him to me. He stayed long after the others left. I wasn't surprised.

I was in my eighties when he came into my life. Sometimes I would talk to myself for company, because all my family was gone away and neighbors weren't close like they used to be. Those little kids loved me, but they didn't want to talk. They didn't want to hear about my memories. They were never interested in how I made my food, or the stories behind how I learned. Like how my mama would sing to her gravy to make it thicken, or how she showed me that bacon fat would make butter taste like a heaven no one had ever dreamed of. Or how cornmeal was better than flour because it had weight, and having weight is how you know your worth, so don't let anyone tell you differ-ent. Mac wanted to know, though. He listened, listened, listened, like he couldn't get enough of it.

When school got back in session, he started staying with me, not going home at all, and I'd wash his clothes and make him grits in the morning and send him off to the bus stop. This went on for weeks be-fore I was mad enough to go talk to his mama about it. Macbaby was a quiet boy, never in the way, never wanting anything but food. He'd sit, all still and shy-like, until I gave him breakfast and supper, never, ever a grabby-grub. How could a mother just let a sweet child like that rot? So I walked to their house, a real old, smelly one set back behind some scrubby palmettos on the corner. When I was a girl, we all said that house was haunted because one of the meanest men I ever knew killed his wife there. Big Willy. We'd tiptoe by the house and whisper, "Don't get us, Big Willy's ghost!" I knocked, but no one answered. So I opened the door, a little scared of Big Willy's ghost still, but there was nothing in there but filth. No electricity, no running water, bugs all over the food his mama had left him weeks and weeks ago. But no mama.

I sat Macbaby down when he came home from school and I asked him outright, "Where's your mama, Macbaby?" He didn't know. She'd been gone for a long time. Well, I didn't know what to do. Macbaby begged me not to tell anyone. He didn't want to leave me. And I know it was wrong, but I didn't want him to leave me, either. So I kept him clean and happy so there were no red flags. But whenever his living situation happened to come up, I would just waltz into that school with some cornmeal sugar crispies for all the teachers, some I cooked for when they were kids, and they'd mostly forget. I told Macbaby that we were just making him slip through the cracks, that's all. He said he was too fat to slip through the cracks. That made me laugh. He's got a good sense of humor, my Macbaby.

When he was sixteen, he got his first job, washing dishes at a bakery here on the island. He got good marks in school, but I got the sense he was lonely. He never talked of friends and he never went anywhere other than his job. He started as a line cook when he graduated—a good restaurant job in Charleston because that's where all the good restaurants were at the time and he was so eager to learn. He would come home at night and couldn't stop talking about everything that went on in the kitchen. He went ahead and moved to Charleston when he was nineteen. I understood. He was big and the house was small, and the bus from Mallow Island took almost an hour each way. A few years later, he moved back after I fell and broke my wrist. I told him not to, but he did anyway. He got the condo at the Dellawisp, then he went to work at the restaurant in the hotel. When he was promoted to sous-chef, he took me to eat there and everyone treated me like a queen.

He doesn't have to show me that he loves me. I know he does. I've always known it.

Children, don't hold on to old love so hard you forget to live. Old love isn't the only love you'll ever have. And I can tell you from this side that it never really goes away, anyway.

So let go.

Whatever you're holding on to, let go.

Chapter Fourteen

I t was so quiet at the camp that the ticking of the clock on the bedroom wall could be heard. There was a girl, just sixteen, on the bed in her parents' cabin, no longer shivering. Another girl was sitting on a hard chair beside the bed. They hadn't allowed her to see the girl in the bed for days, so she'd just crept through the window, tracking in mud that was several inches deep from the spring thaw outside. It covered her shoes and the hem of her baggy jeans. She was crying quietly as she held the dead girl's hand. It felt like she'd died along with her.

Voices suddenly broke through the quiet in the next room, adults. The girl beside the bed turned sharply to the door, frightened she might be caught. She recognized Minister McCauley by his booming voice perfected on street corners where he called dramatically to sinners. Minister McCauley was upset that the death of the girl could mean that so-called authorities would get involved at their camp. He was telling the dead girl's parents that it was everyone's fault but his own that the poor girl didn't survive.

But even the girl sitting by the bed knew that the dead girl could have easily been saved if they'd just taken her to a hospital. These were adults. They should have known better. They should have seen through Minister McCauley. Instead, the dead girl's parents were agreeing with him. The dead girl's father was even telling Minister McCauley that he was sorry.

They were going to bury the dead girl soon. Several men had just gone into the woods with shovels to dig through the wet earth that coated everything during Vermont's mud season. The girl sitting beside the bed knew she had to go. This would be her only chance. But she was petrified. She didn't think she could do this alone. That had never been the plan. The two girls were supposed to run away together. But she couldn't stay, either. She'd just discovered the bag of money in Minister McCauley's office. He was leaving. The bag of money made that clear. He had killed the girl on the bed with his negligence, and he was leaving everyone else to face the consequences.

By taking the money, the girl knew Minister McCauley couldn't go anywhere. Eventually every bad thing he'd ever done would catch up to him, and she wanted people to know exactly where he was when it did.

Trembling, the girl sitting by the bed fell to her knees, not in prayer—she was long past that—but to pry up the loose board and take out the diary. She stuffed it into the waistband of her jeans and then crawled back out the window. The only thing that got her moving, and kept her moving for years to come, was her promise to keep the dead girl's memory alive, even if it meant losing herself entirely.

Especially if it meant losing herself entirely.

———•••———

Charlotte awoke with a start.

She heard a vacuum cleaner, which was strange because she didn't have a vacuum cleaner. She didn't own any rugs to clean.

She lifted her head and found a cat lying on her stomach, staring at her through sleepy, half-closed eyes.

The vacuum cleaner shut off and Charlotte sat up, remembering where she was.

Fig jumped down and went to sit by Mac's bedroom door. If Charlotte left now, she wouldn't have to face him, to talk about things that were so frightening in the dark but seemed completely blown out of proportion now. This was awkward enough.

But then Mac's bedroom door opened and he walked out as Fig sauntered in, as if she wanted to inspect his work. It had the feeling of a well-worn routine.

Mac looked apologetic when he saw Charlotte. "Did I wake you?"

"That's all right," Charlotte said as she stood. She smoothed her hair, which had come out of its braid in the night, and tried to re-arrange her dress into something less messy. She was never at her best in the mornings, even when she hadn't slept in her clothes. It didn't help that he looked so composed with his red hair still wet and neatly styled back. How had he survived what he'd survived and ended up so *functional*? "Do you always vacuum first thing in the morning?"

"Fig's deaf, so it never seems to bother her."

"Oh," Charlotte said, inching toward the patio doors in retreat. "I didn't realize she was deaf."

"I didn't either, at first." Mac watched her progress, his hands in the pockets of his cargo shorts.

She reached the doors. "I should go."

"Do you want to talk to Frasier now," he asked, "or would you like some breakfast first?"

She was running as if he were chasing her, but he hadn't even moved. He wasn't asking questions or demanding answers. He wasn't trying anything. *He wasn't attracted to her.* He was safe. He was only offering her food. And food was touching all sorts of soft spots in her lately. Potato chip sandwiches. Lemon-glazed doughnuts. Corn bread in a glass of milk. She dropped her hand from the door handle. "It's not every day an executive chef offers to make me breakfast."

He smiled, turning toward the kitchen. "Now the pressure's on."

"Can I use your bathroom first?"

"Of course," he said. "It's through the bedroom. You'll probably find Fig there, drinking water out of the bathtub. She pretends her water bowl doesn't exist."

Once Charlotte closed the bathroom door behind her, she put her hands on the sides of the sink and lowered her head, telling herself to get it together. Then she looked at herself in the mirror. It was as bad as she'd thought.

Her brows knit as she reached up and brushed something that looked like flour from her shoulder.

Where had that come from?

When she walked back out, with Fig leading the way, Mac was at the stove. Although their condos were the same size, his kitchen seemed larger than hers, probably because there wasn't a wall separating it from the living room, just a long butcher-block island. She pulled out one of the modern metal stools and sat. Plates and forks were in front of her, as well as syrup and butter and an open clam-shell container of whole strawberries. He had all of this *on hand*. The only thing she was sure to have on hand to serve at a moment's notice was beer and cereal.

She watched as he flipped a golden pancake in a frying pan, then slid it onto a plate. He poured batter from a bowl into the pan and started the process all over again. His movements were agile and he had created a small stack in minutes.

"Help yourself," he said, setting the plate on the island. He moved the pan to a cold burner and wiped his hands on a dish towel draped over his shoulder. "Camille called these johnnycakes. Basically, pan-cakes made with cornmeal."

"You really walk the walk, don't you?" she said. "With cornmeal, I mean."

He shrugged. "It's how Camille cooked. But it wasn't just the cornmeal that made it special. It was her whole philosophy behind food. When I was younger, food was all about trying to fill an emo-tional void. But she taught me food was really about storytelling. It was about creating something good, and then giving it away."

She ate embarrassingly fast. She couldn't pinpoint if it was the food itself or just the act of preparation, but she was suddenly sure that they were the best pancakes she'd ever had. When she was fin-ished, all that was left was maple syrup smeared across the surface of her plate, as if painted with a brush.

She wiped her mouth with her napkin, then folded it and set it aside. "Listen. About last night," she said. "I overreacted to an un-locked door. We don't need to tell Frasier. And we especially don't need to tell Zoey."

Mac leaned against the island. "I get the feeling it wasn't the unlocked door itself that scared you," he said. "It was whatever it represented."

The silence that fell around them was punctuated only by Fig's steady crunching as she worked through a bowl of dry cat food by the Sub-Zero fridge. As Charlotte watched the cat eat, she asked, "Does it ever feel to you like the best things go away too fast, and the worst things never, ever leave you alone?"

Mac didn't answer, waiting for her to say more.

And for the first time in ten years, she did. "When I was twelve, my family sold our house and all our belongings and moved to a small religious camp in Vermont. I say religious, but they really only worshiped one person, the head of the group, Marvin McCauley. That's even what the church called itself, the Church of McCauley. He was fanatically anti-government and was always under investigation—fraud, weapons, you name it." She only wanted to tell the story of Charlotte, but as her mind traveled back, an image of Pepper formed, unbidden. "There were only about ten children there, but one was a girl my age. I didn't want anything to do with her at first. I hated it there and I didn't want to be friends with anyone. But she glommed on to me like I was her lifeline. Like you with Camille. It was like she'd just been *waiting* for me. But it turned out I needed her as much as she needed me. We became inseparable—Charlotte Lungren and Pepper Quint."

"Pepper? Is that her real name?"

"She hated it." Charlotte smiled slightly. "The four years I was there, all I could talk about was running away. I would pore over maps in the school library and make lists of cities where I wanted to live when I finally left. I wanted to travel on a scooter and make money by doing henna." She absently rubbed her thighs under the island counter. She hadn't done any practice work on herself in over a week, so most of the images were gone, but she could still feel them there, like phantom ink. "Pepper was scared to travel, but she was going to come with me. She wanted to be where I was. I made her feel safe."

"Where is she now?" Mac asked.

Charlotte picked up her napkin and refolded it. "She died of pneumonia at the camp when we were sixteen. When she got sick, McCauley told everyone that if they just had faith that she could be cured, she would be. Then when she died, he said it was because they didn't pray hard enough. That's when I finally ran away and never looked back."

Mac frowned. "Is it still there? The camp?"

"No. McCauley was finally arrested on weapons charges about a year after I left. Everyone scattered to the winds after that."

Mac studied her for a few moments before he surmised, "So you're afraid it's someone from the camp who broke into your condo."

"No," she said, "it couldn't be. No one knows where I am." Yesterday was now swirling around and mixing with every other time she'd been meticulous about locking up. Maybe she'd only assumed she had turned the key in the lock before they'd left for dinner. "I probably forgot to lock the door. Zoey was excited and we were in a hurry to leave."

"But you think the people from the camp are dangerous?"

She didn't know how to answer that. She'd spent the first few years after leaving terrified that someone would find her. Not because she'd left—no one was that sad to see her go. But because she'd stolen that money. There had only been a few dozen adults at the camp, and she'd known them all by name, so she used to Google them obsessively. A few had been arrested with McCauley, but most had simply absorbed themselves back into the real world. The only person she'd completely lost track of was Sam.

"I don't know. I just don't want anyone from that time of my life showing up and making me who I used to be. I'm not that person anymore." She paused. "I've never told anyone about Pepper."

"Who better than a chef? I understand condiments." He gave her a reassuring smile that crinkled the skin around his brown eyes. His acceptance, his complete lack of judgment, caught her off guard. "Come on," he said, "let's go talk to Frasier."

Mac let her take the lead and tell Frasier the version of events she felt most comfortable with—that she thought her lock might have been picked last night, though nothing had been taken. And it was similar enough to what Zoey had been saying about Lizbeth's condo that Charlotte felt he needed to know. The only thing Mac added was "Whether or not someone has finally stumbled upon our secret hideout here, it's probably time for our dues to go toward some security."

Frasier nodded as he stood with them outside his office. The birds had surrounded them like Lilliputians. "Could be poachers," he said seriously, stroking his long beard. "Haven't had to deal with them since that book. I'll take care of it."

When Frasier went back inside, Mac said, "Poachers? Do you get the feeling he thinks the birds' safety is more important than ours?"

Charlotte surprised herself by laughing.

"Hey, what's going on?" Zoey asked from her balcony.

They both looked up. "Frasier just told us that he's going to improve security," Charlotte said. "For the birds."

Zoey walked down the steps. "Who do *they* need protecting from?"

"Good question."

When Zoey reached the landing, she said, "Mac, I'm glad you're here. First, thank you for last night! Dinner was amazing. I've never had anything like it in my life."

"You're very welcome."

"Second, do you have a copy of *Dancing with the Dellawisps*?"

"No, sorry. I never read it."

"Darn. I can't find a copy anywhere. I was up for hours last night looking for it online. I was going to buy one for my birthday next week."

"Your birthday is next week?" Charlotte asked. Zoey nodded. "Then we need to celebrate."

Zoey sighed. "Well, I've got nothing but time now."

"So, the great condo cleanse is over?" Mac asked.

"Yes."

Mac nodded. Then he hesitated and turned and walked away.

"Have you noticed that he doesn't seem to know how to say goodbye?" Zoey asked.

A man who doesn't know how to say goodbye. There were worse things in the world than to have a man like that as a friend. Just a friend, for however long she was destined to stay in this place.

"I need to get ready for work," she said, turning to go. Her bank account wasn't going to grow by itself.

Zoey followed, saying, "Isn't that what you were wearing last night?"

———

When Mac got back to his condo, he washed the dishes in the sink, a meditative chore he'd always enjoyed. But this morning all he could think about was tiny Charlotte and her voracious appetite as she'd eaten the johnnycakes. Leaving the dishes drying in the rack, he grabbed his tablet and went to the couch. When he sat down, Fig immediately jumped in his lap. He rested his tablet on her, which she liked because of the warmth of it, and typed in *The Church of McCauley.*

There weren't many mentions, and most of them were from local Vermont media reports a decade ago. He clicked on a short editorial piece whose headline read: THE CHURCH OF MCCAULEY, ONE YEAR LATER.

> This week marks the first anniversary of the federal raid on the camp run by The Church of McCauley in Hunter's Run. The church's leader, fifty-two-year-old Marvin McCauley, went quietly and the small arsenal he'd managed to acquire was seized without incident. Most who knew him would never call rangy Marvin McCauley a particularly charismatic man, but he did have a knack for attracting local residents at low points in their lives. He recruited them at bus stops and food pantries, promising them a loving, religious family who would be fully self-sufficient on his twenty acres of wooded land. We all know the famous ones. Branch Davidians. Heaven's Gate. A few years from now, no one will remember The Church of McCauley. It was small, and so much less brutal. But one thing we should never forget, if only for the sake of the handful of malnourished children who were taken from the camp that day, is that we always need to protect the most vulnerable members of our society.

Mac read everything else he could, most of it sketchy. The conditions at the camp were apparently poor—no electricity or running water except in the church building where Marvin McCauley's well-appointed living quarters were located. The thing that stood out to Mac was how many times the underweight children were mentioned. Camille had taught him that food was love. So to him there was no clearer indication that love was lacking in those children's lives than the fact that they went without food.

He moved Fig off his lap and went to the kitchen. It was muscle memory, learned from years of being at Camille's side. This is what you do when you don't know what else to do. This is how you show you care.

He turned on the oven and started bringing out ingredients.

———•••———

When Charlotte got home from work, she found a Tupperware container on her patio table. On it, Mac had taped a note that read, *Just because.*

She opened the container, and the scent of chocolate and butter burst from it like from a Christmas cracker. She gave a startled laugh. Inside were the biggest chocolate chip cookies she'd ever seen, each the size of her whole hand.

She automatically turned to Mac's condo, even though she knew he was at work. Lucy Lime's curtain moved slightly.

Charlotte took a cookie out and held it between her teeth while she turned back to unlock her door.

Smiling around the cookie, she closed the door behind her.

Chapter Fifteen

Oliver sat by the pool trying to focus on a breathing technique his therapist at school had taught him. Breathe in for seven counts. Hold for four. Breathe out for eight. Over and over. He hadn't had to use the technique in a while, but the Rondo had done something screwy to his head, ever since he'd shown up for that interview. He didn't like how desperate it made him feel, and how fixated he was.

He took his phone out of his pocket and checked to see if the listing for environmental manager was still up on the Rondo's website. It was, and that made him feel marginally better. Maybe there had been a lot of applicants to go through. He decided to go with that, because otherwise it meant they weren't totally sold on Oliver and they were waiting for someone better to come along. Everything would fall into place as soon as Garland's father got home and Garland put in a good word for Oliver. Everything was going to be fine.

Garland came outside alone with a Bloody Mary in her hand. Her sunglasses were hiding her hungover eyes from the vicious morning sunlight. She sat in a lounge chair beside him, still pretending that she hadn't just spent another night with Cooper. Cooper would follow in a few minutes, keeping up the ruse. The Heathers weren't up yet, but Roy was already sunbathing in a tiny bathing suit, two lounge chairs away.

Garland was growing more and more on edge as their week together neared its close. Oliver knew enough about anxiety to recognize it, and he'd tried a few times to get her to talk to him because all this subterfuge was obviously exhausting everyone. But she'd shut him down.

Before Oliver could say anything to her that morning, his phone dinged. Garland frowned. He lifted it to see that it was a text from Zoey.

> I'm on a quest. Do you know where I can find a copy of Dancing with the Dellawisps?

He watched Garland turn her head slightly toward the open French doors, surreptitiously looking for Cooper. Oliver quickly typed a response.

> There's this great thing called The Internet, ever heard of it?

She answered before he could put away his phone.

> College graduate AND a comedian. You're such a Renaissance man.

Oliver smiled despite himself and he felt his shoulders relax a little.

It's a gift.

My birthday is next week and I wanted to treat myself to a copy. But they're so rare. The last one sold on eBay two years ago.

Ask Frasier.

I did. He said he gave away all his copies.

Yes, and one of those copies Frasier had given to Oliver, a long time ago. Oliver remembered having to hide it from his mother, who had hated having a book in the house that wasn't *Sweet Mallow.* The book was now in Oliver's car, somewhere. He'd forgotten that he'd brought it with him to California until he'd found it while moving out of his dorm last week. It had been an unexpectedly emotional time for him, leaving his home of four years. He'd never been able to achieve the real happiness he thought he'd find out here, but he'd at least been able to live between the past and the future, weirdly protected from both, while in college. He envied that Zoey was just starting that journey.

Oliver glanced at Garland. She was still preoccupied with watching for Cooper, so he focused on his phone and typed:

When does school start?

August.

He remembered her earlier text about not knowing what she wanted to do. Oliver had known that he'd wanted to work in hotels since he was sixteen, but college had taught him so much more than what he thought he'd wanted to learn.

I'm glad I went to college. You will be, too.

Why did you go so far away?

You just cleaned out that condo. You already know the answer.

Do you miss Mallow Island?

"Who are you texting?" Garland asked, bringing Oliver back to California. Her sudden interest meant Cooper was near.

"Someone from home," he said, starting to put his phone away.

But Garland grabbed it from him and started scrolling. "Who is Zoey?"

"I honestly don't know. That old friend from home gave her my number. She's just starting school." Garland handed the phone back to him as if disappointed. "Have you heard from your dad?"

"No. Be patient, Oliver. I told you."

"I can't afford to wait much longer."

Cooper said from behind them, "Afford? You're not paying for anything." He leaned over and swept Garland up in his arms. "You look way too hot in that bathing suit. You need to cool off."

"What are you doing?" Garland squealed, kicking her legs. She dropped her Bloody Mary and the glass smashed on the concrete. "Don't you dare! Oliver, save me!"

Cooper ran to the pool and jumped in with her, causing a great arc of water to splash on both Oliver and Roy.

Oliver immediately stood, checking to see if his phone had gotten wet.

Roy sat up on his elbows to watch Garland and Cooper. Garland screamed as Cooper splashed her. She retaliated by jumping on his back. Just minutes ago, she'd been too hungover to talk. But she obviously wanted to put on a good show.

"You know what's really going on, don't you?" Roy asked him.

"Yes," Oliver said.

Roy pushed his water-beaded sunglasses down his nose to look at Oliver. "You seem like a nice guy."

Oliver gave him a wry smile. "Don't let the accent fool you."

"You've made no secret how much that job at the Rondo means to you. She's using you to get to Cooper, but don't be fooled into thinking she's going to help you in return. That's not how she operates. You should cut your losses now before it all hits the fan."

There was a sound of someone yelling Garland's name from inside the house. Oliver turned and his first thought was *Too late.*

Heather Two had just come running out to the pool in her pink robe. Her hair was up in one of those sky-high buns she favored, the ones that looked like she was trying to get Wi-Fi from them. "Garland!" she yelled. "Your dad is home!"

"What?" Garland stilled in the water. "Stop it!" she said to Cooper, pushing him away when he lunged at her playfully because he hadn't yet noticed Heather Two.

"I was smoking some of Roy's weed on the front porch," Heather Two was saying quickly. "I think he saw me as he drove up. He looked angry."

"That's what you get for going into my room and stealing my stuff," Roy said as he stood and gave a catlike stretch.

"Hide it better if you don't want me to steal it," Heather Two said.

"Shut up!" Garland said, using the nearest ladder to climb out of the pool. "He said they weren't coming home until tomorrow evening. You guys were supposed to be gone by then!"

"Wait," Oliver said, his ears twitching with this news. "Then you *have* talked to him?"

"The stepmonster isn't with him," Heather Two said. "He's *alone*." Oliver was beginning to see that what he had initially thought was Heather Two's panic was actually a sort of thinly veiled glee. She was enjoying this unexpected turn of events.

Garland wrapped a nearby towel around her. Cooper got out and stood behind her, his hand on her shoulder. "Showtime," he whispered to her, and she nodded as Harry Howell strode through the open French doors.

"What in the hell is going on?" Harry asked. He looked tan but tired, his white suit rumpled. Using a combination of his blue-collar work ethic and his Stanford-scholarship smarts, Harry Howell had taken his late wife's family's last struggling hotel in the Rondo chain and turned it into a world-class destination resort. He was a legend in the California hotel world.

"Hi, Daddy," Garland said. Her hand holding her towel together was clenching and unclenching nervously. "How was your vacation?"

"Don't 'Hi, Daddy' me. I told you to get a job while I was gone, and instead you invite your friends over to stay in my house and eat my food and drink my booze? What happened there?" he demanded, pointing to the red splash and smashed glass on the concrete where Garland had dropped her drink.

"Just my Bloody Mary. It slipped."

"And of course you left it there to be picked up by someone else." Harry turned to go back inside, nearly mowing over Heather Two, who had been lurking behind him.

"It only happened a minute ago." Garland hurried after him. Everyone else followed, helplessly drawn.

Harry stopped at the brunch table, looking it over, shaking his head.

"Where is Jade?" Garland asked as they all gathered around him like a Greek chorus.

Harry grabbed a cup and poured himself some coffee. "Don't ever mention her name again."

"Did something happen between you and *Jade?*"

His flat blue eyes fell on his daughter, then on everyone around her. "Everyone, out. Get in your cars and go. I can't even get into my own garage. Whose Toyota is that, packed to the gills like a homeless person's?"

"That's mine," Oliver said, "sir."

Garland shot Oliver a look, as if he'd purposely tried to make her look bad.

"Don't think you're going to move in," Harry said. "Garland isn't even going to live here if she doesn't get her act together."

"You don't have to worry about me disappointing you anymore, Daddy. You're not going to see me for a long time. I'm moving in with Cooper." It was obvious that Garland thought this bombshell was going to do something, anything, other than what it actually did.

It made her father laugh.

"It's true! Unlike you, he loves me." Her eyes filled with tears. Real tears. Complicated ones, full of hurt, anger, resentment, and fear. Garland had planned for only one outcome. But she'd failed to understand that as long as other people were involved, you were never fully in control.

"I thought you had more sense than that, Cooper," Harry said. "Do your parents know about this?"

"I know you're good friends with them, but it's none of their business," Cooper said in a pretend sort of grown-up way, not helped by the fact that his Corona-beer boxer shorts were plastered to him and he was dripping all over the Spanish tile floor. "I've got my own money."

"Your own money?" Harry repeated. "None of you have your own money. You *earn* your own money. Get out, all of you."

"I hate you," Garland said. But she didn't leave right away. She stood there as if hoping her father would say something more—beg her to stay, apologize to her, say he loved her. That last one probably most of all. Oliver knew that she had a long road ahead of her, learning to accept that the one person you wanted to love you the most was the one person who never would. When Harry didn't respond, Garland turned and ran out of the room. Cooper followed, then Heather Two and Roy.

Oliver lingered, thinking something might still be salvaged from this. "Sir? I wanted to introduce myself. I'm Oliver Lime."

"Is that a real name?" Harry said, taking a croissant off the table. "It sounds like a cocktail."

"I interviewed for the environmental manager position at the Rondo, and I haven't heard anything." Harry looked at Oliver blankly. "I went to school on scholarship, like you. I'd really like to get my foot in the door."

"And you thought *this* was the way to do it?" Harry asked. "That position was filled weeks ago, Oliver Lime."

"But the listing is still up on the website," he said.

"Yet, instead of placing a follow-up call, you decided to hang out with my daughter," Harry said as he left the room, shaking his head.

Oliver stood there, letting it sink in. Was that really it? It was over? What in the hell was he going to do now?

He didn't have much in Garland's room. He packed his duffel and walked out to find Heather Two waiting by her car. Heather One was sitting in the passenger seat, quickly typing something on her phone. Roy was asleep in the back seat. He hadn't bothered to change out of his bathing suit.

"Where are you going to go, Oliver?" Heather Two asked.

Oliver didn't respond as he tossed his duffel into his 4Runner.

"You can crash on our couch if you want to. Hotel jobs are a dime a dozen. I don't know why you had your heart set on the Rondo, anyway. You'd be wasted out here. Come with us to LA."

Yells came from one of the open upstairs windows; then something crashed. Oliver looked up, alarmed.

"You didn't think that was it, did you?" Heather Two asked. "That was just round one. She'll make her exit as dramatic as possible. Then she'll stay with Cooper for about a month—"

"Try two weeks," Heather One said, without looking up from her phone.

"—and she'll get sick of him, or vice versa, then she'll be back here like nothing happened. You'll see," Heather Two said, sliding behind the wheel.

"Why do you stay friends with her?" Oliver asked.

Heather Two paused. "I know you just met us, so it's easy to assume that we only exist inside Garland's world. But Heather and I are opening a boutique this summer. We just signed the lease. And Roy is going to law school in the fall." She closed the door and started the car, then rolled down the window. "Spending time with Garland is like acting in a very long play. I have my role. Heather and Roy have theirs. Cooper is still playing his role. But eventually the curtain goes down, the lights go up, and we all go home. The only person who thinks any of this is real is Garland. Come on. Follow us."

She drove to the gate and stopped, watching him in her rearview mirror.

He took a deep breath and got in his car and backed out of the garage. As he approached her car, she turned left.

He watched her car disappear around the corner before he took out his phone. The screen came alive, showing Zoey's unanswered question:

Do you miss Mallow Island?

That had always been such a complicated question to answer because of how closely it was tied to his mother. He didn't miss her. But he missed Frasier. He missed the way sugar seemed to float out of every open door on Trade Street. He missed trying to find fiddler crabs with a flashlight on summer nights. He missed being able to drive around without GPS because he knew every road by heart. He missed the good things. He thought the job at the Rondo would give him a taste of himself again, but he knew now that he was never going to find himself here.

He'd left too much of himself behind.

And now he just wanted to go home.

Chapter Sixteen

The Dellawisp turned into a construction zone overnight, which surprised everyone who woke up that morning to a cacophony of hammering and sawing and the bright scent of newly cut wood. Zoey stepped onto her balcony, Pigeon zooming out with her to see what was going on. She looked down and noticed that Mac and Charlotte had already emerged from their condos, looking as disoriented as Zoey felt. Charlotte had drawn a robe around her. Mac's red hair was muted with a coating of what Zoey assumed was cornmeal.

They each stared, disbelieving, at the tunnel of plywood and scaffolding being erected through the garden.

Frasier was in the thick of it all. He had a tool belt around his waist and was helping to hammer up a sheet of plywood, his long white beard swaying against his chest with every stroke. He had a bird on his head, but the rest of the dellawisps were swarming around angrily. The construction workers kept ducking away from them and giving each other faintly alarmed looks.

"Frasier!" Zoey called. He didn't hear her, so she called again, "Frasier!"

He finally turned to look up at her.

"What's going on?"

He smiled. "It all came together overnight. There wasn't time to call you."

"What came together?" she asked, confused.

"I arranged for renovations on Lizbeth's place to start sooner than I told you they would. It's on a fast track, so it'll only be about five days of work. Sorry about the last-minute change."

"Why the rush?" Zoey asked.

"Oliver called yesterday. He's coming home!"

Zoey's brows shot up. "Really? When?"

"He didn't say. But I want the place to be ready for him."

Mac called from his patio, "I hate to tell you this, Frasier, but I think you missed the mark by several feet." He pointed across the garden. "Lizbeth's condo is over there."

Frasier laughed, a full-bellied laugh, more joyful than Zoey had ever seen him. It altered the entire character of the man. This, Zoey thought, is what loving someone must do to you. It changes you completely. "No, no. This is just a temporary shelter to keep the birds from attacking everyone as supplies come in," Frasier said, getting back to hammering.

Well, it was a nice theory. But once the tunnel was completed, the dellawisps hopped inside and chased the workers anyway. Zoey spent the whole day watching the spectacle.

But the novelty of this new development at the Dellawisp grew old very quickly. In fact, the only person who remained consistently happy with it all was Frasier. He got to work earlier and stayed later, supervising the work on Lizbeth's condo and overseeing the installation of the new keypad gate lock and the security camera in the parking lot. For everyone else, the noise every morning was a rude awakening, and remained pervasive throughout the day. Mac and Charlotte had work to escape to, but Zoey was stuck in the chaos without a car or a job, joined by an invisible bird who was even more cranky than she was. Even the initial thrill of the news of Oliver coming home was diminished when Frasier told her that it could be weeks, or even months. He wasn't sure.

Every day after lunch Zoey would leave to visit Charlotte at the trolley tours just to get away from the construction. When she and Charlotte got home, they would check out the progress being made at Lizbeth's place before Frasier locked up. Every day there was something new to marvel at—snowy white drywall, sinks with elaborate fixtures, shiny appliances, glass-paned cabinet doors.

"I wonder who's footing the bill for all this?" Charlotte asked one day. "Surely not Oliver."

"I don't know. Frasier? He seems very fond of Oliver."

"Who knew he had this kind of money?" Charlotte said. "The mystery of Frasier deepens."

As promised, most of the larger, noisy work was completed by Friday. There was only painting and detail work to be done, which Frasier said he was going to do himself. So the tunnel was deconstructed and hauled away.

Then, on Saturday morning, Zoey finally got the call that her car was arriving from Tulsa.

Things were definitely looking up.

She'd been cleaning her studio, which had reached a ridiculous level of messiness. It was even beginning to bother Pigeon, judging by her recent nighttime activity of picking up dirty clothing and depositing it on Zoey's bed while she slept, so that Zoey woke up to a pile of it on her chest. It was so bad that Zoey couldn't even find her phone when it started ringing that morning. She ran around looking for it until Charlotte, who was sitting on Zoey's couch, dug it out from between seat cushions and extended it without once looking up from Zoey's copy of *Sweet Mallow* she was reading.

Zoey gave directions to the Dellawisp to the courier, then dragged Charlotte down to the alley to wait with her. When she saw her little gray Honda turn from the street, she jumped up and down and waved as if her car must be glad to see her, too.

The woman courier got out, gave Zoey some paperwork to sign, and handed her the keys. Then the courier walked back to Trade Street, where there was a car waiting for her.

Zoey led Charlotte over and made the introductions. "Charlotte, my car. My car, Charlotte."

"Nice to meet you," Charlotte said as Zoey opened the driver's door and slid inside, smiling. She'd really missed having her own transportation. She'd even taken the trolley tour again yesterday, just to see some of the rest of the island again, someplace that wasn't the Dellawisp or Trade Street, which she knew by heart now.

Zoey was showing Charlotte how much room the trunk had, which wasn't really all that fascinating, but to her credit Charlotte pretended that it was, when Mac appeared in the alley on his way out.

"My car," Zoey said.

"Nice," he said with a nod.

"I don't know where to go first."

"You need a local tour, where the trolley doesn't take you," Charlotte suggested.

"That's exactly what I need," Zoey said.

Mac clicked his key fob and his Tahoe's lights flashed as it unlocked. "Climb in."

"What? Really?" Zoey asked. "Aren't you going somewhere?"

"Just to the grocery store before work."

Zoey looked at Charlotte questioningly.

"I didn't lock my door. I'll be right back," Charlotte said, going back through the garden gate. When she returned she had on her aviators, and Zoey was fairly certain she'd brushed her hair.

"You sit in front with Mac," Zoey said.

Charlotte shot her a look but Zoey tried to look innocent and jumped in the back seat before Charlotte could argue. Mac's Tahoe smelled like clean aftershave mixed with something fried, like from the restaurant kitchen. It was exactly what a hug from a chef would smell like.

When he left Trade Street, Mac turned toward the center of the island. "For such a tiny island, we have a big tourist economy, most of it toward the shores. Think of it like a theme park. The outer part is for visitors. The inner part is the employee break room where we go to get away from them. There's the grocery store I usually go to," he said, indicating a store chain as they passed.

"I shop there, too," Charlotte said. She turned in her seat. "Zoey, it's so much cheaper there than at the corner market on Trade Street, for exactly the same things. Don't throw away your money."

"Yes, Mom."

"There's the library," Mac said of a small, beige clapboard building near the high school. It looked like someone's grandmother's house, that it might smell like sugar cookies and Rose Milk lotion inside. "Maybe they have a copy of *Dancing with the Dellawisps*."

"I already checked online," Zoey said. "They don't."

"I Hate Mondays is the only place I know that's open twenty-four hours on the island." Charlotte pointed out the café, which was decorated in classic fifties diner. "They have decent coffee."

"I know the owner," Mac said.

"Of course you do. Do you know everyone here?"

"It's a small island."

This went on for the next half hour. Zoey sat back, enjoying their banter almost as much as seeing the places on the island that were just about day-to-day living. But even the most ordinary thing was made somehow exotic in this lush setting with ponds of cattails and tropical palmetto trees dotting the landscape. After Mac drove by an old-fashioned drugstore, which he said once had to shut down for a few days when fiddler crabs decided to take over the parking lot like a gang of juvenile delinquents, he drove past the island's only two local fast-food places. He hilariously rated their ketchup packets according to ease of opening.

He seemed to hesitate at the end of the street, where turning left would take them into one of the many residential neighborhoods that branched off into deep green recesses. "Would you like to see where I grew up?" he asked.

Charlotte studied him from behind her sunglasses. "If you want to show us."

He turned and they entered the neighborhood. The houses at the head of the street were small but newer, interspersed with brick apartments and low-slung, white-painted churches. The buildings turned significantly more run-down the farther along the street they went. Mac eventually turned in to a cul-de-sac where the road was just sand. There was a large sign indicating that this was the future site of a new Habitat for Humanity community. Here, old houses were dilapidated and boarded over and covered in vegetation, obviously waiting for demolition. Some had already collapsed in on themselves, as if they'd grown tired of waiting. Mac stopped at an empty lot where only a few cinder blocks remained of a foundation.

"I have the craziest feeling I've been here before," Charlotte said.

"Me, too," Zoey said, looking around.

Charlotte turned, her brows lifting curiously above her aviators. "Really?"

Zoey nodded, and a thought occurred to her. She quickly took out her phone and called up her photos.

Mac had been quiet for a while, but he finally said, "Camille's house used to be in that empty lot. It's amazing it stayed up as long as it did. Sometimes I think she kept the walls standing by the sheer force of her will."

Charlotte reached over to him, her palm hovering just inches over his plaid shirt. She finally set her hand on his shoulder and patted. He turned his head and smiled at her.

"*It is!*" Zoey exclaimed, looking up just in time to see their surprisingly tender exchange.

Mac and Charlotte both gave a start, and Charlotte dropped her hand immediately.

"That house right there." Zoey pointed to a small green house with a collapsed roof across the road. There appeared to be a tree growing out of it. "Do you see the concrete step? It's got one jagged corner, and the street number fourteen looks like it was spray-painted on it."

"We always called it the lime house. For the color, I guess," Mac said.

She passed her phone to him with excitement. "It's the same house in the background of this old photo of Lizbeth and Lucy Lime I found in Lizbeth's condo! What if that was *their* house?"

Mac used his fingers to zoom in on the photo while Charlotte leaned over to see. He smiled in a *That's interesting* kind of way, as if it weren't the most incredible discovery. "It was before my time, but I bet Camille knew them. She fed the neighborhood children around here for generations."

"Maybe that's what seemed familiar to you, too, Charlotte," Zoey said as she took the phone back from Mac. "You remembered me showing this to you."

"That must be it," Charlotte said, though she didn't sound convinced.

"Did you know Roscoe Avanger grew up in this neighborhood?" Mac asked.

"Now you've done it," Charlotte said at the exact moment Zoey exclaimed, "*What?*"

"I can't remember which house Camille said belonged to Roscoe's grandfather. It might be gone already. Roscoe apparently used to run away a lot, and sometimes ended up on her porch."

"Was his home life bad?" Zoey asked.

"I don't know," Mac said. "But this was a rough neighborhood, and I got the impression from Camille that he was something of a hoodlum. She said she wasn't surprised that he turned into a writer. She said stories chased him like ghosts."

"Roscoe Avanger and ghosts again." Charlotte shook her head. "Everything on this island seems related to those two things."

"Even us," Zoey said. "Roscoe Avanger bought and renovated the Dellawisp. We met because of him."

"And ghosts?" asked Charlotte. "How are we connected to ghosts?"

Zoey put away her phone. "I don't know, but I bet we are."

Mac laughed. "This is like the Mallow Island version of Six Degrees of Kevin Bacon."

"Who?" Zoey asked.

"Ah, youth," Mac said as he made a U-turn and drove out of the neighborhood.

Zoey turned to watch the houses as they faded from sight.

Everything around her was suddenly stitched together by unseen threads, as thin as gossamer. She'd come here wanting to feel a connection, but she'd always thought that connection would be to her mother.

Instead, it was to these people.

And it felt more substantial, more real, than she could ever have dreamed.

———•——

Early in the predawn hours of the next morning, Oliver parked near the boardwalk at Wildman Beach, where the souvenir shop and the New Sea Food Paradise restaurant were located. He turned off the engine, but he could still feel the buzz of the road fluttering along his skin like the tiny wings of insects. He couldn't remember the last time he'd slept. He'd run out of money for motel stays a few days ago. At his last stop, which had been over twenty-four hours ago, he'd had to scour his car for change for gas, finding quarters under seats and in an old coffee mug he'd kept in his dorm room to use for the school washing machines.

And now he was here, finally back on Mallow Island.

He stared out over the water. The white foam from the waves, visible in the darkness, glowed like long strands of blurry Christmas lights.

He was so damn tired. His eyes felt grainy every time he blinked. It was too early to wake Frasier, but even if he'd had enough fuel to do so, he couldn't keep driving around until daylight. He was an accident waiting to happen. He wondered if the Mallow Island police still did their overzealous patrols canvassing for the homeless sleeping in public places, or if he could get away with sleeping here.

His eyes had just begun to close when he caught the headlights of a patrol car as it entered the far end of the parking lot. He reluctantly started the engine again and reversed, giving a wave of acknowledgment to the patrol car as he pulled back out onto the coastal highway. He considered going to I Hate Mondays, if it was still open all night. But then he ruled that out because he didn't have the money for even a cup of coffee.

He could think of only one other place to go.

And, really, there was no use putting it off.

He would have to face it sooner or later.

Trade Street was still like a fairy tale at night, with its old-fashioned streetlamps shining like lemon lollipops in front of the candy-colored businesses. He was so short on sleep that he was on autopilot, less anxious about seeing the Dellawisp than he would have been if he were going on full steam. He turned by Sugar and Scribble Bakery, drove down the bumpy alley until it opened into a parking lot, and then there it was.

The glow of the garden lights through the foliage behind the gate gave the impression of crackled mercury glass. There were only two cars in the lot—a gray Honda and a big SUV he remembered belonged to a man named Mac. He backed into a space next to the Honda, then turned on the overhead light in his car so he could root through the glove compartment, where he'd tossed his old house key years ago. He hadn't thought about it in a long time. It had hung on his key chain for months after he'd left, until he hadn't been able to look at it any longer.

He finally found it, turned off the light, and got out.

His shoulder muscles began to bunch the closer he got to the gate. He'd felt this way every day coming home from school when he was younger. Talking with his therapist at college had helped him understand that it hadn't actually been dread he'd been feeling—dread at facing all those boxes, or the walls that were literally closing in on him, or another argument with his mother, which he would sometimes pick on purpose to try to get her to say something other than "You think I had a *choice?*" when he demanded to know why she'd had him in the first place.

No, it hadn't been dread at all.

It had been hope. Hope that, somehow, things would be different.

Every single day that hope had buoyed him, and then sunk him.

When he got to the gate, he pulled on it, but found that it wouldn't budge. He tried again. Nothing. He looked down and saw that it now had a keypad lock.

He leaned forward and put his forehead against the bars in defeat.

Back to sleeping in his car. At least no one would see him or notice a strange car here until morning. He turned and took a step, but stopped abruptly when he heard a tinny, muffled thud. It sounded like a knock against one of the dumpsters, as if his sudden turning had startled someone and they had backed away.

His first thought was, alarmingly, that it was his mother going through the dumpster as she often did. That maybe she wasn't really dead and he'd been somehow tricked into coming back here just to have his hopes dashed again.

Or, worse, she *was* dead but her ghost was still here, which meant he would never be free of her.

"Who's there?" he asked, his voice low and dry from too many convenience-store corn chips and too little water.

There was no answer.

He took out his key fob and turned on his car lights by remote.

It was a particularly genius move, because the lights were facing him and away from the dumpsters, so he was temporarily blinded.

He immediately clicked them off and waited, listening.

Maybe it had just been a cat.

He jogged to the car and got in and locked it. There was too much stuff in the back to recline, so he rested his head against the upright seat and closed his eyes, but kept opening them again to focus on the dumpsters. He thought he saw a shadow moving around the back of one of them.

He couldn't take it any longer. He needed sleep or he was going to turn to cinder.

He started the car and drove to Julep Row. There, he parked outside Frasier's house and stared at the imposing gates before taking out his phone.

It rang a half dozen times before Frasier's foggy voice answered. "Hello?"

"Hi, Frasier. It's Oliver. I'm sorry to wake you. I tried the Dellawisp, since I knew Mom's place had been cleaned out, but there's a lock on the gate now. And then I thought I saw . . . I'm just really tired and I need someplace to sleep. I'm outside your gates. Can I come in?"

There was some fumbling, as if Frasier was getting out of bed. "You're already on the island?"

"I pushed through the past couple of days on the road."

"Hold on," Frasier said; then the gates opened as if pushed by an invisible hand. "Come on up."

As the large blue house came into view, the light over the front door popped on and illuminated the front porch with its Doric columns. All of a sudden it came to Oliver in a flash of insight.

He knew what the Rondo resort reminded him of. It reminded

him of *this house*. And the relentless feeling that everything was going to be okay once he started working there was the feeling he always got when saw this place. Because inside was the one person he knew would be there for him, no matter what, the embodiment of the hope that Mallow Island had always represented—the hope that we truly could change.

Way to ignore the obvious, he told himself as he parked in front and put his head to the steering wheel with an incredulous chuckle. He was at risk of bursting into full-blown, punchy, so-tired-you-can't-stop-even-though-it's-not-funny laughter, when he looked up again to see that the front door was now open.

Frasier had stepped outside, his dark skin glowing under the yellowy porch light. He was wearing pajamas with the initials RFA embroidered on the breast pocket, for Roscoe Frasier Avanger. Only those closest to Roscoe Avanger called him by his middle name. Oliver had never thought of him as famous, but he'd seen him interact with adoring readers, one of which used to be his own mother, enough to know why he valued his secret identity so much.

Frasier smiled through his long white beard, a much more convincing beard than the fake one he used to wear years ago to try to do errands on the island. He'd finally grown out his own hair and beard, obliterating the bald head and clean-shaven jaw made famous by every author photo ever taken of him, which had once been a source of great vanity to him. He lifted his knobby hand high in the air in welcome.

Oliver got out of the car and wearily climbed the steps. Frasier held out his arms and Oliver walked into them. He stayed there a long time, until Frasier finally clapped him heartily on the back a few times and stepped away to motion him inside. Oliver wiped his eyes and walked past his old friend into the quiet stillness of his home.

Frasier then closed the door against the claggy night air.

And the porch light went out.

GHOST STORY

Lizbeth

So, he's back. That should make Frasier happy.

Something stirred in me when I saw him, something uncomfortable I didn't want to think about. Oliver always made me feel this way, even when he was a baby. He never reminded me of his father, Duncan. If he had, it would have been easier. Instead, Oliver has always reminded me of *my* father, which is strange because I don't remember what my father looked like. I destroyed every photo of him a long time ago.

If I think very, very hard about it, the only real interaction I can remember having with my father is the one time I was sitting on his lap and he whispered to me that all the men in his family lived to the age of one hundred and three, as if it were a temperature they had to reach. I remember the notion gave me a profound sense of unease, though I don't recall why.

I was ten and Lucy was sixteen when he died. Our next-door neighbor went off his meds and got naked on his lawn one night and he shot my father when he confronted him. In the autopsy notes, which I later requested and put in one of my boxes, the medical examiner held up my father's heart for all to see and said, "Will you look at this? A heart like a twenty-year-old!" He would also later say to me, when I tracked him down to put more notes in my boxes, that he remembered he could almost feel the heart beat in his hands, just faintly, as if my indomitable father was still fighting death.

I lost that report, all of Lucy's arrest records, and dozens of old policies I'd taken out and let expire, when my kitchen flooded several years ago. Frasier took the ruined boxes and threw them away somewhere other than the Dellawisp dumpster. He wouldn't tell me where.

After my father's funeral, there was no controlling Lucy. And that's saying something, given how unpredictable she'd been before. It was like only *she* got to react to losing him. Typical. She stayed out all night, getting high. She was arrested eleven times for possession, public intoxication, and solicitation, both on the island and off. She went to the ER almost every weekend with made-up maladies and tales of accidents, all as a con for prescriptions. Mom and I eventually stopped showing up, coats over our pajamas, when the hospital called. Lucy then went in and out of rehab so frequently you'd think there was a sale. Mom finally had enough and changed the locks on the doors. I loved that. When Lucy would pound on the door, Mom would just stare at the wall, but I would yell at her to go away, that *we* didn't need her. I wanted her to know how it felt, all that time she spent with our father behind closed bedroom doors, leaving me out.

It was just me and Mom for a long time and I clung to her, as much as she would let me. She was never a particularly lovey person. I remember her staring at walls a lot while fights went on around her, not doing a thing about them. After high school, I could have gone off to college with scholarships. But the real world scared me and all I wanted to do was stay at home with my paper collection. That's why I started taking classes at the island tech extension. I had to do something that looked productive or I was afraid Mom would make me leave.

And that's when I met Duncan, and every good thing I'd ever wanted to happen finally did.

As I waited for the city bus to take me home, Duncan—beautiful, in his forties, with eyes the color of pool water—would talk to me. He told me he was living in a halfway house and that he'd been clean for over a year. He said he was finally getting his life together, going to school and working part-time at the Quick as a Wink gas station on the coastal highway. As the days passed I found myself looking forward to our bus-stop time. I was flattered by his willingness to tell me so many personal things about himself, even though I was fairly certain he didn't even know my name for at least half the semester. When it came time for him to leave the halfway house, Duncan asked me if I had a room to rent. I knew exactly what he'd been doing all this time, chatting me up. He saw me as someone sheltered and easy to manipulate. But by that point I didn't care. I was already in love with him. I took him home to meet Mom, and she liked that Duncan could fix the leaky sink and have a wildly imaginative meal on the table when she got home from work. She rented out Lucy's old room to him, and we lived in perfect contentment together for a whole year.

Immediately after moving in, Duncan started coming into my room every night to sit at the foot of my bed and talk to me about classes, sometimes reading to me his favorite passages from *Sweet Mallow* while rubbing my feet through my blanket. He would go a little higher each night and I would lie motionless, every muscle contracted from the intimacy of it. I was eighteen and I felt like I was finally being completely rewritten.

But of course it didn't last. I had one year with him, one wonderful year of someone wanting only me, then Lucy ruined everything when she got kicked out of rehab again for trying to break into the prescription cabinet.

In a fit of goodwill, because Duncan had made our lives easier in many ways, Mom let her move back into our house and sleep on the couch since Duncan was now in her old room. I *hated* it. I was scared of the way she looked at Duncan, of the way she could make him laugh when they shared worldly stories. She was beautiful and captivating, but he didn't know the real her. He didn't know what a sinister magician she was.

Lucy and I fought like we were kids again. I told her she was damaged and useless and I wished she would just go away because we didn't want her there. She told me I had no life, that only ugly girls still lived at home, weird girls that no one liked. I told her that wasn't true. Mom had never kicked *me* out. And I had Duncan—who did she have? I realize now I never should have said that. She couldn't stand to see me happy. And just to punish me, Lucy seduced Duncan with both her body and her addiction. She won, even though it meant we all lost.

He stopped coming into my room at night. Then he started missing classes, using work as an excuse. Eventually he and Lucy would disappear together for days at a time. They would come back high, though they would claim not to be. Addicts always think they're as good at manipulating when they're high as when they're *trying* to get high. They fed off each other for nearly half a year. Mom checked out and let it happen, as she always did when things got hard. She didn't do anything, just like when my father was alive. It got so bad that Lucy stole a prescription pad from a doctor's office and she and Duncan went on a reckless tour of pharmacies, trying to fill forged prescriptions until they were finally caught.

I never blamed Duncan. I never thought that it was ever anyone's fault but Lucy's. I tried to tell him that, how I understood. When they went to prison, I wrote to Duncan all the time. He never wrote back, not even when I told him about Oliver, which my mom had made me *promise* not to do. He was the wrench in her perfect plan.

Because, you see, Duncan was the only one besides me and my mom and Lucy who knew that Oliver wasn't actually mine.

It was Lucy who had gotten pregnant, not me.

You thought you knew my whole story, didn't you? Everyone does.

After they were arrested, Mom paid Lucy's bail and let her come home while she awaited sentencing. I was livid. Why didn't she pay Duncan's bail? He was stuck there! That's when they told me Lucy was going to have Duncan's baby. Lucy had been ignoring it, denying it, but time was running out. And, here's the kicker, they needed *my* help. Even though she was pretty far along, she wasn't sure exactly, Lucy wasn't showing in a way anyone could really tell because the baby was so small and Lucy was so curvy. It would get complicated, they said, if people found out. She was going to have to serve time, that much was clear. And when that happened, the baby could go into foster care, it could be taken away from *us,* unless *we* did something. And that something was to let Lucy pretend she was me when she had the baby. It would be easy, they said, because I was still on Mom's insurance. Then my name would go on the birth certificate and the authorities wouldn't get involved. The baby would be all ours.

All Mom's, more like.

I didn't understand all the subterfuge. Lucy didn't care anything about the baby. I knew the only reason she told Mom about it was to manipulate her into paying bail. I was sure she would pop it out and then take off and never be seen again in order to avoid going to prison. There was no reason they had to involve me, but of course they did *because they didn't care.* I was surprised as anyone when Lucy stayed, then when she actually showed up to serve her sentence a month after Oliver was born.

But Lucy didn't do well in prison, in part because Mom never sent her photos or letters about Oliver like she'd promised. Early in her incarceration, Lucy got into fights with other inmates. Then she tried to break out with a guard who had fallen in love with her. They were caught five minutes later when they'd pulled to the side of the road to have sex. She told everyone that the only reason she'd done it was because she wanted to see her baby. No one believed her because no one knew the truth about Oliver. They all thought she was crazy.

Duncan was released much sooner than Lucy. Away from her, he was just fine. I knew he would be. And I knew he would come back to me when he got out. I would give him a place to stay—Mom couldn't stop it because of what I knew—I'd give him *everything,* just like before.

But three days after he was paroled, he died of an overdose. He was found by an early-morning jogger on Wildman Beach, lying in the sand, facing the rising sun. There was evidence a woman had been with him—some long strands of hair, a cheap golden hoop earring, a used condom—but no one could ever find her. I hate that woman, whoever she is. He should have come to me, not to her. He was cremated and his ashes sent to his elderly mother in Boca. I didn't even know he'd had an elderly mother in Boca.

Camille keeps saying that we never know the deep-down reasons people do the things they do, so we need to be gentle with each other. We need to forgive. She says I need to let go of all of this. I wish she would stop bothering me. That other ghost here at the Dellawisp doesn't try to give me unwanted advice.

I asked Camille why *she* doesn't let go.

She says she wants to, but Mac is the one holding on to her.

I told her that's what I want, too, for someone to love me so much they can't let go of me.

She says it's about the love you give, not the love you get.

But the way I see it, it's not really love if you're not loved back.

It's just something you make up.

And if no one ever reads my diaries, then no one will ever understand and finally love me.

And all I'll ever be is something I made up.

Chapter Seventeen

A tropical, three-blade fan was spinning overhead. It confused Oliver when he opened his eyes, because Garland's room didn't have a ceiling fan. He turned his head and looked around the room with its coastal blue walls and white wainscoting. It slowly came to him that he was no longer in California. He was back on Mallow Island. He sat up, achy from a week of travel, and took his phone from the bedside table to check the time. It was just past noon.

He got up and showered, then went down the grand staircase in search of Frasier. The squeaking of his sneakers on the hardwood floors was the only sound in the eerie quiet. He used to love the cleanliness of Frasier's house, but it had been a long time since he'd stayed here and he'd forgotten how quiet it was.

Oliver eventually wound his way into the kitchen and found Frasier's longtime housekeeper Rita wiping down countertops that were already spotless. A haunting song was coming from the radio over the sink, something gospel. Oliver cleared his throat and she turned. She immediately went to him, enveloping him in a fierce hug. It made him smile, because she was a large, soft woman and it made him remember the alarming feeling of being swallowed when she would hug him as a little boy.

"You're a sight for sore eyes," she said, pulling back and holding his face in her doughy hands. "I was so sorry to hear about your mama."

"Thanks," he said. "Is Frasier around?"

"No, but he left you a note." She patted his face before pointing to the whiteboard by the walk-in pantry. On it, Frasier had written: *Oliver, come to the Dellawisp when you get up so you can see the work that's been done. Rita, for God's sake, NO MORE CHICKEN BOG TONIGHT! I'm tired of it! Make something special for Oliver.*

"You don't have to make anything special for me," Oliver said.

But she was already fussing, bringing things out of the refrigerator. "I want to. When was the last time he had visitors? He's excited. Sit down," she said, indicating the sunny kitchen nook overlooking the pool. "I'll make you some fried ham and tomatoes."

"You don't—"

"And have you show up there hungry? I don't think so," she said.

An hour later Oliver drove away from Frasier's house, full of food and local gossip, of which there had been plenty. When he arrived at the Dellawisp minutes later, he parked next to Frasier's old pickup. Frasier owned a Mercedes that probably had less than ten thousand miles on it because he drove it only when he had to be Roscoe Avanger. And that hadn't been for years. When Oliver got out, he glanced over to the dumpsters. Had he imagined it all last night? There was room enough for a person to hide between them and the alley wall, but who would do that? At the Dellawisp gate, he pulled on it to see if it had been left open, but it was still locked. He wondered if this new security had something to do with trespassers. The Dellawisp was so hard to find that it had never been a problem before. His mother had been hyperaware of everything that had gone on, so they would have known.

He took his phone out of his jeans pocket to call Frasier to let him in, but before he could, he heard a man's voice call out, "Can we help you?"

Oliver angled his head to see through the bars. He could make out three people—a man and two women—standing on the patio beside his mother's. "I'm here to see Frasier," he said.

"*Oliver?*" That could only be Zoey. She was dark-haired like he remembered her mother, with those same arched eyebrows. But she was a lot taller and thinner, with legs that didn't seem to have a beginning or an end. They made her seem as fluid as a jellyfish moving through water as she ran across the garden to the gate. The birds swooped at her and she put her arms up like Tippi Hedren in a Hitchcock movie, but she didn't break her stride.

When she reached him, she put her hands on the bars and looked at him through them, her dark eyes wide. "It *is* you! Frasier said you were coming back, but he didn't know exactly when. It's been forever since you've answered a text. I was getting worried."

Her presence blew over him like a fresh breeze. He found himself smiling at her, a little goofily. He must still be travel-drunk. "It was an intense road trip."

The two others finally approached, having taken the longer way around to avoid the birds. Oliver knew Mac by his red hair and beard. He'd moved in about four years before Oliver left. But he didn't know the other one, a short, bohemian blonde. "Mac, it's good to see you again," Oliver said.

"You, too, Oliver. Sorry I didn't recognize you. You've grown up."

"This is Charlotte," Zoey said. "She lives in the condo beside your mother's."

Oliver figured she must be new. The unit beside theirs had never stayed occupied for long. But Oliver had loved when it was empty. He used to take a sleeping bag and sleep there in between owners, basking in the sheer emptiness of it.

Frasier suddenly opened his office door, as if he'd been watching. Although how, Oliver didn't know. His office didn't have windows. "That gate isn't the Berlin Wall," he called. "Let him in."

Zoey punched in the key code and opened the gate for him. As he passed them, he thought how strange it was for everyone to be out of their condos like this, socializing. His mother would have come out long before now, telling them to stop loitering, spittle collecting in the corners of her mouth as she yelled that she had notes on all of them, that she *knew things*.

This wasn't the same place. It looked the same, but without his mother here it was as if a fog had lifted, revealing a place he'd always hoped he'd find.

———•◦•———

Roscoe Frasier Avanger had been a wild boy because he thought no one loved him.

He'd turned into a dishonest young man because he thought no one cared.

Then he'd become an arrogant adult because he thought he deserved it when suddenly, because of his book, everyone did love and care.

He'd selfishly never wanted children, resenting even the thought of having to be responsible for someone else's happiness. He'd enjoyed his share of relationships with women, but he'd had a vasectomy years ago. He hadn't realized until Oliver left just how much having him in his life made it better. How Oliver made *him* better. He wished he'd done things differently now, but it was just another regret he'd collected.

He watched as Oliver walked through the garden, looking around as if seeing it for the first time. One of the birds landed on Oliver's head, and Frasier smiled. He was obviously not the only one who had missed the boy.

He could remember the first time he'd ever set eyes on Oliver. It was when Lizbeth had recognized him as Roscoe Avanger that day at the bakery and had run up to him with Oliver in a ratty stroller. Frasier hadn't needed anyone to go through his reader mail when he'd met Lizbeth. He'd always just thrown it away. But he'd offered her the job anyway, because he'd seen something in Oliver that he had always felt in himself, an in-betweenness. Oliver had been living in a gap that existed between Lizbeth's mental illness and the real world, just like Frasier had always felt in between the living and the dead, sometimes losing sight of which was real.

He stepped back to let Oliver enter the office.

"How is Aunt Lucy?" Oliver asked as he stepped inside.

Frasier looked over to her condo before he closed the door. Her curtain moved, as if she'd been standing close by. "I talked to her on the phone after your mother died, but I haven't set eyes on her in a while. The last time was when an electrical short made her lose power, probably three years ago. That's when she told me her shower had stopped working and her refrigerator had been broken for over a year. I fixed it all at once. Having people in her space made her anxious. She had maybe three pieces of furniture, and the place reeked of cigarette smoke. She looked frail."

"Why do you think they never talked?" Oliver asked.

"I don't know. But I think your mother wanted to tell me."

"Let me guess," Oliver said. "The mysterious story you were looking for."

"She always said she had a story she wanted me to know." Frasier shrugged. "If I found it, I thought it might give her some peace."

Oliver rolled his eyes. "If she had wanted you to know a story, it wouldn't have been so she could've found peace. It would've been so she could've caused as much chaos as she possibly could, with her in the center of it. I'm glad you didn't find anything, though I'm not surprised."

Frasier glanced to the corner significantly, making sure Lizbeth heard that. Oliver saw the gesture and looked at him curiously.

"Otis remembers you," Frasier said, by way of distraction.

Oliver laughed as if he'd forgotten, then reached up to take the bird off his head. "Normal birds don't act this way," he said as he set Otis on the desk, where he hopped around, picking up and dropping colored pencils.

"Who ever said they were normal? Have a seat. How did you sleep, son?"

"Good," Oliver said, sitting in Frasier's desk chair. His hair was longer than Frasier had ever seen it, falling into his green eyes. He looked tired. His skin had the kind of dull tone that bespoke not drinking enough water. This hadn't been a trip he'd enjoyed making, that was for sure. "Rita made me lunch when I got up."

Frasier leaned against the filing cabinets. "Any idea how long you're going to stay?"

Oliver shook his head. "I'm going to find a job and make some money first, then decide what to do." Frasier waited for him to say more, because he knew there was more. Lizbeth was hovering beside him, but her focus was not on Oliver. It was on something she thought was going to happen now that he was here, something she thought was going to benefit her in some way. She still couldn't see what was right in front of her—an extraordinary child who was kind and smart and funny and who deserved all the love the world could give him. "I was counting on an environmental manager position at a resort in a small town outside Santa Barbara, a place that reminded me of Mallow Island, actually. But it fell through and I ended up without anywhere to stay after graduation." He paused. "I never really found my footing out there. But I couldn't come back while she was still alive, Frasier. I'm sorry, but I couldn't."

"I know that, son." Frasier, too, had spent a long time away from Mallow Island as a young man. He'd run away to New York at seventeen. He'd been fed up with his grandfather, who was always drunk by noon and unable to deal with his wild grandson. Frasier hadn't known it at the time, but his grandfather only drank to make the spirits go away, and Frasier had inherited his ability from him. Frasier had ended up working odd jobs around the city, barely getting by, sometimes having to leave in the middle of the night when rent was due and he couldn't afford to pay. He'd made up names for every job he'd had, which had been an easy enough thing to do in those days, trying on new personas to see which one fit. His grandfather had died while he'd been away, but no one had known where Frasier was to tell him. But they didn't need to tell him. His grandfather had found him. And his ghost hadn't given Frasier a moment's peace, keeping him awake at night with stories of Mallow Island and his time during World War I, stories he hadn't stayed sober long enough tell Frasier as a boy. His was the only ghost Frasier had ever been able to hear, an experience he never wanted to repeat. Frasier had written *Sweet Mallow* just to make him go away, in an intense eight-week period when he'd slept little and ate less. And sure enough, as soon as he had finished, his grandfather disappeared. Frasier had been as surprised as anyone by the book's success when it had been published. But he'd quickly gotten used to the adoration. He had even come to expect it, which had led to the whole *Dancing with the Dellawisps* debacle decades later. It had been so long since he'd written *Sweet Mallow* that he'd forgotten that his gift, and his curse, was that he could tell other people's stories so much better than his own.

"I've been thinking a lot about your mother since it happened, and all the junk that came out of her condo," Frasier said as he watched Oliver move a pencil around the desk and Otis chased it. "I knew it was bad. But I always thought, as long as I was there to watch out for you, you would be okay. I thought there was a way for you to live between the world your mother lived in and the real world. But there wasn't, and it never should have been expected of you. I should have taken you and raised you myself, to hell with the ruckus Lizbeth would have made. If I had, maybe you wouldn't have felt the need to go so far away. I'm sorry I failed you, son. I hope one day you'll be able to forgive me. I hope that one day you'll be able to forgive us all."

Oliver looked up in surprise. "You didn't fail me, Frasier. You *did* raise me. I wouldn't have survived without you."

Frasier blinked a few times, then took a handkerchief out of his pocket and started wiping his runny nose. "I don't know what's wrong with me," he said, embarrassed, as he stuffed the handkerchief forcefully back in his pocket. "Suddenly I'm this old man with all these . . . emotions."

"You? Human?" Oliver smiled. "I don't believe it."

Frasier laughed and patted him on the shoulder. "Ready to see your place?"

"As long as there are no boxes," Oliver said. "I could live my whole life and never see another box."

"Not a single one," Frasier said as they stepped out and waited while Otis took his time hopping out after them, complaining the entire way. "Zoey was very thorough."

Charlotte and Zoey were sitting on Charlotte's patio, Charlotte drawing henna on Zoey's hand, when Frasier and Oliver walked by. Zoey watched them disappear into Lizbeth's condo. She had imagined their first meeting being a much more mature one than screaming Oliver's name and running to him. She couldn't believe she did that.

"Someone that handsome should be on stage." Charlotte smiled. "He certainly has a fan in *you*."

"Shut up," Zoey said with a laugh. "He caught me by surprise."

"But I think the feeling is mutual. I know that kind of tired. It numbs everything in you. It feels like you're never going to feel anything ever again. But something brightened the moment he saw you."

Zoey shook her head, embarrassed. "It's not like that. It just feels right, his being here." Charlotte was still smiling. "What?"

"I was trying to remember the first boy I fell in love with."

"I'm not in love with him," Zoey said quickly.

"Not yet."

Okay, so she didn't know exactly what she felt for Oliver. It wasn't like she had tons of experience in this area. She did love the *thought* of him, of what his being here meant. He was another invisible thread, another connection.

"Why don't you invite him to your birthday party tonight?"

That gave Zoey pause. She didn't want to overwhelm him with

too much attention. She'd spent so much time with his mother's things and so much time staring at his photos that she had imaginary memories of actually knowing him. He was familiar to her without being familiar at all. She had to keep telling herself that he hadn't spent nearly as much time thinking about her. "Do you think I should?"

"Misfits only. I think he'd fit right in. There," Charlotte said, sitting back and studying her work on Zoey's left hand. Satisfied, she set down the soft plastic squeeze bottle filled with henna paste she'd used to draw with.

"It's beautiful," Zoey said, holding her hand up. The design was a lace glove of flowers and paisleys with a single vine trailing down her middle finger. She'd chosen it from a binder of example photos Charlotte had shown her. Zoey had known how good Charlotte was, of course. She'd seen the work on Charlotte's own skin. But there had been something hypnotizing about actually watching Charlotte draw, the way her brows knit and her eyes flicked around the design, the way she would lean away every once in a while to study it. It was like Charlotte was somewhere else, a place where she was wholly herself, when she was drawing. Zoey had never seen her that comfortable without a bottle of henna, around anyone, ever.

Frasier and Oliver stepped back outside to Lizbeth's patio and stood there, talking. Zoey could only guess what Oliver thought of his mother's place now, so empty, so different from the last time he'd seen it. That made her think of the box of Lizbeth's things she was keeping for him in her studio. "I'll be right back," Zoey said.

"Aren't you going to invite him?" Charlotte asked.

"Yes, but there's something I need to give him, too," Zoey said, trotting to the steps to her studio.

"Be careful with that hand until the paste dries!" Charlotte called after her.

By the time Zoey retrieved the box, which had taken some maneuvering to pick up because she could only use one hand, and then stepped back out onto her balcony, Oliver and Frasier had already parted ways. She caught Oliver's back as the gate closed behind him.

She ran down the steps. "Oliver, wait!" she called to him through the gate, making him stop where he'd opened the door to a dark blue 4Runner in the parking lot.

She set the box down to punch in the gate code; then there was more maneuvering to pick the box back up. When she finally made her way to him, it was obvious he was wondering why on earth she had decided to do everything one-handed. "I wanted to get this part out of the way, in case you were dreading it. Here's the box I saved," she said breathlessly. "I know you don't want it, and I get that now. But I didn't think it was my right to throw it away, so you'll have to." He took the box without a word as she looked in his car with interest. There was a lot of luggage in it, tumbled around with small appliances, desk lamps, and books. "Are you unpacking?"

"No," he said, "not yet."

"But you're moving into your mother's old place?"

"I think so. For a while, anyway."

"I bet Lucy will be glad," she said, even though she had no way of knowing what Lucy was feeling. But Lucy had taken the photos. That had to mean something. "Where are you staying in the meantime?"

"With Frasier. What is that?" he asked, indicating her hand, which she had at an awkward angle to her side, as if holding the hand of an invisible child.

"Oh, it's henna." She wiggled her fingers. "It's not dry yet. It's my birthday present from Charlotte."

"Is today your birthday?" That made him smile, the same smile from his early school photos. She found herself thinking, *There you are.*

"I'm nineteen. And I finally got to meet you in person on this day, of all days. That's a pretty good present." Oh, God. Did she just say that? She made a pained face, which made him laugh.

"I'm glad I could oblige," he said.

"Listen, feel free to say no, because I'm basically just a well-meaning, slightly excitable stranger, but Mac and Charlotte and I are having a get-together tonight. If you don't have anything planned, would you like to come?"

"You want me to come to your birthday party?"

"Open to all Dellawisp members, free of charge. We're meeting on Charlotte's patio. If you come, I promise not to scream your name and run to you, like I've done twice already," she said. "Think about it."

"I don't know, that's a nice way to be greeted."

"You say that now, but wait until I do it to you in public."

He stared at her before saying, "You're exactly how I imagined you."

"Thank you," she said, delighted with the idea of him imagining anything about her. But then, "Wait. Was that a compliment?"

"Yes," he said, "it was a compliment."

Oliver smiled as he watched her walk back through the gate. Then he realized he was still carrying the box and his smile faded. He didn't know how much time passed as he debated what to do with it before he finally got into his 4Runner and put the box beside him on the passenger seat.

But then he thought, *What good would keeping this do?* He didn't want the cheap painting or the flower vase or the signed book or the necklace with his father's name on it. He certainly didn't want to read her childhood diaries. This box was all about her, what she cared about, *who* she cared about.

And he was absent from it. He would always be absent from it.

He had to make peace with that, finally.

He got out with the box and went to the dumpster and threw the box in. He jogged back to his car and tore out of the alley as if the box were about to jump back out and chase him. He was glad no one saw him.

Chapter Eighteen

Frasier watched Oliver on the new security monitor in his office, watched him throw away the box before running off. Lizbeth's reaction to it was immediate and frantic. Whatever she wanted to happen had something to do with that box.

But what was in the box? Just some cheap knickknacks and her diaries.

Oh, Christ.

The story she wanted him to know.

It was in the diaries.

But whatever it was, Oliver *didn't* want to know.

And here Frasier was, caught in between, as he always was.

With a deep sigh, Frasier left his office and went to the dumpster. He dug out the box and retrieved the diaries. There were ten of them, some palm-sized and girly with flimsy locks, others simply spiral-bound notebooks. He carried them all back to his office and put them in an old birdseed bag.

"There. Safe and sound," he said as he stuffed the bag inside one of the file drawers, not intending to read them right away. He thought it would be enough for her to know that he'd saved them.

But a gust of air blew around the office, fluttering papers on his desk and lifting the edges of the bird sketches tacked to the wall, almost as if they were taking flight. Oliver was right. Lizbeth didn't want peace. She wanted chaos. And whatever was in those diaries was going to cause it.

He took them back out, irritated. It was a familiar feeling, as he'd often been irritated with Lizbeth when she was alive. The lines were blurred in the in-between, making him sometimes forget which side he was dealing with. He dumped the diaries on his desk, and then he sat down and found the oldest one and began to read.

It took him a few hours, but he finally finished the last one, written just after Oliver was born. He sat back in his chair and closed his tired eyes. Lizbeth's expectation was palpable, filling the small office with humid air and making him sweat.

She'd had a terrible childhood, which didn't surprise him. Frasier had grown up in that same neighborhood, years earlier. If it hadn't been for the bright spot of Camille, shining like a ray of light through the darkness with her food, many of the neighborhood kids would have spent their whole lives not knowing what love looked like. But that was only outside their homes. What went on inside was not something even Camille's light could penetrate. Like with Frasier and his alcoholic grandfather. And Lizbeth with her tales of sitting on her father's lap as a child, and her vitriolic jealousy of the supposed playtime her father had with Lucy behind locked doors. Lizbeth never seemed to make the connection between their childhood and their struggles later in life. Frasier had known them both for years and he'd never had to know the details to understand something must have happened.

But then there was the part that did surprise him.

Lucy was Oliver's birth mother.

But it was Lizbeth on Oliver's birth certificate because of an elaborate plan concocted by their mother, who had wanted another chance to raise a child. Lizbeth had only ended up with Oliver because her mother died. And in true Lizbeth fashion, she'd kept him because she lacked the ability to give anything away.

Frasier had always assumed that Lizbeth wanted him to know her story because she wanted a book written about herself. But it made no sense to him now that she wanted him, and ostensibly the whole world, to know yet she had never bothered to tell Oliver the truth. And Oliver was the *one* person who should have been told. But the boy had been, and still was, so lost among her other things that she thought it was perfectly fine if Oliver found out with everyone else when the story was discovered.

Frasier knew what he had to do. He had to protect the boy. There were no halfways about it now.

There were only two times in a person's life when a family secret should be revealed—at the very beginning, or at the very end. When a bomb like this is dropped in the middle, it forces the person to spend the rest of their life struggling to live a life redefined, because everything they'd known as truth was suddenly false. This secret had gone on for so long that sharing it with Oliver now would only derail him.

"I'm sorry for your pain in life, Lizbeth," he said. "I truly am."

Oh, that made her happy.

"But it's time for you to leave that pain behind and go. I know what you wanted me to know now."

That confused her for a moment. Then she started spinning around the office again. She clearly wanted him to say more, to react more. But he couldn't.

He wouldn't.

As sad as it made him, as sad as this whole damn situation made him, he knew that ignored spirits eventually went away. That was why they were drawn to those like Frasier, who acknowledged them. It would take her some time, but Lizbeth would eventually leave.

And she would find the peace he wanted for her, the peace she'd never known how to find because no one had ever bothered to show her, if she did it sooner rather than later.

Later that evening as Charlotte and Zoey were helping Mac carry in platters of food and a birthday pie with an enormous dome of whipped cream, Charlotte said, "Look who showed up."

Mac continued on through Charlotte's open doors, but Zoey stopped on the patio. Oliver had just used the keypad to enter the garden. She watched as he walked to Frasier's office and knocked. Frasier opened the door and beckoned him inside. "Oh," Zoey said. "He's only here to see Frasier again."

"With a wrapped gift?" Charlotte asked.

Zoey quickly followed her inside with the platter she was carrying of tiny cheese biscuits so light they almost hovered above the plate. She deposited the platter on the kitchen counter, then hurried back outside to find Oliver walking toward her. He stepped onto the patio, but neither of them said a word, each apparently waiting for the other to say something.

"I had to stop and reschedule dinner with Frasier," Oliver finally said, pointing over his shoulder. "It's not every day someone turns nineteen."

Zoey laughed. "You and Charlotte should start a club and call it I Think I'm Really Old. You're only what, twenty-two?"

"Going on ninety," he said. "Here. This is for you." He held out the gift, something thin and rectangular wrapped in a fold-out road map. It was obviously a small book. Book lovers could spot a wrapped book from a mile away. "Sorry about the paper. It's all I had to work with."

"Can I open it right now?" she asked.

"Of course."

He watched her carefully as she opened the map. The book inside had a gold watercolor background with a single turquoise feather floating down from the title. She gasped when she realized what it was. Oliver smiled, as if that was exactly the reaction he'd wanted. "*Dancing with the Dellawisps*! How did you get a copy so quickly?"

"It's a copy I had from a long time ago."

"And you're giving it to *me*?"

"It seemed fitting," he said. "You're the only person besides Frasier who seems to actually like those birds."

"Thank you, Oliver. I *love* it." There was another awkward pause. She wanted to hug him. Was that weird? Would he think it was weird? No one was around to see if it turned out badly except for Pigeon, who was in the garden. Zoey could hear her rustle in the ferns. Her bird was still keeping her distance, but she was nearer tonight than she had been lately. She seemed worried about something.

It would be easier if Pigeon weren't watching, but Zoey took a step forward anyway. Charlotte chose that moment to call from the kitchen, making Zoey jump back in surprise, "Oliver, do you want something to drink? A soda? Or a beer, if you're legal?"

"A beer, thanks," he called back. "I can show you my ID. Or my I Think I'm Really Old membership card." He winked at Zoey as he passed.

"I don't want to hear it," Zoey whispered to Pigeon. Still clutching the book, she had turned to join Oliver when she saw Frasier emerge from his office. He had his lunch box in one hand and a piece of paper in the other. She was surprised when he crossed over to her. "Oliver told me it's your birthday," he said. "I wanted to give you this on my way out." He held out the piece of heavy-stock paper.

This was an embarrassment of riches. She set the book on Charlotte's patio table and Frasier's eyes followed the movement, frowning when he saw what it was. Zoey took the paper from him. It was a sketch of a fat dellawisp sitting on a thin branch. The bird's weight was bending the branch so far down that he had to cock his head sideways to see the world straight from his awkward perch. Frasier had managed to perfectly capture both the bird's annoyance and its beauty.

"That's old man Otis," Frasier said, his eyes finally leaving the book. "He's the last of the original birds found nesting here."

Zoey looked at him with surprise. "I didn't know he had a name."

"They all have names." He shrugged. "But I'm the only one they've told."

"Will you sign it for me?" she asked, handing it back to him.

He hesitated, then slid a pen out of his shirt pocket. He initialed it "FA" in the lower right-hand corner.

"Thank you," she said. "This means a lot to me. Will you join us? There's enough food for an army."

"No, but thank you for asking. And thank you for giving Oliver a distraction tonight." He looked up at the darkening sky, which was a foggy plum color. "There's something in the air tonight. Do you feel it?" he asked, and Zoey shook her head. "There's a lot to be let go of."

Zoey watched him walk away. When he disappeared through the dark gate, she didn't hear the now-familiar sound of the electronic lock clicking into place behind him. She thought she saw a shadow move across the garden but, distracted, Zoey found herself looking back down at the drawing. There were more threads here, important stitches, but she couldn't quite make the connection.

And then it dawned on her.

She picked up the book Oliver had just given her.

Dancing with the Dellawisps by Roscoe F. Avanger.

She turned the book over to the author photo on the back. She'd seen it hundreds of times on copies of *Sweet Mallow* at Kello's bookstore. In the photo, his head was bald and his face was clean-shaven. He wasn't wearing glasses, either. And he was decades younger, of course.

But it was *Frasier*.

"Don't tell the others," Oliver said from behind her, his breath soft on her ear. Zoey turned quickly. He was very close to her, so close she could smell his cologne, but she didn't step back. Neither, interestingly, did he. "He doesn't want anyone to know."

"He's Roscoe Avanger?" she whispered.

Oliver nodded conspiratorially.

She gave an incredulous laugh.

This might already be the best birthday she'd ever had.

Charlotte hated her dreams. They were always about the camp, or her mother, or Minister McCauley. The very things she wanted to forget.

But this week, all of a sudden, new ones began to present themselves. She would wake and catch the tail of dreams about the Dellawisp, or the birds, or the sandy road where Mac grew up, or wispy, warm presences like ghosts.

And Mac himself.

It was hard to wrap her mind around the fact that only a few short weeks ago she'd had to leave the Sugar Warehouse, Benny had stolen her money, Lizbeth had died, and Zoey had just moved to the island. She'd had no idea that the confluence of these things would lead to this point, where she actually looked forward to coming home to people she considered friends. She liked these people. She even trusted them, inasmuch as she would ever be able to trust anyone. She had been profoundly lonely for as long as she could remember. She'd begun to wonder if she had finally satisfied enough of teenaged Charlotte's unfulfilled longings that she could stay here. She wanted to settle into something that felt more like herself. She didn't know what, or who, that was yet. But it was the first time she'd ever thought it might be possible to find out.

Later that evening, as Charlotte and Mac stood side by side in her galley kitchen putting candles on Zoey's pie for dessert, she broke their companionable silence and said, "I had a dream about you last night."

"Oh?" he asked with a quirk of one red eyebrow.

"Not like that." She bumped him with her hip playfully. He'd recently started walking to the trolley tours every day with Zoey to hang out early in the afternoons before going to work, sometimes playing foosball with Zoey. One day he'd shown up on his own when Zoey, with the first day of school barreling down on her, had gone panic shopping for things on her college list. While the tour bus was out, he and Charlotte had sat on one of the couches and talked. She couldn't even remember what about now. She could only remember how they'd faced each other, mirroring the other's body language, and that there had been one moment when she'd thought, *I could stay like this forever.*

"It was snowing in the dream," she said. "But it wasn't really snow.

It was like flour, and you were covered in it. Camille was sprinkling it over you."

A flicker of something crossed his broad features as he turned back to the pie and changed the subject. "I hope Zoey likes this."

"Zoey eats potato chip sandwiches. Of course she'll like this."

"Camille used to make it. It's an old Southern icebox pie called millionaire pie, because it's so rich. Basically, it's just ambrosia in a pie shell. But I thought it was magical when I was a boy."

"I usually don't like my dreams. But that one, I liked." She didn't want to make him feel uncomfortable, but she needed to say this. She wanted him to understand. "I know I'm not an easy person to get to know. There'll always be a lot that people won't know about me. I just wanted to say thank you. You and Zoey have made these past few weeks surprising. Surprisingly nice, I mean. I'm not used to that."

"Do you think if we knew everything about you, we wouldn't feel the same way?"

That was definitely something she didn't want to get into. "It's complicated."

"We all feel that way. For one reason or another."

"Do you?" she asked.

"Yes," he said. "Of course." But didn't elaborate.

"Well, anyway," she said with a wave of her hand, trying to dispel any awkwardness, "thank you for your friendship. It means a lot to me."

Mac paused as he took a lighter out of his pocket. "Is that how you see me, a friend?"

"Isn't that how you see me?"

He set the lighter down and turned to face her, crossing his arms over his chest. She liked when he did that. She thought it made him look like a genie about to grant a wish. He considered her seriously before he said, "I remember the day you moved in. I remember you were wearing jeans and a pink shirt. After Lizbeth chased the movers away, you stood alone on your patio with your eyes closed. There were glints of sunlight on your hair, and I remember thinking that it looked braided with stars." He reached out to touch her hair, but he dropped his hand with just inches to go. "You looked so relieved to be settled, as if it were the best feeling in the world. I could've stared at you like that for hours." He turned away and picked the lighter back up. He flicked it, lighting the first candle on the pie. "That's how I see you, Charlotte."

She went very still as the impact of what he was saying hit her.

He'd seen her that day, the real her, in one of her rare, unguarded moments. Charlotte never acknowledged that person, even though she kept pushing through the cracks. But Charlotte clearly remembered that no one had loved that little girl, so somewhere along the way she'd made herself believe no one ever would.

"But I thought . . ." She didn't know how to say this without sounding ridiculous.

"What did you think?"

"Since you hadn't made a move . . ."

He gave her a funny look. "You've been *waiting* for me to make a move?"

Had she? Had she been waiting all this time? She was used to bottling everything up until she fell with a white-hot intensity that felt like the hunger of her childhood, when she would quickly fill herself out of fear of not getting enough. She'd never had this kind of slow attraction to a man before, something that felt like she didn't need any more than this.

It was the strangest sensation.

It felt like finally being full.

"What's the holdup? I'm going to be twenty by the time you guys finish lighting candles. Oh! Sorry!" Zoey said as she quickly backed out, hitting her shoulder on the doorjamb in the process, having caught Charlotte and Mac leaning in so close now that their faces were only a whisper apart. "Sorrysorrysorry."

Mac held her eyes for a few seconds longer, not moving, making her wonder if he was going to lean in those last few inches. But then he pulled back. "Okay. Pie first," he said.

Charlotte shook her head as if to clear her thoughts. She looked around for something to do. She grabbed the pie plates and forks. "Right," she said. "Pie."

"Charlotte?"

She turned to him.

"Just to be clear: I'm going to kiss you later."

That made her smile as she walked to the patio, leaving him to light the rest of the candles. When he emerged, they sang "Happy Birthday" as Mac set the pie in front of Zoey. The spray of light illuminated her young, beautiful face like the pale moon in the sky as she closed her eyes, forming a wish.

The possibilities of what was to come for all of them made it hard for Charlotte to catch her breath as she watched Zoey.

This is what being full feels like.

She was going to stay here and be happy and full.

But then she felt an odd chill.

Mac reached out and put his arm around her, as if he'd felt it, too.

Oliver, who was standing behind Zoey with his phone up to take a photo, looked around as if he was also aware of the sudden change in atmosphere.

Zoey finally took a deep breath and extinguished all the candles but one.

And at that same moment there was a crash from inside Charlotte's condo.

The four of them looked at each other, surprised, then immediately went inside to see what had happened. Nothing had been disturbed in the living room or kitchen. Charlotte opened her bedroom door and turned on the light. When she stepped into the room, something crunched under her sandal.

"I found it," she called.

"What happened?" Zoey asked, appearing at her side.

Charlotte held her arm out to keep Zoey from entering. "Careful. The witch balls broke."

"How many?"

"All of them," Charlotte said.

"All of them?" Zoey looked up, confused. "How did that happen?"

"I have no idea."

Mac appeared with her broom and her trash can, and they stepped aside to let him sweep a path to the bed. Charlotte followed him and carefully folded her comforter, keeping the pieces of glass that had fallen there inside. Zoey and Oliver brought up the rear and started picking up some larger pieces off the bedside table and the television.

"How could all of them have broken at the same time?" Mac asked. "The window isn't open and the AC isn't even on."

"I don't know," Charlotte said, feeling uneasy. Something about this felt portentous, almost as if she'd caused it by the audacity of finally feeling like she could let go of the ghosts of her past.

"I didn't blow out the candles *that* hard," Zoey joked. She suddenly waved her hand above her head, then looked up with a frown.

"I feel kind of silly asking this," Oliver said, "but what is a witch ball?"

Before any of them could answer, a voice from the bedroom doorway said, "Look at Princess Pepper, getting her friends to clean for her."

Zoey, Oliver, and Mac all turned.

But Charlotte, who'd had her back to the door as she'd pulled the bundled-up comforter off the bed, froze.

She knew that voice.

And every single crack she'd tried to seal over since leaving the camp split open at once.

Chapter Nineteen

C harlotte," Mac said as he held out his hand to her, "come here."

He hadn't taken his eyes off the person behind her. Zoey and Oliver had gone unusually still. She didn't understand. She had every reason to fear that voice. What reason did they have?

"*Charlotte,*" the voice said. "I should have known. I should have figured that out a long time ago."

She slowly turned.

Her mother stood in the bedroom doorway with a large, tattered backpack at her feet. She smelled strongly of body odor and cigarette smoke. If Charlotte was shocked by her being here, it was nothing compared to the shock at her physical appearance.

When Charlotte ran away ten years ago, the hard life of living off the land at the camp had been starting to take its toll physically on her mother, but Samantha Quint had still been a beauty. Now, the only thing recognizable about Sam was her china-blue eyes. She was heavier, but most people who had once lived at the camp were probably heavier now because there was easier access to food on the outside. Sam's face was a road map of dirt-caked lines, her hair was in a long, oily braid, and she was missing several teeth. Everyone else from the camp Charlotte had ever looked up seemed to have rebounded and moved on in some way, like the camp had been nothing but a bad dream. But not her mother. No one at the camp had loved Marvin McCauley more than Sam had, which was probably why she had fallen so far. She looked like she'd completely lost her direction, her only momentum being memories and resentment.

Charlotte understood that her once-beautiful mother had grown up poor and uneducated and abused, which was why she'd been so susceptible to the allure of Minister McCauley. The Church of McCauley had been a magnet for people like her. The church had made them feel important, probably for the first time in their lives. Minister McCauley had encouraged their belief in an us-against-them world, and he had convinced them that by building their own community they were going to win. These were people who had never won at anything in life. But moving there came at the price of their children, because Minister McCauley had hated children. Children couldn't do the same amount of work as the adults, they couldn't bring in money, so servitude to the adults was the price they'd paid for the privilege of living there.

"You always wanted to be like her, didn't you, Pepper?" Sam said, lifting her hand to point at Charlotte. Charlotte realized now why the others seemed so wary. Sam was holding an old butcher knife, the wooden handle covered in black tape as if to prevent splinters. "The moment you met Charlotte, she was all you could talk about. Charlotte this, and Charlotte that. Charlotte, Charlotte, Charlotte. I should have known you would take her name, you little thief."

Charlotte willed her mother to stop. *They don't know*, she silently said. *Don't tell them.*

"I thought you were dead. Hell, I wanted you to be dead. But I never once thought to look up Charlotte Lungren. Then one day I happened to type in her name at a library, and up came a blog post by a woman who had gotten henna done by a *great* artist named Charlotte Lungren on Mallow Island. And, lo and behold, there was a photo of *you*."

Charlotte remembered the client. She remembered the photo. She normally never let her photo be taken. One mistake. One little mistake. That was all it had taken.

She dared a look over her shoulder at Mac and Zoey and Oliver. They didn't yet have a reason to believe that Charlotte's name was really Pepper Quint and that she had taken the name of her best friend, the real Charlotte Lungren, after she'd died at the camp. And she didn't want them to know, not ever.

"I've been watching you in this pretty place, with these friends," Sam was saying, using the old knife to indicate Zoey and Mac and Oliver. Charlotte automatically shifted slightly to put herself more fully in front of them. "Once your neighbor died, I started sleeping next door because there's no place on this damn island to camp without the police finding you and making you move. But then that lock went up on the gate. Do you want to know where I've slept since then? *Behind a dumpster.* While *you* got to live in here. What a sweet little life you've made with the money you stole."

It suddenly became clear what the events leading up to this meant. Her mother had been the one who'd taken the cash out of Charlotte's purse, not Benny. And she'd broken in a second time, but couldn't find anything else. Her mother had been on the island for *weeks*, while Charlotte had actually begun to think she could stay.

"You don't deserve this," Sam needled at Charlotte's continued silence. "You don't get to live this way after what you did."

That finally lit something inside her as, no doubt, her mother knew it would. She was never happy until she had pushed every button. "After what *I* did? That place nearly destroyed me! It did destroy Charlotte. And you did *nothing*. You were my mother. You were supposed to protect me. That was your one job. I deserved every cent of that money I took. Charlotte deserved it." She paused to try to calm down. Her anger wasn't going to do anyone any good.

"He had to start selling the guns because of you!"

Charlotte had figured as much. If Minister McCauley's plan had indeed been to leave after the real Charlotte Lungren died from his failed attempt at faith healing, his plan had been foiled by small, meek, sixteen-year-old Pepper Quint breaking into his office and taking all his cash that night in retaliation. He would have been forced to sell the guns he had amassed illegally to get more of the money he needed for a new start.

"How much do you want?" Charlotte asked, the only path she could see out of this.

"I want it all," Sam said.

"You can't have it all. How much to leave?"

"You think I'm going to leave?"

Charlotte paused. "Then how much to let them go?"

Sam smiled and Charlotte realized she'd just let her mother see her soft spot. All she'd wanted was to get Sam away from them, but now Sam knew that hurting them would hurt her. "Do you really think it will be that easy?"

They stared at each other for what felt like eons. Continents shifted. Glaciers melted.

Then a quiet voice came from the living room. "Excuse me."

Sam leapt to the side, her knife swinging toward the voice, then to Charlotte, and back again. "Who the hell are you?"

A thin, broken-looking woman had appeared in the living room from the patio. It was hard to determine her age. Fifties? She gave an overall impression of yellow—sallow skin, stained teeth, crew-cut blond hair. In the light of day, she would probably blend in with the sunshine and disappear completely. "I'm no one," she said. "I live across the garden."

"*Lucy?*" Zoey whispered, taking a step forward to try to see around the door into the living room.

Oliver caught her by the arm and said, "Don't, Zoey."

Charlotte watched Lucy's eyes dart to the bedroom door at his voice. There was absolutely no doubt in Charlotte's mind that Oliver was the reason Lucy was here.

Her mother was assessing Lucy. It wouldn't take more than a single breath to knock her over. "This is none of your business," Sam said. "Get out. And don't you dare call the police. This is between me and my daughter."

Lucy just stood there.

"What's the matter with you?" Sam said. "Go away!"

Lucy's eyes again went to the bedroom door, where Oliver was hidden just out of sight. "I thought you'd want to know that the last bus off the island leaves soon."

"I know what time it leaves," Sam snapped.

Lucy paused, pressing her lips together. "What's your name?"

"Her name is Sam," Charlotte said quickly. "Samantha Quint."

"Shut up!" Sam yelled, making Charlotte wince. She had almost managed to forget her mother's yells, how nothing Charlotte ever did would make them stop. Sam yelled if she was too loud, and if she was too quiet; if she laughed or if she cried.

"I've watched you come and go here for a while, Sam," Lucy said. "I know what it's like to be without a home. I know from experience that there's no place to camp on the island. The nearest shelter is about an hour away. If you leave now, you can catch the bus. I'll go with you, if you want, and show you where it is."

"I'm not catching the goddamn bus. This place is as much mine as it is hers. It was bought with the *church's* money."

"It wasn't the church's money," Charlotte said. "It was the Lungrens'. They sold their house for him before they moved to the camp. They were the only reason he had that much."

"You ruined *everything*."

"No, I didn't," she said. "He was planning to leave the night she died. The camp wasn't going to survive."

"That's not true!"

"Sam, do you mind my asking what your plan is?" Lucy interrupted. "There are four people in the bedroom. And I'm out here. But there's only you and the knife in between. It's just a matter of time before one of us gets to a phone. But if you leave now, you can catch the bus."

"Stop it with the bus! I'm not taking the bus! I'm staying right here! She doesn't get to have this!" Charlotte put her hands up to try to calm her mother down, but at the movement Sam swung the knife to point it at her. "Don't move, or I'll kill you. I swear I will."

Charlotte slowly lowered her hands. She knew what she had to do. She had to save the others the way she should have saved the real Charlotte. She should have told someone back then. She should have called 911 when the real Charlotte got so sick. She should have done *something* for her best friend. Instead, she was too afraid to openly go against the adults at the camp. But she wasn't afraid anymore. Nor was she angry. In fact, she felt an incredible sense of peace come over her. Come what may, Pepper Quint was finally going to find some redemption.

"You can't kill me," Charlotte said.

"Why not?"

"Because I died a long time ago."

That made her mother go quiet. Charlotte calculated the distance it would take to get close enough to Sam to lunge at her, giving the others time to escape and call for help. She started to move incrementally forward. Sam looked suspicious, as if knowing what Charlotte was about to do.

But before Charlotte could do anything, Lucy leapt forward and seized Sam's wrist, jerking it quickly down to connect with Lucy's lifted knee. Sam, caught by surprise, dropped the knife. Lucy then grabbed Sam by the hair and Sam reached up to scratch and claw at Lucy's face. Lucy didn't back down even though it was clear Sam had the superior strength. Lucy didn't seem to need strength, though. She was quick and wily. She fought like she'd fought before, like this wasn't fear or adrenaline. This was experience. Charlotte could see a faint impression of Lucy's youth, something dark and unstable, crackling around her now. When they both staggered back in an undulating knot, Charlotte was able to snatch the knife off the floor. That seemed to be all Lucy was waiting for. As soon as she saw that the weapon was taken care of, Lucy let go of Sam and the darkness around her disappeared. She was again so pale she was almost translucent. Sam wasn't through with Lucy, though. She let out a primal scream and tackled Lucy. Lucy didn't fight back. She went limp, her hands at her sides, and let Sam take her down. Then she just lay there on the floor while Sam hit her.

Charlotte felt Mac brush by her as he ran into the living room and grabbed Sam by the waist and pulled her off of Lucy. He held Sam's back against his chest, her arms pinned, while she screamed and kicked like something feral.

Charlotte looked away.

Once again, Pepper Quint had failed to save anyone.

"Oliver, get your phone and call the police," Mac yelled over Sam's wild screams. "Calm down, lady! I'm not going to hurt you!"

Oliver dashed past him to the patio, where he grabbed his phone. He came back inside while dialing. He knelt by Lucy as she rolled over onto all fours. "Aunt Lucy, stay still. You're hurt."

"I'm all right," she said as she got to her feet.

"Come sit down," he said, touching her arm.

She backed away from him as if scalded. "I'm fine."

He looked like he was going to say something more to her, but then the line obviously picked up. Oliver put his finger in his ear as he turned away to try to hear over Sam. "Yes, we need the police . . ."

Zoey was the only one left in Charlotte's bedroom, and Charlotte heard her saying, "Pigeon, stop it! Let me out!"

Charlotte turned to see Zoey making her way across the broken glass, waving her hand in front of her as if swatting away gnats. She finally reached Charlotte, her color high. "What happened?" Zoey said breathlessly. "I couldn't see anything from in there."

"Lucy got the knife away from her," Charlotte said, putting her arm around Zoey and drawing her near. Just the thought of Zoey getting hurt made Charlotte feel sick to her stomach.

"Thank you," Oliver was saying. He hung up and turned to them. "They'll be here soon. The police station isn't far away."

"Where is she?" Zoey asked.

"Where is who?" Charlotte said.

"Lucy."

Even Sam stopped screaming at that.

They all looked around and realized that Lucy was gone.

Sam's screams amped back up when Oliver left the others to walk around the garden to check on Lucy. The dellawisps were shooting in and out of the trees like bottle rockets, alarmed.

He stepped onto Lucy's dark patio, but then stopped and spun around.

He'd just had the strangest sensation his mother was right behind him. He even put his hand to his hair, as if she'd touched him, which was odd because she never used to touch him.

He suddenly remembered a particular conversation he'd had with his therapist in college. She'd asked him, "What would you say to your mother if she were here?"

He'd answered, "It wouldn't matter. She wouldn't listen."

"This isn't about her. This is about you. What would you say?"

He'd thought about all the things he'd already said. The questions he'd already asked. He'd realized then that wanting something she could never give was only ever going to hurt him. He had to focus on what he had to do to move on.

"I would say goodbye."

"You didn't say goodbye when you left?" his therapist had asked.

"I think I said something like, 'Well, I'm leaving now.'"

"Why didn't you say goodbye?"

"I kept thinking that if I just waited a little while longer, she would change."

The moonlight cast ghostly shadows around him, moving and rolling in the ocean breeze.

He put his hand to his hair again. *Had* she changed?

He shook himself out of it and turned back to knock on Lucy's door.

It took a long time for her to answer.

But finally the door opened.

And somewhere far away, another door closed.

GHOST STORY

Lizbeth

I couldn't go with Frasier when he left this evening. He didn't want me. So I was stuck here feeling angry and wondering what I could do to change his mind, to change Oliver's mind, to change *anyone's* mind.

And then that woman appeared, and Lucy took action.

I spent so much time wanting people to hate Lucy that I never stopped to realize that no one actually loved her, not even our father. That wasn't love, though I thought it was at the time. And the control I wielded in order to survive, the conditions I put on everyone, were never hers, either. She was never in control—of herself, of others, of anything. Even so, look what she just did. If she had waited like me for someone to love her back before giving love herself, Oliver might have gotten hurt tonight.

I think I hate her a little less. I'm not sure what I'm feeling right now.

There was a moment when I saw what was happening that made everything that was left of me feel like it was going in a thousand different directions at once, breaking me apart and putting me back together in ways I never was before. I didn't know what to do. I felt hopelessly pulled to Oliver, but unable to help him. All of us ghosts here felt pulled to the people we loved. The force of us broke all those glass balls trying to trap us once we got too near. I was scared for Oliver. It frightened me with its intensity. What if something happened to him? If I had felt something this intense while I was alive, it surely would have killed me.

Camille says it wouldn't have killed me. It would have given me holes. And the holes are where the love comes through.

Now you know, she says.

She's beckoning me. She wants me and that other ghost here to leave with her. That other one says she won't go yet, but I will.

I'll go for Oliver. I'll do this for him.

He'll never know I'm doing it for him, but that's okay.

It's okay, it's okay, it's okay, it's okay.

Because *he's* okay.

Something is lifting me, and I'm soaring.

I see things so clearly now.

How wrong I'd gotten it.

It is love, even if you're not loved back.

It *is*.

Chapter Twenty

When Lucy had gotten back to her condo, she'd barely made it to her creaky papasan chair before her legs had given out from under her. She'd taken out a cigarette, and the bright spark of her lighter illuminated the photos of Oliver that Zoey had given her, spread out on the TV tray beside the chair.

Night and day, she spent most of her time here, watching the garden. At first it had been so she could watch Oliver without Lizbeth knowing. But after Oliver had left, it simply became habit.

She'd been aware of the woman, Sam, for weeks now. She would watch Sam pick her way into Lizbeth's place late every night, probably to sleep, which was why Lucy hadn't been too concerned at first. She'd even felt a certain sympathy for the woman. Before prison, Lucy had become homeless every time her mother had kicked her out for using. She'd assumed Sam had stumbled upon the Della-wisp by happenstance, found Lizbeth's condo empty, and decided it wouldn't do any harm to have a roof over her head for a while. Lucy had done the same thing. She'd once had an eerie sixth sense for finding empty houses on the island to crash in.

Sam had disappeared when the new keypad lock had been put on the gate. But a few hours ago, she'd reappeared as Frasier had left, catching the gate before it closed. And as Lucy had watched Sam lurk in the dark near the hippie girl's place, an uneasiness had lifted the hair on her arms.

Sam had looked furious. Seeing happiness did that to some people. Money, a place to live, transportation to get you where you were going—these were all sources of envy to someone with none of these things. But nothing, *nothing*, could make someone who didn't have anything angrier than witnessing actual happiness.

Lucy had watched as Sam finally walked into the condo after the group had all hurried inside, as if they'd heard something in there. And that's when Lucy had seen the knife Sam was carrying.

Lucy had been up and out the door before she'd even realized she was doing it, thinking only one thing.

Oliver.

Once Lucy had approached Sam, she'd tried to get her to leave on her own, but Sam's hatred of the hippie girl had made it impossible for her to leave now that she had shown herself. She was only going to be satisfied by doing harm, by tearing down any happiness in her path. So Lucy had had no choice. She'd had to call upon a past she'd spent more than twenty years trying to forget. Lucy knew from experience that if you get hit, you can call the police. If there's physical contact, you can press charges. When she was younger, it had been a tactic Lucy had used as punishment for lovers and drug dealers if she felt ill-used or betrayed. She would pick fights, always making sure that she ended up wounded but the other person bore no marks so the blame would appear to be entirely on them.

Once Sam's knife had been confiscated by the hippie girl, Lucy had stopped fighting and had simply fallen to the floor and taken Sam's blows until they'd pulled Sam off. But Lucy's body wasn't as resilient as it used to be. She'd treated it too badly over the years. She almost hadn't made it home. In the old days, she'd be high when she would fight, so she hadn't felt pain. She hadn't felt *anything*, which had been the whole reason for using in the first place—for that blessed, beautiful nothing. Now the pain was so intense it made her teeth chatter.

But Oliver was safe.

And that was all that mattered.

She'd just taken her first drag of her cigarette, hoping the nicotine would take the edge off, when there was a knock on the door. She went still, her cigarette frozen at her lips.

"Aunt Lucy? It's Oliver."

She waited for him to go away. But he knocked again.

"Please, Aunt Lucy. I just want to know you're okay."

She finally stubbed out the cigarette and lifted herself heavily from the chair, wincing. She wondered if she had a broken rib.

She opened the door only a sliver but concern bloomed across Oliver's face when he saw her. "She hurt you," he said.

She put her hand to her cheek, to the long scratches there. The sweat from her palm made them sting. "I'm fine."

"Thank you," he said. "For what you did."

She nodded.

Oliver hesitated. She could see all the questions he wanted to ask. His eyes darted past her into her dark living room. She angled herself slightly so he wouldn't see his photos on the TV tray.

She began to tremble again, but not from the pain this time.

She had a dream, once. It was the only reason she came back to the island after prison. She was going to take Oliver. She was going to save him. First her mother betrayed her by not sending her updates and photos like she'd promised, then Lizbeth took over after their mother died. They were always so happy to let Lucy bear the brunt of things, as if Lucy were stronger, meaner, and better able to survive than them. How else to explain the way they just let her father abuse her? And then they seemed to blame her because of how messed up she became as a result. But she hadn't messed up with Oliver. He was perfect, her one good thing, her tiny baby with dark curly hair and bottle-green eyes. She held him every day for a month before she left to serve her sentence, committing everything about him to memory. Once she got out, a DNA test would prove Oliver was hers, and she would scorch the earth with her vengeance. She didn't stop to consider how this might affect Oliver. She remembered how small and vulnerable he was, so she figured all she would have to do was grab him and hold him to her like she used to and everything would be fine.

She looked all over the island for him. She didn't find either him or Lizbeth—they were no longer in the house where Lucy and Lizbeth had grown up—but she did find people from her old drug life, far more than she had anticipated. *They* were right where she'd left them. Her head felt muddied when she was around them, her skin itchy. She stayed on a few couches at first, but she had to leave before she gave in to temptation.

Then out of the blue, one day Frasier found her. He said he knew her sister and understood that Lucy needed someplace to stay. He led her straight to Oliver! She set eyes on him for the first time since he was a baby right here in this magical garden. He was twelve, a young man, nearly grown. She didn't recognize him. She didn't know her own child as he peered at her from around a tree.

She'd seen enough counselors in prison to know about bipolar and borderline personality disorders. Childhood abuse. PTSD. Addiction. She could recite all the recovery steps by heart. But none of it had ever really sunken in, like words someone else had written on her skin. She was fine. Everyone else was the problem. Agreeing with the counselors had only been a means to an end. If she agreed, then they would let her out.

But those words on her skin, Oliver could read clearly that day.

The world outside of prison was unexpectedly frightening, from the moment she walked out. She suddenly had the freedom to do *anything she wanted*. It would be so easy to go back to old habits, as easy as slipping into a warm bath. Oliver was supposed to be her shield from all of that temptation. If she didn't have Oliver, she didn't know what would happen to her. She realized in that moment that coming back wasn't about saving him at all. It was about saving herself. And the only way she could possibly do both was to be as close to him as possible, while staying as far away as she could.

"Aunt Lucy?" Oliver said when she was silent for many moments, one eye peeking at him from around the door. "Are you hungry? Do you need food?"

"No."

"The police will be here any minute. They'll probably want a statement."

She nodded.

"Mom left me her place. I'm going to stay for a while, if that's all right with you."

She nodded again. Of course it was all right with her. She would get to watch him every day, just like she used to before he left—a reminder that she was capable of at least one good thing.

He was her one good thing.

He was written on her skin, too. But no one would ever see that but her.

"I'll be right over there, if you need me."

"All right," she said, closing the door and going back to her papasan chair. She reached for her cigarettes again. She lit another one, the flame shaking so badly this time that the light made a zigzag pattern in the darkness.

She picked up one of Oliver's photos and set it in her lap, not looking at it, just letting it rest there as she patted it comfortingly.

Chapter Twenty-one

When she gave her statement, Charlotte tried not to seem too nervous, saying as simply as possible, "She raised me, but I ran away when I was sixteen. I don't know where she's been, or what she's been doing all this time. I cut ties with her a long time ago, for obvious reasons. She wanted money tonight. That was the reason for the knife. But I don't have any money. I just have this condo."

Sam screamed the entire time, "She's not real! She's not real!" Until she was finally led away.

An officer walked across the garden to talk to Lucy, who spoke to him through a half-opened door. She apparently refused medical attention, because the paramedics, who arrived shortly after the police, left without seeing her.

Charlotte, Zoey, and Oliver then silently cleared the rest of the broken glass from her bedroom while Mac remained outside, talking to an officer who had stayed behind, someone he apparently knew from school.

He walked back inside after the officer left and at last those strobing emergency lights, which had been making the entire garden look like a carnival, disappeared. "He told me this in confidence," Mac said, "but Samantha Quint is apparently wanted for felony burglaries going back several years. She's probably looking at some serious time."

"Was that really your mom?" Zoey finally asked.

"Yes," Charlotte said. "But I haven't seen her in a long time."

"Why did she keep calling you Pepper?"

They were all looking at her. "It's just a name she gave me," Charlotte said. "I always liked Charlotte better. It's late. You should go to bed." She turned to Oliver. "Will you walk Zoey home and stay with her awhile? I don't want her to be alone."

"Of course," Oliver said.

Charlotte then pointed a warning finger at him. "Just stay with her. Nothing else."

"*Charlotte*," Zoey said, embarrassed.

"Come here," she said, drawing Zoey into a hug. "I know that must have been scary for you," she whispered into Zoey's hair. "I'm sorry."

"You're hugging me," Zoey's muffled voice said into Charlotte's shoulder, where she was holding Zoey's face to her.

Charlotte pulled back. "What?"

"I didn't think you were a hugger."

"Come on," Oliver said, taking Zoey's arm.

Zoey seemed to sense that something had changed, had shifted. The crack was open and there was no sealing it back. "I'll see you in the morning?" she asked, but Charlotte just smiled.

As soon as they left, Charlotte turned to Mac. "Look after her for me."

"What are you talking about?" He followed her into her bedroom, where she opened her closet and grabbed a tote bag. She tried to be deliberate, thinking of just what she needed, but she ended up stuffing random clothing inside. She'd sort it out later.

"I stayed too long and I got careless." What she really meant was *I stayed too long and I got happy.* Either way, the result was the same. "I have to leave."

"Where are you going?"

"I don't know. The next place on the list, I guess." She grabbed a small box and put some henna supplies inside. She would empty her account when banks opened in the morning, but she couldn't close the account with Charlotte's name on it yet, because she needed to sell this place first. Then she would have to change her name, her whole identity, again. The thought was too overwhelming to fully grasp yet. It was like losing the real Charlotte all over again.

Like losing *herself* all over again.

"You don't have to do this," Mac said. "She's not coming back."

The last thing she did was pull out the basket from under her bed to take out Charlotte's diary. She put it in her backpack, hesitating when she saw the menu from Popcorn still in there. She brushed by Mac, not looking at him. She went to her scooter in the living room and strapped the tote and the box to the back. Then she slipped her backpack over her shoulders and kicked up the stand.

But Mac stepped in front of the scooter. "There's nothing you can do tonight that can't be done in the morning," he said. "Come with me to my place."

She knew he deserved answers. And she would be lying if she said it wouldn't be a relief to finally tell someone her whole story, even if it was on her way out the door. She let go of the scooter and walked outside with him. She stared at the millionaire pie left on the patio table as he closed and locked her doors. The single candle Zoey hadn't managed to blow out had burned down into a tiny pool of wax on top of the whipped cream. Mac led her the long way around the garden to avoid the birds, and then he opened his door and guided her inside.

She took off her backpack and went directly to the couch. She sat back and covered her eyes with the palms of her hands, rubbing so hard she saw dark spots. "So how much have you worked out?"

"Just the obvious. That you're really Pepper in the story you told me, and that it was Charlotte who died. Here, take this."

She lowered her hands to see him extending a glass to her. She took it without a word and drank. It tasted malty as it burned down her throat. Scotch.

"What money was your mother talking about?" he asked as he sat beside her. Fig crossed from the far side of the couch and climbed into his lap, curling herself into the shape of a shell.

She looked down into the glass. "The night the real Charlotte died, I picked the lock on Minister McCauley's office door. I'd seen Charlotte do it dozens of times. She'd tear his papers, empty his stapler—small stuff that would bother him, but not really draw his attention. Because if he found out, there would be hell to pay. There was so little power the kids had at the camp, but she found ways. I was going to destroy everything that night because of what he'd done to her. But when I got into the office, there it was, a bag of cash he'd not locked up. He *always* kept the money locked up. He was good at preaching about communal living, but he kept all the money to himself. He'd been planning to leave that night. There'd never been a death at the camp before, so he probably thought he couldn't control the fallout. I took it and ran, just like Charlotte always wanted to do. I used it to buy my first place. That's what I do every time I move. I buy a place that's all mine, something no one can take away." She raised the glass to her lips and downed the rest of the Scotch in one gulp. Then she slapped the glass on the coffee table harder than she'd intended, like something from a movie. "I don't regret it."

"And I don't blame you," Mac said. "But are you saying that all this time no one but your mother has been looking for you and the money?"

She shrugged. "That place meant more to her than anyone else."

"Then I don't understand why you think you have to go. She's not coming back."

Of course it would never occur to him. He was too decent. He didn't know what it was like to be this broken. "Because one day she might start making sense and reveal I've been living under a stolen identity for ten years." She reached for her backpack and took out the diary. "Charlotte kept this when she lived at the camp. She listed all the places she wanted to go and everything she wanted to do when she finally ran away. I've tried to do it all for her." She removed the photo tucked in the back, her hand shaking slightly. She'd never shown this to anyone. "That's her."

He took the photo and stared at the skinny girls—Pepper, short and blond with lips pinched nervously together, and the real Charlotte, tall and dark-haired with a smile so wide it caught everyone in her orbit. She was sure he was going to see what she saw and finally understand why it was so important to go on living as Charlotte: Of the two, clearly Charlotte should have been the one to survive.

"You told me what Charlotte wanted, but what did *you* want?" He handed the photo back to her.

"It doesn't matter." She turned away as she put the diary and photo back in her backpack.

"It does matter," he said.

Still not looking at him, she said, "I just wanted to feel safe and settled somewhere." In a quieter voice she added, "I wanted to feel loved."

"Everyone wants those things. It's not wrong."

She shook her head.

"Look at me," Mac said. He waited for her to finally turn to him. "You don't have to do this alone anymore. We're better because you're here. Now let us be here for you."

"You don't need me, Mac. You're already so put-together."

"I'm not put-together." Mac scrubbed his beard. It made a sand-papery sound. He picked up Fig and set her aside, then went back to the liquor cabinet. He poured himself a Scotch and drank it quickly, making a pained face at the stinging in his throat. "Do you want to know how un-put-together I am?" he finally asked. "Camille is here. Right now. I know that sounds crazy, but she is. I'm keeping her here, even though I know she wants to go. I've put her ghost between my-self and everyone else because her love defined me for so long that I don't know who I am without it. But then you came along and made me realize I can't hold on to the past and grab for the future at the same time. I have to choose. Eventually, we all have to choose."

She automatically turned to look at the photo on the wall of him and Camille. "That's not crazy, Mac," she said. "But it's not the same."

He walked back to the couch and sat, taking her hands in his. "It's *exactly* the same. It's as scary as hell to think of letting go. But I'll do it," he said, "if you do it."

"Mac—"

"We'll do it together."

She hesitated.

"On the count of three. Okay?"

His eyes held hers, and she couldn't look away. Emotion was welling in her, making her unable to speak. She was so tired of running. But could she really trust herself to stay, to be the person Mac and Zoey needed her to be? She hadn't been Pepper in a long, long time. She wasn't sure she remembered how to be herself anymore.

"One," Mac said.

Slowly, Charlotte leaned against him and rested her head on his shoulder. He put his arm around her and held on tightly, as if they were about to jump off a cliff.

"Two."

Charlotte began to cry. She knew who Mac was saying goodbye to. But was she saying goodbye to Charlotte or Pepper? Her mother or the camp? Maybe she was saying goodbye to everything.

"Three."

Mac opened his eyes. Watery morning light was shining through the gaps in his patio-door curtains. He squeezed his eyes to clear his vision, wondering what he was doing in the living room. He never slept here. It was nearly impossible to get the cornmeal that fell on him during the night out of the couch cushions, and Fig would track it all over the condo. He winced as he started to get up and go for the vacuum cleaner. He'd slept in an awkward position, his arm draped over something.

He lowered his chin and saw Charlotte's blond head resting on his chest.

He first felt an overwhelming sense of happiness, lifting him as if he were feather-light. She hadn't sneaked off in the night. She was still here.

Then the panic set in.

He'd convinced her to stay, but now what was she going to think of all this cornmeal? *He'd told her he would let go.*

He was trying to figure out how he could disengage himself from her and silently clean what he could before she woke, when he felt Fig, who had been asleep on the back of the couch behind him, jump down to get water from the bathroom now that he was up, per their routine. He watched the cat walk across the living room, and she wasn't trailing cornmeal on the pads of her feet.

He slowly looked down at himself, then around.

There was no cornmeal anywhere.

For the first time in five years, the memory of Camille hadn't snowed on him, covering him in grief.

He felt his eyes go wet as he realized what this meant.

He really did let go.

GHOST STORY

Camille

So it's time for me to go now.
  I'm happy about it, so don't you be sad.
  Because going doesn't mean all gone.
  We'll meet again one day.

Chapter Twenty-two

The night before Zoey was set to drive the hour to school for her move-in day, she said a tearful goodbye to everyone at the party Charlotte threw her. It was a bit of an overreaction when she thought about it later, because she would be coming home in exactly five days for the weekend to tell them everything. But when her phone alarm went off in the morning, Zoey got out of bed and went straight to her balcony doors because there was someone she really *did* need to say goodbye to. She might not ever get another chance.

She passed the refrigerator with Pigeon's empty cage on top, and the menu and new photos tacked to the door. One new photo was of Oliver with a pink butterfly on his head. He'd recently gotten a job at the Mallow Island Resort Hotel as part of their ecotourism team, and he gave daily tours of the hotel's Butterfly Walks. Zoey had gone on his very first tour last week, during which that butterfly had landed squarely on his head and stayed there. Oliver had just kept talking, unfazed. Everyone had loved that. He was still living with Frasier, but the two of them spent every weekend painting inside Lizbeth's old place, reinventing it and, Zoey suspected, themselves a little, too.

Another new photo was of Mac watching Charlotte draw henna on a client's hand on the first day at her new table at the Trade Street gallery. Mac and Charlotte were spending a lot of time together, often staying overnight in each other's places and thinking Zoey didn't notice. Whatever had happened that night with Charlotte's mother had changed Charlotte. It was like she was settling into a version of herself that made so much more sense. One day she had come home from a salon, having had several inches of length cut from her hair. And she was in the process of selling her scooter on Craigslist and comparing prices on used cars. Maybe Zoey would never know Charlotte's whole story, but she'd bet everything she had that Mac knew, and that made Zoey happy. It was one less story that would disappear.

Zoey stopped at her balcony doors, her hand on the knob, willing Pigeon to be waiting outside. She hadn't come in again last night. She was hiding in the garden most of the time now, so distant that she felt almost gone.

She thought she heard something out there, so she put her ear against the doors. Was someone whispering? She threw open the doors to find Charlotte and Oliver on the balcony.

"Surprise!" they said in unison.

"What are you two doing here?" Zoey asked with a laugh, her eyes going to the garden, surreptitiously scanning for any sign of Pigeon.

"Four," Charlotte said. "Mac and Frasier are down there. We were waiting for you to get up. We didn't want to wake you."

Zoey stepped onto the balcony and looked down. Mac and Frasier waved to her from Charlotte's patio. On the table were a silver carafe of coffee, cups, and muffins the size of small melons. "Is this a going-away breakfast?"

Charlotte smiled. "It's a we're-coming-with-you breakfast. We all took off work to help you. You said it was family move-in day, right?"

"Right."

"So, we're your family. Did you really think we were going to let you do this alone?" Charlotte looped her arm in Zoey's and led her down the steps. "See, I told you she slept in her clothes," Charlotte said over her shoulder to Oliver.

"And I told you I already knew that," Oliver said as he followed. "I spent the night with her that night. You told me to."

"I didn't tell you to pay attention to what she wore to bed."

"I'm stopping while I'm ahead."

"Smart man," Charlotte said.

Oliver winked at Zoey, who almost tripped down the stairs. Sometimes the dynamic of their relationship was so comfortably platonic that she wanted nothing to change, like when Oliver sat with her on her balcony in the evenings after work. Most of the time they simply stared out at the garden, every once in a while turning to smile at each other as if they couldn't quite believe this was their life now, that they were actually adults being trusted to navigate this world on their own. But once, he'd reached over and taken her hand and kissed it for no reason she could think of. It was as if she'd touched something electric, and she'd found herself thinking she would be perfectly okay if *everything* changed.

Pigeon hadn't so much as dive-bombed her at that.

After breakfast, they packed Mac's SUV full of everything Zoey had spent the last few weeks buying, which included a mother lode of pillows that made the Tahoe look like there was a slumber party going on inside of it. Just before they headed out in a caravan, Zoey ran back to her studio to make sure she hadn't forgotten anything. Then she locked her doors, her stomach feeling fluttery.

She got to the garden gate but stopped before she opened it. She stared at the motley crew gathered in the parking lot—the magically large redheaded man, the blond woman with her painted skin, the beautiful green-eyed boy, and the famous writer with his Rip van Winkle beard.

Her family.

She glanced over her shoulder. She caught the movement of Lucy's curtain, and she knew she was watching. Ever since the night Lucy had appeared to save them, Mac would leave by her door small containers of the most exquisite food. Oliver would leave cigarettes. Zoey bought her marshmallows from the Trade Street candy shops, never the same flavor twice. And Charlotte left small bottles of bath oil that smelled like patchouli. Zoey always stayed awake as long as she could when these things were left out, hoping to finally see Lucy. She'd been the only one that night who hadn't actually set eyes on her.

Zoey turned her attention to the garden, where the dellawisps were arguing. Pigeon was there, somewhere. She was watching, too. And, like Lucy, she wasn't coming out.

Zoey wondered if one day she might wake and think Pigeon was just a dream. She decided right then and there that if that ever happened, it wouldn't matter.

A dream, a story, an invisible bird—it was all the same thing, really.

Not everything has to be real to be true.

"Goodbye, Pigeon," she whispered, then opened the gate and walked through.

GHOST STORY

Paloma

It is strange to me to speak now. I was not sure I would remember how.

My name is Paloma Fernandez Hennessey. You may call me Pigeon. Zoey does.

My thoughts lately have been of a song my grandfather used to sing to me. It was an old, old song his own grandfather sang to him and that I, in turn, sang to baby Zoey, though she does not remember this. It was about a woman who died giving birth to a son. She loved her child so much her soul went to live in the body of a bird to watch over him while he grew. She would warn the boy when there was danger and lead him to food in the forest. Then one day the bird was killed by a hunter, and the mother had no choice but to leave her son for good. The last lines of the song were:

I go now to settle in a place where there is always happiness.
But how can I be happy when my soul still needs to fly?

We have always had a curious connection to birds in my family.

My grandfather was even called the Birdman of Havana because he kept pigeons. He named them after family members long since gone. I spent my childhood believing the birds were actually these people, simply transformed. I remember the musty, sweet scent of them. I remember the bloom of dust on their wings. My favorite was the one named after my mother. When my grandfather died, my brother set the birds free and I hated seeing them fly away. I did not want them to leave me, as nearly everyone I had ever loved had left me. But my brother said we were free like them now, and we left to cross the straits that very night.

I know he loved me, my brother, but he was always in control and his idea of freedom meant he had it all and I had none. He promised me great things in America. He promised everything. As I lay in the boat that night, I remember several birds followed us, silhouetted like ghosts against the velvet night, and I reached my hand up as if I could touch them. I lost sight of them in the storm.

The storm.

It felt like being born again, the rush of water, the struggle to breathe. When it was over, I was left clinging to the overturned boat. The water and the horizon blended into one entity, and I felt suspended. My brother was gone, and I remember calling for him until I had no voice left. At some point I felt, but could not see, a bird land next to me. I knew at once it was my brother, assuring my safe passage as he had promised.

I was glad for his presence, at first. But even in death he tried to control me. He did not like that I did not stay in Miami, as he had wanted. He did not like when I moved to Charleston. He did not like what I did to make money. And he did not like when I met Zoey's father, Alrick.

But I was not taken advantage of by Alrick, despite the fact that

I was only a teenager and he was much older when we met. I knew exactly what I was doing.

Alrick was more insistent than most, that I see only him, that I do nothing but wait for him. He bought me the beautiful Dellawisp condo and I fell in love with this island. I would walk and walk and walk and just see. I had pretty clothes, and could buy a strawberry pastry whenever I felt like it. I imagined I looked like an American movie star. I said goodbye to my brother on Mallow Island. I set him free and finally became the person birthed by that storm.

I was in control.

The moment I knew I was pregnant, I understood that between my love and Alrick's money, this baby would have everything. I knew he did not want a child, so she would be *mine.* I waited months before I told Alrick. I said I did not know how far along I was, that I was irregular and often missed my periods. He wanted to be mad at me, but knew he could not. I stroked his chest and told him it would be all right. I purred to him that we were practical, if nothing else, and that this child would not make me different, and it would not make him different. We will get married, I told him, and put my finger to his lips when he started to protest. Our child will be legitimate. And if things do not work out, then we will separate. It was simple. I convinced him that nothing would change. Nothing at all.

But, of course, it did. Two months after we married at the courthouse, his partners voted to sell their business. I did not know what he did specifically, just that it involved imports and large, noisy ships that came to dock in Charleston. I did not know when he was away from me on Mallow Island that he went home, to his family home, somewhere in the great middle of America. Zoey was only three months old when Alrick took us to his Tulsa to live, because he had no more reason to stay in Charleston now that he did not work. His business was gone, sold, and there was money, money, money, always money, but not happiness, because he did not have anything to do. He did not look at me the same way. I was annoying and childish to him now. And so very out of place in his Tulsa. I often left for weeks at a time with Zoey. We went back to Mallow Island and stayed at the Dellawisp, where I had been so happy. But I always returned to him. If having me as a wife was embarrassing to him among his Midwestern family, having me disappear with his child was even more so. We argued and I would scratch his face with my red fingernails. I demanded a divorce several times. He always said no, because he did not want to part with his beloved money. It was only after he met the snotty woman with the young children of her own that he finally agreed. I challenged him with everything, because I wanted as much as possible for Zoey.

But I died just after the divorce was final.

Alrick hated that. He hated that the settlement money went into a trust for Zoey and not back to him.

Oh, my precious Zoey. My gift to the world.

I never wanted for her to be left with him, and certainly not with that judgmental woman he married, the woman who thought her own children could do no wrong, who made Alrick love them, but who resented that anything from his previous marriage was still in that house. I often knocked over her tiaras and pageant trophies in her glamorous closet, once even breaking a perfume bottle, just to vex her.

I had to stay with Zoey, just as my brother stayed with me.

But just as I let go of my brother to follow my own path, Zoey is now letting go of me.

I see her happy and hopeful and settled, but *I* am feeling restless. I wonder if this is how my brother felt. I am spending more and more time with the dellawisps in their trees. I did not like them at first, but now their energy excites me. I feel alive again when I am with them.

Some of the younger ones want to fly away to new adventures, and if this happens, I know I will go with them. Zoey does not need me and this saddens me. But I do not want to leave this world yet.

I am like that song my grandfather used to sing.

My soul still needs to fly.

Acknowledgments

To Andrea Cirillo and everyone at JRA, and Jennifer Enderlin and everyone at St. Martin's Press, for being there for the long haul. To my dad, Zack, and my niece, Hanna, for the strength it took to get through the hard stuff. To Michelle Pittman and Heidi Carmack for your friendship—and to the memory of your sweet moms. To Billy Swilling, Erin Campbell, and Tracy Horton for your support. To Pam Palmer and Alexandra Saperstein for your gifts of kindness. To the staff at Givens Estates for the care you gave my mom. And so much love to my readers for your well wishes and patience. I lost my mom and my sister days apart while writing this book, so I was away for a while. When I finally began the process of finishing *Other Birds*, it wasn't because I had managed to say goodbye to two of the most influential people in my life. No, I was able to write again because they were still with me, and I know they will be for as long as I need them. My mom sustained catastrophic brain injuries after her sudden strokes. She couldn't move, and often spoke in an unknown language. But one day as I was sitting on the edge of her bed, talking to her about this book, about Zoey and her mother, who came back as a bird after she died to watch over her daughter, my mom said to me with surprising clarity, "Oh, you have to write that."

And so I did.

I finally did, Mom.